ONE ON ME

Tim Huntley

DAW BOOKS, INC.
DONALD A. WOLLHEIM, PUBLISHER

1633 Broadway
New York, N.Y. 10019

Copyright ©, 1980, by Tim Huntley

All Rights Reserved.

Cover art by H. R. Van Dongen.

FIRST PRINTING, JANUARY 1980

1 2 3 4 5 6 7 8 9

DAW TRADEMARK REGISTERED
U.S. PAT. OFF. MARCA
REGISTRADA. HECHO EN U.S.A.

PRINTED IN U.S.A.

I WAS A SURPRISE TO MY MOTHER...

she being sterile. Uncle Benny accompanied her to the receiving terminal to argue her case. *"She's sterile, dammit! Sterile, sterile, sterile!"* He knew a thing or two about the law. *"We're all sterile!"*

It's on tape. I've seen it a hundred times— Uncle Benny beating on the dispenser with his little fists. Mimi Jo (my mother) in a fit of tears, hiding her face from the camera. Uncle Michael was there too, but we don't see him because he's taking the pictures. Mimi screams, "Please, please, not a child. God help me, not a child." Her sobs echo through the empty chamber.

On the word "child," Michael pans to reveal *me,* moving up on the conveyer, a plumpish, pinkish little meat-like creature, but lovely as babies go, floating in my bowl of primal goo, all smiles and happiness.

Mimi Jo lets out a screech. Michael pans suddenly to catch her reaction, misses, pans around looking for her, finally finds her fainted dead away on the floor and zooms in for a close-up. Next thing, there I set, dry and pleased to be alive, ready for pick-up. In going for the reaction shot, he missed the actual birth.

That's the first page of a novel you won't ever forget!

1

I was a surprise to my mother, she being sterile. Uncle Benny accompanied her to the receiving terminal to argue her case. *"She's sterile, God damn it. Sterile. Sterile. Sterile."* He knew a thing or two about the law. *"We're all sterile!"*

It's on tape. I've seen it a hundred times—Uncle Benny beating on the dispenser with his little fists, Mimi Jo (my mother) in a fit of tears, hiding her face from the camera. Uncle Michael was there too, but we don't see him because he's taking the pictures. Mimi screams, "Please, please, not a child. God help me, not a child." Her sobs echo through the empty chamber. On the word "child," Michael pans to reveal *me*, moving up on the conveyer, a plumpish pinkish little meat-like creature, but lovely as babies go, floating in my bowl of primal goo, all smiles and happiness. I arrive at the unloading chute. Two spongy calipers dip into the pool and surround me lovingly. Mimi Jo lets out a screech. Michael pans suddenly to catch her reaction, misses, pans around looking for her, finally finds her fainted dead away on the floor and zooms in for a close-up. Next thing, there I sit, dry and pleased to be alive, ready for pick-up. In going for the reaction shot, he missed the actual birth.

What we see next is the terminal screen displaying Mimi Jo's genetic code and mine side by side. For anyone who understands such things, the proof is there. I am the son of Mimi Jo.

"But she is, was, and always has been sterile," Benny insists. "Her God damn organs are in the organ bank. I was there when she had them out." Exactly true. To be as far on the safe side as she possibly could and still satisfy so many so regularly, she had her reproductive apparatus surgically removed, all but the fun parts, and stored pending a change of style. But of course, I wasn't nurtured in a womb of flesh, so that particular argument was worth very little. Nevertheless, to add an air of feasibility to the situation, in the way of an

5

explanation, the computer in charge offered up Mimi Jo's medical records on the display screen for all to see. It seems that nine months prior to my announcement, Mimi Jo, complaining of cramps, had submitted herself to Medcomp for a routine check. And woe to Mimi Jo, because sure enough, during the examination an intra-uterine growth was discovered. It was removed. It was examined. It was found non-malignant. Mimi Jo was given the okay. She thanked the machine and went home. And that, as far as she knew, was that. In the meantime, however, the growth, having failed the cancer test, was given a second chance, another test, the test for human potential. Apparently I was not fated to become a cancer, but a human being, for the growth was found embryonic and genetically sound. It was classified as such and transferred to the egg bank in Zurich, there to grow into what I became. It was entered into the records as the son of the one known parent, Mimi Jo Hornblower. The other parent never came forth. That position remained open. There was no rush of volunteers.

Against all odds, a child was born.

The growing or mere possession of children was considered to be in the poorest taste. It simply was not done. Even so, the law allowed it. Worse, there remained on the books a body of law protecting children from death. Infanticide was out and out illegal. It carried a penalty of up to twelve (but no more than twenty) minutes on a TV show called *Tongue Lash*, on which a panel of one's peers, after due consideration, would chew one out royally in front of everyone tuned in. It was an archaic law, rarely enforced because there were so few babies to kill. In my own lifetime infanticide dropped from a prime time offense to a daytime offense, and from there to the early morning slots, simply for lack of use. But Sunday evening prime time or Tuesday morning early, everyone on earth would have tuned in to watch poor Mimi Jo wither up and die of shame.

To avoid that fate she spared me, and raised me in the strictest secrecy. To the world at large there was only one child alive, a fellow by the name of Ted Wasserman, who was ninety-four years old at the time of my birth and still somewhat famous for his youth. His parents had misjudged the times. They thought they could lead off a new baby trend, and maybe win some fame that way. They hit much too early and flopped. They committed suicide. But there was Teddy. Nice Teddy. No one dared adopt him, so he was raised and educated in an automatic room full of good sounds, sights, tastes, smells, and touches—everything perfect from the day he was put in until the day he walked out, no doubt the happiest man alive. God, was he dull though. Not stupid exactly, just so perfectly content with life and thoroughly pleased with himself that it seemed that way. He got all the coverage, all the interviews, all the media attention, while I wasted away in captivity. Teddy Wasserman, the only child! Pure crap. *I* was the only child (the only living one, that is. There were several dead cutaways in the Museum of Natural History).

Mimi Jo couldn't get access to the machinery that raised Teddy without risking public exposure; besides which the law wouldn't allow it while even one parent lived. So she raised me herself, with the help of the seventy-two uncles and twenty-nine aunts who comprised her community of lovers. Like Teddy, I was raised indoors. Unlike Teddy, who was allowed to leave any time, I was kept a prisoner in Mimi Jo's slightly larger than usual sky house, which by unrenounceable order to the navigation system floated far away from the general cluster. The system was programmed to shy the approach of any and all flying objects except those transmitting the entry code, a code known only to Mimi Jo and her regulars. The phones were removed all but one, which was locked in the master bedroom. It was wired to a switch on the bedroom door so that on the chance that I might break in and yell for help in the middle of a call, it would disconnect.

My crib had a locking top and a feed trough. They put it in the bathroom off the pool deck, which became my room. It was completely hoseable. When I did uh-uh, instead of changing me they'd hit me with a shower.

Until I was eight Mimi Jo wouldn't talk to me directly—always through an interpreter. She was Swedish. She had me convinced that she couldn't understand English. We had speakers in the ceiling connected to a computer which made translations. Apparently, when I was still a baby I wandered in among the company, where I let out a string of goo-goo's and ga-ga's or some such baby drivel. The computer gave forth an interpretation in Swedish: "Pardon me, but I wish my bottle now, and if you please, my pants are full." And that gave her the idea. From then on she left the machine running continuously all through my formative years, when I might otherwise have developed if not a loving attachment then at least a verbal affinity to my mother. Instead I ended up unable to understand or speak my mother's tongue. She planned it that way, anticipating the day when I would be full of annoying questions. And when that day came she shut me off with a switch.

One night when I was about ten or eleven, she sneaked into my room, stuck an anti-gravity pad under my crib, put me into free fall, and woke me in the darkness, yelling, "Man overboard! Man overboard!" again and again, each time softer. I remember screaming my guts out, expecting any minute to smack the ground. Then she flicked the lights on and said to me, "Next time, kid, for real, you betcha." And next time I woke up thinking this was really it. And the time after that. I never really learned. I asked why once, just out of curiosity. She suggested that it was good exercise for my heart. I said, "I think it's broken." She quit doing that.

And then I'd wake up to find myself dressed in a plastic plant suit, arms painted green, hands and face pretty flower colors, my feet secured in a pot of hardened cement. I was to suppose that I had died in the night and been reborn accordingly. She'd leave me standing in my pot like that for hours, ignoring me completely except to water my shins and prune my nails. Occasionally she would threaten to harvest me. I'd scream. She'd pretend not to hear me. I'd call to the other plants for help. She'd taste me, biting, licking, chewing, without actually injuring me, physically, that is. I can't account for any mental damage. I know for sometime after I couldn't eat vegetables.

I can't count the number of nights I spent on my back trussed in a shell trying to right myself. This turtle phase went on for months. Followed by a brief fish phase. I woke up once dressed in fish scales inside a flushing toilet. I was too big to go down. I distinctly remember trying.

They weren't intentionally cruel. They just didn't know what else to do with me. Mimi Jo and her friends were of a generation so far removed in time from their own beginnings that they knew nothing of the subtleties of child growth and development. I was like a dog or a cat, a small creature born to be teased. More than anything else, I suppose, it was a problem of size, for as I grew bigger, and perhaps more cautious, their ways changed. Little tasteless pranks were replaced by subtler amusements. The holograms Uncle Michael cast into my room at night evolved from a rudimentary monster-executioner format to something a shade more religious in character; radiant beings would appear at my bedside with questions of a moral spiritual nature, such as, "What are you doing under there?" or invectives like, "Come and you die," until my tolerance for apparitions exceeded the power of his transmitter.

Escape was my constant preoccupation—escapes of the mind. I spent perhaps twenty percent of my early life in the swimming pool, not because I liked the water so much, but because the pool offered me the best view of the place I most wanted to be—earth. When extended, the pool hung down from the bottom of the house like a giant scrotum, a crystal-clear semi-flexible plastic sack full of warm, super-oxygenated water. I could remain submerged as long as I cared to, absorbing oxygen through the membrane of my mask. The bottom of the pool was curved in a particular shape to complement the lens of my mask, so that the view below was brought up close. By raising and lowering myself in the water I could adjust focus to match our altitude, and that's where I spent the best times of my life, at the level of good focus, taking in the glories of good mother earth below, pretending to flit from tree to tree as the house drifted. I used to think of myself as a sort of flying prune which all the wild things of the forests loved and brought their problems to.

No one ever understood my love for nature, except maybe Michael. They told me that the forests were just old pieces of carpet that people had thrown overboard, and that the oceans and lakes were merely accumulations of discarded tile and glass and broken mirrors. I knew better. I'd actually been there, both feet on the ground. My secret. Mine and Uncle Michael's. He took me down once, briefly, making me promise I would keep it to myself. I couldn't have been more than three, but I remember every detail. I was amazed at how huge each tree was, amazed that there could be so many, each one standing right there on the ground with nothing to hold it up, no straps, no lift engines, nothing but its own magnificent strength, which I assumed was magical. And I remember having to take a shit and Michael telling me I could shit right there if I wanted, right on the carpet. It was wonderful. I remember that too. It could very well be that my love of nature extends from the association made between what I saw and a most satisfying BM. Or it could simply be my love of that thing most certainly denied.

I had no friends my own age, of course. My closest and dearest were the bathroom fixtures that shared my space. Mimi Jo gave them all names for me. There was Chiticaca,

Geronimo, and Nantucket, three giant copper cobras which brought water into the bathtub. Water trickled like tears from the eyes of three little duck-billed creatures: Hewi, Dui, and Lewi. The wash basin was Chelsi the Clam, the crapper Perky Pelican. (Perky, by the way, could be made to snap its beak and flush with a button located *outside* my room.) These were my childhood friends, these and the aunts and uncles. I preferred the faucets.

Between teases and dips in the pool, I slept and watched television. I was very good at both. I could sleep on a dime, which is to say fast. Immediately. On request even. I was something of a champion go-to-sleeper. But television was my forte. I could watch twenty pictures on a subdivided screen with nearly seventeen percent comprehension. Beyond that, I had the near-psychic ability to *know,* just *know* exactly what was on any channel at any given time. With me around no one needed listings. And I mean *any* time, day or night, all fifty-three channels. It was uncanny. Three o'clock? *Ornery Cousin* on one, *Oh, Too Solid Wall* on two, *Sex* on three and four. *Let's Play Cards* on five, *Sex* on six, seven, and eight, *Sigh With Me* on nine, *Party Party* on ten, and so on for fifty-three stations.

I had my favorites, of course. *Party Party* allowed me to put a card table up against the one on-screen and join in the celebration, with big name stars to toast me, different stars every week. For whatever reason, I greatly preferred these upbeat, lively shows to what everyone else seemed to like. *Mombo Zombie* was the number-one rated show most of my life. Mombo Zombie did nothing. Absolutely nothing. He was dead for all I knew. He'd sit there and not move, a pose which was intended to put the viewer in a mood to do likewise, without fear of interruption. *Baseball Game* was another such show. *Let's Go To Heaven, Deep Breathing, Yoga, Test Pattern,* all of them highly rated shows.

Sex shows were of the same order of dullness until I acquired the taste. Along came puberty and I developed an outstanding preference for a certain computer-generated three dimensional cartoon figure on channel forty-three. It was an exaggerated variation on a female theme, called, simply, *Emmy Lou.* Her opposite number was *Mr. Big,* but for whatever reason, the figures of men did not arouse me, my one concession to nature's way. These computer-generated figures had one great advantage over the more fleshly realities ... well, actually several advantages, but one in particular. They changed. Emmy Lou was never the same girl, strictly speaking, from one moment to the next. The computer which provided her image was programmed to evolve it slowly, in unnoticeable increments from one gorgeous shape to another, always just one critical step ahead of the viewer's own rate of boredom. All the sex shows had evolving images, but Emmy Lou was fast; exactly suited to my personal needs. Just as I started to feel that I'd had enough of her, she'd roll over and be someone else. *Emmy Lou, Mr. Big,* and dozens of others were run continuously, day and night, on the sex channels; alone, in groups, doing or not doing unto other images, but always one thickness of glass away from being there in person. Which suited me fine.

The uncles and aunts found the separation painfully frustrating. They wanted what they called a "personal tactile olfactory experience" with what was known to be an "unobtainable nonexistent on-screen personality." They wanted *actual bodily contact!* Whereas I could be completely and entirely satisfied with the untouchable media image. That and my good right hand was all I ever needed.

This difference between us was no accident of nature, by the way. Chance alone might have made me thus, but they wouldn't leave anything so important as my sexual development to chance. No sir. I was conditioned. Psychologically conditioned.

The uncles and aunts didn't want me hungering after some cutie-pie in the classifieds, that is, someone outside the house. Faced with the eventual maturing of my sexual urges, and not wanting me plotting escapes day and night, they devised a little plan to keep me satisfied at home, where I could incur no threat to their social standing.

They started me at age eleven. They bought me a beanie cap with antennae and had me wear it whenever I watched TV. They told me I was the new antenna. I held out my arms for good reception and thanked them for the opportunity to be of some use. It turns out that all the while they were sending signals to the motivational centers of my brain by way of the hat, little yes's and no's. Yes's for girlish images, and no's for men, animals, objects of art, and the like. In very short, a liking for the female form. And then when I matured a little more and the urge blossomed full, it attached itself to the female images on TV, reinforced thereafter and evermore with every orgasmic reward my little hand could deliver.

Still, it was only natural for me to wonder about touch and

personal contact, so on my twelfth birthday they married me off to a big pillow-girl, a doll, lifelike in every respect, patterned after my current fancy on the TV screen. They made a big occasion out of it, full ceremonies, cake, the works. Come evening, the doll and I were sent off to the guest bedroom for our honeymoon. Already I wasn't too happy with it. But I did what I was expected to do, and the very instant I struck home the doll gave me a terrific electric shock and belched up bad smells in my face, nauseating gases that made me throw up. We didn't last the night. At my insistence the marriage was annulled and the doll thrown overboard. From that day till this I have an aversion to anything female which is solid, tactile, present, and real. No matter how visually pleasing, I don't want to touch it. Or smell it. Or have it touch me. Which is exactly how they wanted me to feel regarding sex. I don't recall ever desiring to leave home on account of sex. For other reasons, certainly, but not for sex. Their efforts were completely successful. *Too* successful, in fact.

In time they regretted having done it, for I matured beautifully, without need of plastic surgery. I became magnificently desirable. They hungered after me, the aunts and several of the uncles too, all of them except Mimi Jo, and every so often I'd catch even her looking at me shitty. But let one of them so much as touch me, and they'd have one mess to clean up. I got to where I could actually aim my vomit, and they soon learned in much the same way I did to keep their hands to themselves.

All except Uncle Alfred and Aunt Caroline. They took it very hard. Alfred couldn't get his mind off my virginal buns, and made vague threats to expose my existence to the press if the others wouldn't allow him to bind me and have a go. The others, to protect both themselves and me, got ahold of him one night and injected him with about fifty cc's of Esternot, a medication which relieves one of all sexual desiring. They held him down until it took effect, and afterward he thanked them for relieving him of the madness. From then on Alfred was not only able to do without *me*, he further declined all enticements to join the others. For days. Weeks. He even got self-righteous about it and began to chastise the others for their endless pointless orgies. Then one day he woke to discover that during the night, without waking, he'd chewed the toes off his right foot. He nearly bled to death.

Aunt Caroline was another one they had to subdue with medication. When Uncle Alfred showed up with his toes gone, they all looked to her for signs of the same behavior. But she seemed none the worse for it, and continued to take her medicine and preach against our evil ways, picking up the banner from poor Uncle A.

I was the first to notice anything amiss. She came into my room one evening, apparently bursting at the bladder to relieve herself in Perky. Mine was the only crapper in the house not exposed to full view. Apparently she had something she wanted to hide. I was asleep, or so she thought. I eased my hand out from under the covers, and when I heard that whistling sound of a woman pissing I snapped on the sun lamp. She screeched and quickly covered up, but not before I caught a glimpse of what seemed to be a small green shrub between her legs. It seems she'd packed her vaginal cavity with dirt and grown a carrot there. Word got around, naturally, and pretty soon everyone knew. She absolutely insisted it had nothing whatsoever to do with repressed urges or anything at all sexual. She maintained that she was pure. But tease her or try to pick it and she'd cut your hand off.

For my own protection I learned the cosmetic arts and made myself look ridiculous. With the daily application of creams I was able to prevent the appearance of any and all bodily hair—eyebrows, peach-fuzz, pubic thatch, absolutely everything but what grew from my scalp. That I kept long, down to my shoulders, blond with a flip. It was the style of the time to have big floppy ears, so I kept mine to the quick with a special solvent. I did my teeth in steel gray, and kept my skin bright and shiny with a high-gloss shellac. Most of the time I wore short skirts, lacey blouses, and thick black galoshes. For a time no one bothered me much. But as my luck would have it, each and every one of these styles and cosmetics became high fashion, and ultimately I was considered more beautiful than ever.

From the very first day, Mimi Jo refused to accept me as her son. Even after I became gorgeous. In fact, *especially* after I became gorgeous. She'd rage at me, "You're someone else's kid." I'd scream back, "And you're a sex fiend," which generally pleased her and had a calming effect. She enjoyed a tendency to go off on imaginary binges for days, weeks, years at a time—as did they all—and I would be included in her scenario, not as her son, but as some kind of slave or employee. While she was Queen of the Nile I was the food taster, and as such offered all sorts of unlikely delicacies to sample.

For my own safety I confined my diet to food tabs right from the dispenser. Tabs were safe, and untampered with. Where she got onto Egypt is beyond me. She'd wear sharp prongs on her nipples, call herself the great Nympho-Titty, and strut back and forth in the sand box hour after hour, pronouncing edicts, admonishing priests, and putting down unruly slaves, which could be anyone standing too close. I was promoted from food taster to chief architect, Builder of Pyramids, offered a plot in the Sahara and promised a good supply of stone to keep me busy. I declined.

I declined several opportunities for employment, both real and imaginary, throughout my early years. Uncle Nudgle wanted me on his moonball team, me first with the promise to organize the rest of the team later. Uncle Jack offered to set me up with a Sno-Cone concession on the cold side of Nix Olympicus, the biggest volcano on Mars. He was a member of the Rocket Club, and every seventh year he'd be looking for long distance volunteers. "How bout it, kid? You could be Adam to some slick Eve out there among the stars. Worth a try, don't you think?" I declined. Again and again I declined any and all such offers.

Until Uncle Michael gave me a chance at being farm boy on a snazzy new farm he'd "hacked out of the wilderness of North America." Actually it was a rental, something he'd run across in a catalog, a vintage "Dust-Bowler," with its very own windmill (guaranteed toppled), tractor (rusted), farm house and barn (both collapsed), all very authentic according to the period. Which appealed to Michael. It was isolated and therefore safe for me if I cared to join him. *Any* chance whatsoever to touch ground was thoroughly okay with me, so I went along.

And it was there that I learned the ways of our fathers: how to "till the soil," for example—not that we actually tilled any; it was in the little booklet along with instructions on how to "pray for rain," "husk the corn," "slop the pigs," and "hump the sheep." I got shots of Michael in his spiffy overalls beating the tractor with his wrench; Michael in the outhouse; Michael reading lines like, "Yep," and, "Looks like nother dry summer. Gall durn. Sand a-blowin, dust a-blowin. When will tever end." It was pouring down rain when I shot that scene. We were supposed to be having a drought. Neither one of us knew what "drought" meant. Michael thought it was some kind of boat. It was right there in the glossary too, if we'd bothered to look it up.

And then, on my nineteenth birthday, it was school. "Ya, ver finden a schoole for you to go to at last, unt get schmarter." A few years back I would have jumped at the chance. Now older, bigger, a wee bit wiser, I knew enough to know better. In a childless society, the word "school" had a mythological ring to it.

"Bullshit school."

Michael was in on it too. "Seriously, kid, we got a letter from your Uncle Theo. You remember Theo?" I did not. "Look, I have it right here. Read it yourself. He's agreed to become your teacher and open a school, just for you ."

"Bullshit letter. You wrote it and mailed it to yourself."

Michael and Mimi Jo both swore up and down it was authentic. I wanted out of the house, certainly, but on better terms. At nineteen I was legally entitled to free credit, a house of my own, and all the other customary artifacts of living. I knew it. They knew I knew it. The time had come.

"No, no, no, no!"

"But I'm tall."

"Yes, of course you are."

"You said. You said." They'd always said, "tall is all." "You promised." That single promise, that one day when I would be on my own, drew me on into life year after year more than any instinct to live. All that was required of me, they said, was to become *tall*, and hence not so recognizable as a young being, a "son" in the world at large where I just might expose Mimi Jo as a parent. I got myself plenty tall at age sixteen, but apparently not tall enough. I'd grunt. I used to think grunting would make me taller. They'd accuse me of making rude noises to annoy them, and send me to my room. Ten thousand times. Seventeen had me two centimeters taller than Uncle Ben. Still they kept me. I developed a raspy voice and a bleeding hemorrhoid grunting so much. And grew another 3.5 centimeters. *Still* it was no go. After all that, it turned out height wasn't the issue. They confessed.

"Boy, when you open your mouth people are going to wonder. And they're going to ask. And you're going to tell them. Now we can't have you telling them, can we?"

"I won't tell. Please. Daddy, I'm a big person. Just like you. I got control. Please? You promised! I won't tell anyone where I came from. Honest I won't."

"The point is, you're too obviously deficient. Two words out of your mouth and the evidence is simply overwhelming.

You've got no depth. So we're sending you to school, and that's final."

"Daddy. . . ."

"For one thing, *stop calling me Daddy!*"

"Father?" He was neither. Just an uncle, but the closest of them all.

Mimi Jo laid it on the line. "Uncle Theo has offered to make school for you unt you goen. You bet!"

"Where? Pluto? I'm not going."

"Right here on earth."

"Uh-uh."

"I thought you'd be delighted. I really did." Michael began affecting a disinterested stance.

"It's a trick."

"All right, never mind then. Forget I ever mentioned it."

"Isn't it?"

"No. It's not a trick."

"Yes it is. Yes it is. You're trying to trick me."

"What do you intend to do with the rest of your life, if I may ask?"

"*Do?? Do??* What do *You* do?? You sit around the house. You think I can't do that? Just get me a house and see."

"I do *not* sit around the house, although to you it may appear that way. I relate. I relate to the surroundings, to the company of others, to. . . ."

"Mother."

"Go to your room."

"No. I won't go."

"Go."

"You can't make me. I'm nineteen. I'm legal."

"But I can, you see, by virtue of my greater strength."

"Aw. . . ."

"*Now!*"

He was right. I was less than intelligent, less than adult. I did not turn out quite right. I was a twerp and a wienie, and I don't deny it. With my upbringing, how could I have been otherwise? I *was* in need of an education. I could read, but only slowly, sounding out the words. I could not write. I knew the vowels and could draw most of those okay, but not the consonants. I could imagine no use whatsoever for the consonants. I rarely used them in my speech. They slipped my grasp by virtue of their seeming unimportance. And at nineteen I was still prone to soil my pants. I had number one down pat, but it seems I would two any old where. I think this was more due to the fact that I shit so very infrequently than to any supposed retardation. I shit only once a month. No more. I simply lacked sufficient opportunity to learn control. My food tabs were so totally digestible that by the time one reached bottom there'd be nothing left to pass. What did pass, once a month, was a normal intake of dust, which my system converted to tiny pellets, which were nevertheless smelly enough to announce their presence every time. Impossible to deny.

I had no depth. Michael was right. Even my dreams were empty. I tended to dream, not in dramatic episodes the way others did, but in colors. Solid colors. Blues, mostly. Greens I considered a good night. I used to hate any shade of yellow. Yellow was my nightmare, don't ask why.

I had no talents either, other than those I've mentioned. I couldn't even play the games of the day, except to bet against a coin flip, and even at that I would lose half the time.

I might have killed myself. I was certainly given plenty of opportunity and inspiration, but on those rare occasions when I contemplated the Great Beyond, I saw in my mind an eternity filled with souls with nothing whatsoever to do but roam the infinite in search of diversions. I assumed the earth to be one such diversion, an amusement park for the soul, a body to take a ride in, a place to kill time. I reasoned that the Beyond could not possibly be a better place than the earth, for why would the powers-that-be go to so much trouble to make a worse place? Or go to such lengths to keep us in ignorance of the hereafter if the hereafter wasn't an unpleasant thing to know? So even in my cosmology I found no hope. If I'd killed myself, I knew with unshakeable certainty that I'd wake up on the other side surrounded by the souls of the departed, pointing, laughing and shouting, "You thought you had nothing to live for? Let me tell you, *this* is nothing to live for. And it's *forever*."

On the other hand, I didn't have all that much to look forward to in mortal life—nothing but a slow assimilation into society at large, which, after all, was just more of what went on at home. I asked them once why they kept at it so, with their imaginary games and their endless fucking. They said when I got to be their age I'd understand. They were all pushing nine hundred some. Apparently, the older one gets the more basic the wants, instead of the other way around as one might suppose. I am becoming more contemplative myself, but I'm only twenty now, so who am I to say?

By way of introduction: my first given name was Octopus, out of Jocasta, a tragic Greek phase Mimi Jo went through shortly after my birth. A later Roman phase saw me renamed Marcus Aurelius. Michael, the uncle I called Dad, maintained an old last name which he allowed me to use. Since in a manner of speaking we three comprised a family, we were all of us Hornblowers, with various and assorted first names to suit the trends and moods. But of all the first names, Michael stuck with Michael, my mother hung on to Mimi Jo, and I remain to this day, yours truly, Marcus Aurelius Hornblower.

How do you do!

2

"Mark, where are you?" I was available by intercom any time, any place in the house. I was required to answer promptly.

"In the pool."

"Well, dry yourself off and come upstairs. We got a surprise for you."

"What kind of surprise?"

"You'll see."

"I'll pass, thank you."

"It's a birthday present. Happy birthday."

"My birthday was last week."

"Well, hey, yeah, I know. And look. We forgot to get you a present. So to make up for it, we went out and bought you the most wonderful surprise."

"Sleeping pills?"

"You needn't be sarcastic."

"Whatever it is, I don't want it."

"It's your wings."

"................"

Only a week to think about it, and I'd already put it together in my head that the offer of school and my coming of legal age (both on the very same day) was no coincidence. At nineteen, by ancient but unchanged law, I was due my place in the Free Market—a house, a credit number, and a terminal to the system of automatic supply, these being the three necessities of life, the birthright of every Free Marketeer no matter how recently born. But the granting of my rightful estate would have been equal to the spilling of the beans. Given that I might have somehow managed to sneak my house in unnoticed among the others and then initiated a few purchases without arousing curiosity, sooner or later I would have made that first human contact, and the big stir that Mimi Jo and her friends dreaded would inevitably have followed. The moment I turned nineteen they were faced with that problem: how to maintain the secret and at the same time comply with the law.

Uncle Theo, an uncle whom I did not know but who obviously knew about me, came through at the very moment of need by offering the best and perhaps only solution: school. The catch being that my consent was needed. At nineteen, as a legal person, I could choose to go or not to go to school as I desired. Therefore, and in recognition of this set of circumstances, I knew I should expect a bribe. I anticipated a bribe. I might even have anticipated the precise item if I'd been mathematical, for there was one thing that carried a very high desirability quotient with me, relative to cost. For the same reason that a bird in the hand is worth two in the bush, I could be counted on to give up my birthright for a pair of kiddie wings.

"Yeah . . . bullshit."

"Oh . . . well, all right. We'll send them back."

"NO! WAIT!!!"

I surfaced like a porpoise, slipped into a robe, and ran wet to the elevator, arriving in the living room still dripping.

"Well, don't just stand there. Open it."

"No shit."

I'd been promised wings many times before, in return for my good behavior. Flawless obedience for the specified period of time, and did I ever get my wings? Hardly. "We never said when. You'll get them. Someday. Didn't we promise?" Wings meant perfect freedom, both symbolically and in point of fact. Symbolic freedom they could have lived with, but the real thing was out of the question. Their argument was simple: if we let you out on your own, even for a moment, what's to prevent you from flying away with the secret? I'd argue that they could take me to some unpopular continent and let me fuss around where I wouldn't be seen. Their argument to that was, "You never can tell."

I found Michael settled into the davenport fondling his pipe, with Mimi Jo curled up beside him, pretending to be napping. The act of giving always embarrassed her; she would watch between the lashes. Upon the coffee table sat a big bright lavender box with a red ribbon. And a card: "To Mark from the Hornblowers." I looked to Michael, tears streaming down my cheeks.

"Go on, open it up."

Of course I did it immediately, although I should have known better than to dive too carelessly into an attractively wrapped package. I should have considered, examined, listened with a stethoscope, taken X-rays. Why should I believe that this time, at long last, there would be a wing pack within and not a bomb? Because if there wasn't a wing pack, then I *wanted* the bomb. I tore wildly into the box like a hungry crazed beast at the belly of its prey, drooling with expectation.

"Oh God. Oh God, please let it be."

I exposed in short order a backpack, a pink and gold flecked green false leatherette backpack with bright orange harness straps, and a six-point pressure-lock silver and gold safety buckle. I lifted it up off the table. "Please God. Please." I set the pack on the floor, reached for the side, felt for, found and extended the two over-shoulder hand grips. All was in order so far, but were there wings inside?

I would have to put the pack on in order to find out. I was about to do so when Michael jumped up and came at me, saying, "Uh-uh. It's yours to look at, but if there's any flying to be done, I'll do it. You hear? Now hand it over to me. Come on, gimme the pack."

"NO . . . MICHAEL . . . NO, PLEASE . . ."

Rather than argue, he simply snatched the pack out of my embrace, told me to shut up and watch him. Mimi Jo sat up, rubbed her eyes, saw what Michael was up to and said, "You not gonna fly, are you? Michael, no. You kill yourself."

"Just don't worry now. I know what I'm doing." He hefted the pack to his shoulders, put his arms through the loops, reached behind for the straps and wrapped himself up one strap at a time, jamming the end cleats into the safety buckle, two from the shoulder, two around the waist, two up from between the legs, making a couple of adjustments for size. He positioned the grips for easy reach, walked to the center of the room, paused a moment to test the lift unit. He rose up to the ceiling, hovered a moment, then settled back down on the carpet, full weight.

Mimi Jo got herself up from the davenport, put on a serious look of concern and said, "No, Michael. You no wanna do dat." Too late. He marched boldly across the room, out the door onto the patio, stepped up onto one of the outdoor chairs, from there to the table no break in stride, and leapt clean over the railing. I gulped. Mimi Jo screamed. We looked at each other and dashed to the window.

We missed his plummet. By the time we got to the window he had the wings spread. Beautiful, beautiful, beautiful, peach and burgundy wings in two sets of two, a pair of Binks Butterflies, a brand not known so much for speed as for safety.

I couldn't bear watching him on *my* wings. But I couldn't bear not to watch him. He did some un-fancy stuff, a couple of slow turns, a lazy eight, a stall, a brief tuck and plummet for speed on a half-completed inside loop. I watched intently as he disappeared from sight. I kept my eyes glued on the point of his disappearance, and in a moment there he was again, wings in the pack, rising up on lift power. He came up a few meters out from the patio, continued on up a ways before spreading wings again for a short glide to a point directly overhead. Then he pulled in on the grips, tucked the wings back inside the pack one last time, and made a very nice touch-down on the same table that launched him. A little bow to those inside watching.

Mimi Jo applauded wildly. I said, "PLEEEEEESE."

He got down off the table, popped the buckle, dropped the pack, stepped out of the entanglement of straps and said, "No, Mark. Not around here. Someone's sure to see you." His statement did not carry the usual note of finality. An invitation for me to beg. New burst of joy.

"The ocean. We can go over the ocean."

"No, no. You'll want to touch down, try a landing."

"Oh, Michael, Michael. Anywhere. You name it." I found myself jumping up and down, clapping my hands together.

"I can't imagine where."

"North Pole."

"Too many picnickers. You'll be seen."

"Picnickers?"

"Mark . . ."

"Uh . . . uh . . . North America. South America. Australia."

"Well, which is it?"

"Australia?"

"North America is closer."

"North America. North America. Oh, Michael. North America."

"Wait a minute, no. Too many trees there. Too many trees. You'd get yourself all tangled up and I'd have to call for help. Won't do."

"There's trees everywhere, what do you mean?" He was leading me on. Every choice would appear to be my very own. To me that is. I suggested a clearing, obviously. He thought it over and agreed that a clearing in North America would be suitable. But the time of day where we happened to be put the west coast of North America in the late afternoon, unless . . . "Can we go fast? Can we? Huh?"

"For you, seeing as it's your birthday, give or take a week, well. . . ."

"Michael, pleeeeese!"

"One thing. . . ."

"School." I knew. Of course I knew.

"You've got to promise."

"I do. I do. I promise. Michael, I promise."

"Let's say it for the record, okay?"

"I did. I did."

"You know what I mean."

"Do I have to?"

"Do you want to fly?"

" . . . ."

To the ceiling he said, "System?" A soft acknowledging beep. "Record this, please, and file access under Hornblower, M.A., contractual agreement. . . ." He went on, giving the date and what-have-you; then reading from a little card he happened to have in his pocket: "For valuable consideration (meaning the wings). . . ."

I repeated: "For valuable consideration. . . ."

"I, Marcus Aurelius Hornblower, do solemnly swear that if I am allowed to fly I will go to school."

"I, Marcus Aurelius Hornblower, do solemnly swear that if I am allowed to fly I will go to school, cross my fingers . . . I mean, *heart*, and hope to die. I promise."

Our contract did not specify exactly *when* I would go to school, or where, or what subjects, or for how long. In the back of my mind I figured a couple of hours of Desert Appreciation commencing in about two hundred years would satisfy all terms. It seemed to me that he should have known better than to leave such a gaping weasel-hole. On the other hand, I wasn't going to be the one to point it out to him.

"All right, Mark. I have your promise. Run along up to the map room and pick out a clearing."

I was up there in a shot, calling up North America onscreen. I requested an illumination of all suitable clearings near our present course line. We were already in motion on an easterly heading. I was queried by the navigation system as to the meaning of "suitable" in the present context. I said, "Big enough to land in," and got for my request seventeen blips along the west coast of the continent.

Michael came up beside me. "Go on, pick one," he said, making it *my* choice. In retrospect, I'd say that I could have been counted on to choose the one nearest our present position.

"Can I touch it?"

"Sure. Go ahead."

A touch was all the system needed. An expanded view of the general area surrounding my choice came up on the big screen. I ran over and touched the exact center of what appeared to be a big, round, grassy field, not unlike the sort of place professional flyers used to use in competitive landing exhibitions, long, long ago. Almost too perfectly round, but it was my decision and my choice all the way. I had no reason to suspect anything, so I didn't.

Projected ETA came up: 9:42 local, twilight over there, except I had already been promised a full-speed flight across. "Michael, you said...."

"Would I forget?"

The command for sub-orbital flight was, "Step on it." Michael gave the command; the system took it from there, computing a new ETA of 3:28 local. Travel time: two hours and five minutes.

Immediately the patio, which stuck out from the house like a drawer, slid shut and tucked itself away. Metal awnings closed down over all the windows. The pool retracted, the toilets flushed and drained, various cupboard doors left open around the house slammed shut and locked. Magnetization secured the bric-a-brac and miscellaneous dishes. All chairs swiveled to face forward and inclined slightly to accept the G-load of their passengers. With everything in order, the secure-to-quarters sounded; just a polite word from the ceiling to find the nearest chair and be seated, which we all rushed to do.

After a brief burst of thrust from the seldom-used auxiliary lift engines, we found ourselves in free fall. Mimi Jo drifted around the house picking up loose odds and ends. Mike pushed off after her with lust in his eyes. I went back to the living room, scrambled into the harness of the pack, but refrained from spreading wings inside the house, knowing it was bad luck to do so. I spread my arms instead and flew with my eyes shut, pretending to be outside, where in just a short time I would finally be for real.

The arrival bell rang. We got ourselves sitting down for a leisurely re-entry. At 5000 meters motions ceased, and everything opened back up. Michael cautioned me: "Hold on, Mark. Not yet." I leaned out the window and looked down. I could see directly below us, not more than a couple of kilometers from the coastline, a tiny circle of light green grass amid the darker tree-green of the Great American Forest. My target, winking at me seductively. I was more than ready to go, but there would be some ritual delay, some preparations. A flyer's suit was needed.

"I don't need a suit."

"What if you get lost? You'll freeze to death in that thing. Come."

"Aw, Michael. How can I get lost?"

"Mark, do as I tell you." He led me downstairs one flight into his own private dressing room, the second largest one in the house. (Mimi Jo's was slightly bigger, but then she owned the place. Technically, at least.) "Well, Mark," he said, taking his good old time. He thumbed through the index, came to the section marked "Flying," put up on the display screen miniature outlines of his available stock, chose F.S. 28 as the most practical, punched in the number, and stood back while his wardrobe swept past him on the conveyor. "One of these ought to do. We're about the same size now, old sock, what do you think about that?"

"Michael, do we have to?"

The rack stopped. F.S. 28 was a strictly functional affair, solid white, one piece, tight-fitting around the waist, chest, arms, and legs, everywhere except at the joints, which had accordion pleats for ease of motion. The whole thing was lined with a fine mesh of heating wire for those cold high-altitude ascents. With the suit came a pair of white silken slippers with plug connectors to match.

Fifty-two mirrors couldn't lie. I looked stunning. Michael slapped me on the butt to recapture my attention. "I'll take your picture going down and we'll run it when you get back, what do you say to that? Now strap up, and let's get it right this time." He made more adjustments than I considered necessary, and when I was suited, strapped, buckled and ready to go, he asked, "How's it feel?"

"Kind of heavy."

"You can take off weight with the lift unit, but wait until you get outside so you don't crack your head on the ceiling. Now remember, land like I told you, nothing fancy yet. If you end up over the trees, pull up and fly back over the clearing before you attempt a landing."

"Yeah, I know."

"I assume you know what to do when you get out there. Just push on the grips."

"I know. I know."

"You know about these." He ran his hand under the cords along the shoulder straps. "The left one is the up-cord and the right one is the down-cord. Left up, right down. If you forget, it's automatic. So don't worry."

"Aw, come on." I spent more hours in front of the TV watching the old professionals than most people fifty times my age.

"When you get close to the ground, settle out, get vertical, then kick your feet the way I told you. Get running along with the wind, then ease down. Don't worry about what it looks like."

"Jesus, can I go now?" He smiled.

We returned to the front room where Mimi Jo was waiting. She was dressed for the occasion in a leather jacket, raised goggles, and a long white scarf. "Mark, so hansom, you looken goot. Giff Mimi kiss." She presented her cheek and I pecked accordingly, while Mike hauled out the camera to record that unprecedented event for the uncles and aunts.

The three of us walked ceremoniously to the porch railing. The moment of moments—my life-long dream. And I was scared.

"Oooo, Mike, I don't know. I feel funny."

"Well of course you do, but you got wings now, boy. Wings. Think of it."

"Yeah, I don't know." For after all, the railing was still the railing.

"Giff Mimi anudder goo by kiss, you svell looken ting you."

"Not now, Mimi Jo. I feel funny."

"Just step up there. Atta boy. Now one more step."

I got myself up on the table all right, and then at the last moment the decision wasn't mine. Four firm hands grabbed my two legs and lifted me up and over. I fell screaming: IIIEEeee e e." I knew for sure that somehow they'd switched packs and given me one full of bricks.

Nevertheless, at around 3000 meters it occurred to me that I might at least test my theory. All it took was a gentle push on the grips, and if no wings came out at least I couldn't fall any worse. I pushed out on the grips. From that moment, and for the next few minutes, life flopped around and became marvelous. The big wings shot out of the pack and concerted all that speed I had accumulated into one magnificent huge inside turn. I said, "Oh, Michael. Thank you."

I came out of my loop and flew for a long time in a straight line south, out from the clearing and over the trees, then eased in on my left grip to execute a left turn, a slow, gentle sweep to the east and north again, back over the clearing. Then I retracted both wings, plummeted to pick up speed again. Just a little. I jerked out on both handles, caught the wind with a loud "pop" and shot straight up until I stalled out, whereupon I flopped over on my back, a wee bit out of control, but loving it. A simple left tuck brought me around, no panic, no fear at all. Just immaculate fun.

I spiraled down the last thousand meters or so, tightening my circle on the center of the clearing, getting ready for the tricky part. I wanted to do a power-off touch-down my first time out, but the equipment knew better and took over. The lift unit came on and slowed my descent more and more, until my wings lost the wind and fell slack. This left me hanging vertically one meter above the grass, drifting across the clearing with the wind. So I did it the way Mike recommended, kicking my feet in a mid-air run. When it felt right I eased gently down on the cord, running with the wind until I had enough weight on the ground to bring myself to a stop.

I felt delirious. Ecstatic. I looked up to the folks and waved for the camera. "Thank you, oh thank. . . ."

I was waving to no one. Just a clear and cloudless sky, no speck in the distance—nothing. Well, of course. They'd done it again, but this time they'd done a good thorough job of it. This time they weren't just playing around to amuse themselves.

I'd been ditched.

3

Ditching was an old and settled issue. The law prohibited it. There would be the bi-monthly census, a Zurich inquiry as to the whereabouts of each and every one on the list. Even me. If I were not at home, in person, live on-camera, the Zurich system would switch automatically into a search mode, beginning with a sternly worded request for the legal mother to present herself for immediate questioning. She would be asked where I was. She would say school. A release statement would be requested. She would play back the record, our contract. So far, so good. The computer would open a line to said school and call for my appearance. Then what? No school, no me. She would be in trouble. Only in the meantime, *I* was in trouble.

Serious trouble. I had my wings, but Bink's Butterflies, as gorgeous as they were, had the air speed of a falling leaf; they were entirely unsuitable for a trans-Pacific crossing. For what it was worth, I had the Western Hemisphere at my disposal, but that was an empty, unpopulated place, shunned by the free-floating cluster of homes and shops that made up the Free Market.

I rummaged through every pocket in both pack and suit for a phone; I found nothing but a half-empty canteen and a tube of bug cleaner for the wing struts. Twenty zipper pockets, and not a phone in any of them.

There had to be some trick. My only consolation. The law was the law and they would not risk the secret. My contract was valid only if the place where they had left me would qualify as a school, which . . . well, I did learn to land there.

I learned to take off from there too. I made several trips up on lift power, waving and flapping my big wings to anyone who might see me, perfectly aware that I'd never be seen in a hundred years of flapping except by those who knew exactly where to look. And they knew without my having to flap.

Since I wasn't rescued immediately, or within the first hour, or the next, or the next, I knew that somehow they'd done it. Legally. To the letter of the law. I was a ditched individual, and by the time the day ended, with no sign of help either human or mechanical, I felt pretty sure that that was that.

So what did I care? Hadn't I always wanted exactly what I was getting? Just me and nature nose to nose? I gave it plenty of thought.

No.

Yes to the extent that the earth, its trees and birds and all the furry creatures were aesthetically pleasing to me, a favored decor, so to speak, one I liked to have around, but *no*. I did not want to have to depend on it for survival. I did not want to have to eat it or any part of it to stay alive. It would have been like eating the living room. I would die first.

That's no exaggeration. I've given quite a bit of thought to what would have become of me left alone in the wilderness with just my wings and my wits. I would have starved to death. What I knew of natural survival could have been written on the head of a pin. Longhand. Of farming I knew even less. My two weeks on the farm gave me knowledge only that plants were once consumed as food, a fact I might have missed otherwise. But of their cultivation I knew nothing. I could dress, pose, and speak like a farmer. I could pour endless buckets of water into the well. I could artificially inseminate our stuffed bull. But raise one grain of cucumber, one patch of wheat, one stalk of pumpkin—not in a million years. So it was just as well that in the evening hours, in the center of the clearing, as the long shadows of the forest crept my way, I began to dig my grave.

I'd witnessed the digging of several graves on TV—a spade jabbed in the ground, a dissolve, a hole. What happened during the dissolve was anybody's guess. I managed a rather shallow grave by comparison; only an inch or so deep. Just an impression in the grass, really. For a cross, two sticks that would not join no matter how hard I pressed them together. So I set them across one another in the grass at my side, lay down, shut my eyes, and made every effort to be dead.

I could not die. Nothing seemed to work. Another of the

lost arts, something missed in the dissolves. I tried last lines: "Forgive them, for they know not what they do." Still conscious. "This then is my last good-bye." Nothing. "Tell Carol I forgive her." Strong and healthy. "Give my regards to old Broadway, and tell them I will soon be there." Which got my foot to tapping so that I had to kick it with the other one to make it stop.

Obviously, I didn't know how to die except by inflicting injury on myself, and in scenes like these suicides were never called for. For quite some time I simply lay still, thinking any minute now nature will take her course and I will die. But nature had working against it, in the short run, a perfect balance of nutrients from my morning food tab, and in the long run my inoculations against every possible illness, including age.

I made the usual emotional scene, the cry, followed by the screaming rage tapering off into a whimpering beg, an act which usually qualified me for a laugh and a tease followed by a return to normality. No one so much as sneezed. I began to consider seriously the possibility that I might really be alone, and looked around for a camera. Somewhere there had to be a camera, hovering near, not so easily seen in the day, but night was on. It would ncessarily have a flashing beacon to warn away flyers. And indeed, the moment I looked up I saw a brilliant flashing star of purple hue. Only it wasn't a camera. The color was wrong, and the code, too—four shorts, pause, two shorts. It was the "hi" sign of a free flyer looking for company. A human being on wings coming my way.

I'd studied the fast flicker and dart of the night flyer all my life from the confines of my swimming pool. I knew their codes. I tried once to blink the pool lights in a vain attempt to attract them to me, but we were never so low that they could come to me on wings. But this time, seeing the blink, realizing that I had no watery envelope to stop me, I pulled the up-cord and rose straight up into the sky. My own beacon lit up with the application of lift, one short, one long, "A" for amateur class. At once the other light veered off toward me.

I'd watched enough flyers in competition on TV to know a few things about the art, and this person was good. He flew with a minimum of undulations, a straight-line course through both vertical and horizontal planes—a feat requiring a sensitivity finely tuned to available thermals and up-drafts. I pooped along like a jellyfish, up and down, losing altitude and gaining ground at about the same rate. The other flyer took my inadequacies into account and managed to be waiting where he knew I would be, only I didn't yet know quite how to manage a mid-air stop. I passed him, shouting, "Wait for me!" He *was* waiting. Perfectly still. He understood my problem and followed while I grappled with the up-cord and finally brought myself to a stop. He swooshed past me, cut back sharply, did a perfect Tinkerbell turn followed by an abrupt stop with cup and flare. The draft of his big wings pushed me away slightly. Only then, after coming to a complete stop, did he condescend to use the lift power to hold himself in position. This person was an expert, and for that reason, even before I saw him face to face, I knew that I was about to meet the first human being who was not one of Mimi Jo's regulars. My first stranger.

I didn't know what to say or how to behave. Which alone would have made me nervous, but on top of that he was as far as I could tell a perfect being—flawless. Never mind his character and personality, mere abstracts. Going strictly by what was visible, I found myself in a sweat. He draped himself in perfect posture, loose and limp, bare feet, toes pointing down, head back, Adam's apple foremost. He wore a flyer's suit of the type barred from Olympic competition because it was just too good: a film of hexoplaner, one molecule thick, virtually as light as the emperor's new clothes, worn not for warmth or vanity but to improve the air flow over the skin. He was himself about as thin as surgery could make him, hollowed and shaped, unnecessary organs removed or trimmed, and otherwise rendered more aerodynamically sound than some birds, another Olympic no-no. To top it off, his skin was silver, still another professional trick to avoid the extra weight of suntan lotion.

He had on a pair of the most gorgeous wings—micromembranous Spalding Eight-Eighty racers with hollowed boron epoxy struts, worth easily a thousand Free Marks. Total weight of the pack was less than nine kilograms (including lift unit, which couldn't have been any bigger than a tennis ball). Variable contour wings, with feather tips and touch controls; oh, God. Such a one.

He gave me plenty of time our first moments together to come up with something decent to say. He waited. I thought. He smiled. I sweated. He looked me up and down. "Hello" would have been appropriate. He left it to me to speak first.

It took every ounce of concentration to overcome my intimidation and blurt out, "You angel."

Good enough. He smiled and began a long, beautifully worded reply: "Ah, where the relatively cool moisture-laden ocean breezes contact the warm dry air off the inland basin, there we find our little up-drafts. But I caution you. Beware the occluded front, my friend, for therein lies much turbulence and precipitation, varying in intensity relative to the difference in barometric pressure between the warm and cold air masses on either side."

"Oooooooo."

"We shall speak of these and many other things another day. For now, I invite you to be my guest, fellow flyer. Follow me and we shall fly together, you and I, to my castle on the mountain. There you shall find contentment for awhile. Spread wing, my friend, and fly with me. Fly, fly, fly. . . ."

So saying, he flew and I did what I could. He flew with no loss of altitude, riding the coastal currents north along the beach to the hills, circling back every so often to nudge me along. I went up and down, up and down, the only way I knew how, the only way anybody could have flown on a pair of metal strutted two-by-two butterfly baggies.

We came to a castle, sure enough. Our approach was from the south where the beach turned at the top of the bay. My first sight of the place was a silhouette against the setting moon. It was a turreted, spired, drawbridged, pennanted castle—a ruin, I suppose, spruced up. Someone's hobby.

He led me into the valley below the southern portico. As we came over the top of the last hill, he dove suddenly to pick up speed, then raced straight down to the bottom of the canyon like a hawk. A fraction of a second before crashing into the ground he spread his wings full, caught the ground cushion, and shot up into the air again along the opposite side of the canyon. On the way up, at precisely the correct moment, he folded his wings down flat against his side and let his momentum carry him the rest of the way up to the top of the castle wall. As he coasted to a stop, just before gravity had its chance to pull him back down, he put one foot out and stepped smartly onto the top of the wall, like there was nothing at all to it, another power-off stop *on target*.

I landed the only way I knew how, settling in on lift power, kicking my feet with the wind. He waved me in, and when I touched down he smiled and said, "We were all beginners once. No need to feel ashamed. Come. Walk with me now. It's easy. Just put one foot out and . . . there, you have it. One, two. . . ."

He "one-twoed" me all the way down the stairs, which ran along the outside wall into the courtyard and across the southwest colonnade, which had many rooms, all but one boarded up. He paused in a big archway, posed himself like a Parrish neuter against the moonset, and pointed out to sea. "Behold, standing here on a clear day one can see the Isle of Catalina, where rests the fabled city of Avalon. I have never been there, nor shall I ever. Far better it remain a mystery. Ah, but you are weary. Come. You shall be my guest."

He broke pose, turned, and led me to the one room which did not have slats nailed across the windows, a corner room with two sides to the ocean. The door was open, the light was on. A bed was waiting. "Tomorrow we shall speak of many things," he said. "But for now, rest. The hour is late."

Hard as I tried I still couldn't come up with anything polished to say. The best I could do was repeat my earlier question: "You angel?"

He nodded. "You're welcome," he said, and left me to figure out for myself how to act when for the first time in your life you're someone else's guest.

Sleep and the chemistry of a morning tab, a single tab I found in a cupid-adorned dish by my bed, took away the panic of the night before. In the light of day, recalling the improbable being, the kind stranger, as much as I appreciated his efforts on my behalf I had to admit he seemed a trifle peculiar. As though I had dreamed the question, I woke up answering, "No. He's not perfection personified, despite my earlier opinion, a judgment passed in a moment of desperation. He's a weird creature." I thought and considered very seriously the possibility that I might have been better off in my little grave. On the other hand (and I considered this), here I was, a cloistered child, with direct knowledge of but one hundred and two uncles and aunts, assessing not a TV personality, but a real human being. For all I knew the uncles and aunts were weird and this shiny eunuch plain average. So spoke the voice of reason. In my heart, though, I knew who was weird and who wasn't.

I took my time getting up, lingered in the tub, spent too long in the dryer, fussed overly with my suit, avoiding the duties of my obligation. I didn't know how to behave with people, and wasn't the least bit anxious to learn. Not with a stranger, no matter how kind. Finally, when I'd primped and buffed myself to a glistening shine, I stepped outside. There he was, poised on the turret top, staring off toward the Isle of Catalina, a breeze rippling his long golden gown, sun glistening off his little silver head, waiting for me to catch him posed against the sky. Likely waiting all morning. He heard my door open and stiffened a little. Chin up. Striking pose.

I yelled up to him: "Hi!" He turned to face me, lowered his gaze, beat his chest once smartly (the centurion salute), and bade me join him on the tower so that he and I together might "usher in another glorious day." I figured he'd done pretty well by himself, since according to my watch it was half-past noon. He met me on the way upstairs and diverted me into a room halfway up the turret, a room outfitted with a desk, a few chairs, millions of books and tapes; such a library as I'd never seen before. And a lovely viewport overlooking the bay. A picture window. He offered me a chair in front of him by the desk, continued around to a bigger chair on the other side, and sat down. He brought his hands together, fingers spread tip to tip, swiveled toward the window and back, and said, "Are you well rested?"

"Sorry I took so long getting up, but I usually sleep sorta...."

"Have you fed?"

"Yes, thank you."

"Very well." From the top drawer of his desk he withdrew a sheet of paper and a stopwatch. "Are you comfortable?"

"Yeah, pretty much so. I wish this chair swiveled like yours."

"Perhaps someday. In the meantime...." He pushed the piece of paper across the desk to me but kept his hand on it. "This is your paper. Do not turn your paper over until I tell you to do so. When I tell you to do so, turn your paper over. Then read the question at the top of the page. Select *one* of the *four* answers below. Select only that answer which you believe best answers the question. Any questions?"

"What??"

"You have sixty seconds." He looked down at the stopwatch in the palm of his hand. "Go." He clicked it.

"Go?"

"Time's wasting."

"But..."

"Turn the paper over and read the question."

"Oh. Okay. Sure."

It said: The New Universal One-Question Test of Intelligence, Personality, and Gender. Question: if a stitch in time saves nine, how many are saved by two stitches in time?

Below, waiting for my check, were the four answers:

    A. Eighteen (18)
    B. Eight (8)
    C. None of these (0)
    D. One of these (1)

"Answer the question. Mark the square. Hurry."

I drew my "x" beside the letter of my choice.

"Now turn your paper over and hand it to me." Which I did.

Click. "Forty-five seconds. Not bad."

He slid the paper across the desk without turning it over. He leaned back in his big chair and swiveled slowly to the left for a thoughtful profile. He held a pencil up to his mouth and carefully bit the eraser. He swiveled back again to face me, sat up straight, set the pencil down on the desk, folded his hands, rested them on top of my paper, stared me in the eye, and said, "I haven't looked at your answer, you understand."

"Ah, er, no. Yes. I mean, yes, I understand that, only I don't understand what's going on."

"Did you chose 'A'?"

"No, I chose. . . ."

"Ah, ah, ah—don't tell me."

"No?"

"Of course, 'A' has an immediate appeal. It is given that one stitch has the power to save nine, but one must not infer from that the effect of two stitches. That is for science to demonstrate; it is not yours to infer. Had it been given that two stitches save eighteen, then you would have done well to choose that answer. However, that would have been no test at all. No test, no way to determine your real worth."

"Wait a minute. . . ."

" 'B' seems reasonable, doesn't it? If there are nine stitches pending the one, then the one sewn leaves but eight to sew. Choosing 'B' is your way of saying, 'Certainly the second stitch must save the remaining eight.' But of course, a moment's reflection reveals the absurdity of such a notion. I won't even go into it. I sincerely hope *you* didn't."

"But . . ."

" 'C' is interesting, though. It is uniquely self-exclusive. However, if 'None of these' is correct, then neither is 'C.' Ho ho. That's a fooler, that one. If your answer was 'C,' then, young man, we have a great deal in common, you and I. When I was your age, I chose 'C.' But I was wrong. Oh, yes. I admit it. And I believe I have learned to accept it."

For an instant I found myself in the strange position where a smile or a nod from me might have put *him* at ease. I let it pass, I'm afraid. He turned in his chair and gazed toward Catalina again, then turned back to business.

" 'D' is correct, of course. 'D' states that one of these is correct. Which one? 'D,' of course. I wish I had thought of that when I first took this test. You are quite a bit luckier than I, you know. Yes. You have been born into an age of permissiveness. Bless you, bless your peers, if you have any. Because of the new rules you, my young friend, are permitted to take the test again. There is no penalty for taking the test a second time. Not any more. Go ahead, my child. Do it. Take it over. Please, please. Use that eraser of yours and be glad you don't have to suffer what I suffered in my time. Oh, God . . . never mind, never mind. Take it and be thankful."

"Thank you, but . . . but I chose 'D.' "

He stopped short, looked me in the eye, tapped his finger seriously three times on my folded paper, and said, "I have your paper right here. You *do* know that."

"I know."

"I still haven't looked at your choice."

"I know."

"Let me clarify before we continue further that you are free to take the test a second time, or did I say that? There is no penalty for taking the test a second time. I did. I said that. I won't say it again."

"That's all right. I chose 'D.' "

"Very well." He opened the paper at last, looked at my choice and grimaced. " 'D' indeed. Hmmm. Very good. Very good indeed. Yes. Very, very, very good. You know, I like a bright child (this through clenched teeth). A bright child can do well here. A bright child can do a lot to build the reputation of a school. A bright. . . ."

"*School???? School????*"

My agony at my stupidity for not having realized earlier put the fellow at ease. He smiled. He was pleased. "All this time you never guessed?"

"This is *school????*"

"I find it difficult to believe that a child with your score could sit here and not know where he is."

"Oh, no, no, no."

"She didn't tell you, did she? Oh . . . and there you were in the receiving grounds all afternoon without any idea why. Shame on her for treating you so poorly. I've told her to be a better mother, but would she listen to me?"

"Uncle Theo??"

"You don't mean to say she didn't even tell you about me? Shame, shame. Leaving you in such ignorance, why you might have thought . . . did you think she'd deserted you, left you to die? Poor baby child. It is the great tragedy of life that we cannot know our destiny, even from one moment to the next. But *you*, my son, if I may call you that, may I call you that? You have the most incredible future waiting for you. Can you believe me? *Will* you believe me? It's true. I shall personally attend to your destiny. I shall shape you, mold you, guide you in ways you cannot as yet even imagine, and you shall become a do-er of great deeds. That is my promise. You have what it takes. You are a diamond in the rough. Why yes, I knew the first moment I saw you, you were just an infant—you wouldn't remember, perhaps, but we did meet once, oh, it seems like yesterday, and here you are today, full grown, quite amazing really, but what is important, *you are here*, perhaps not eager, no, but certainly able to learn. We've proved that beyond a doubt, haven't we? Oh, I beg your pardon, do we have something to say?"

"I want to borrow your phone."

"I'll tell you what. Upon graduation, I'll see to it personally that you have a phone of your very own, how's that?"

"Now. I want one now."

"No."

"What?"

"No."

"But . . . but . . . I'm nineteen. You can't refuse me."

"Certainly I can."

Such a look of pain I must have had on, for he was at once all smiles to see me so. He rose up and danced around his desk, chirping, "You and I shall rule Idealand together. I am by far the finest teacher on this entire continent. I am by far the *only* teacher on this entire continent. You may ask, what are we doing, you and I alone in this godforsaken hemisphere? Well, there are certain advantages to isolation. You do understand. Do you understand?"

"How long will I be here?"

"You *do* understand."

"How long?"

"As long as it takes. Ah, to teach again. Do you realize how long it has been since I've had a child in my command? A child? A real child?"

"If I hadn't passed the test?"

"Well, I do have my standards."

"Tell me something."

"Certainly. That's what I'm here for."

"What's a stitch?"

"A stitch is . . . ho ho. Nice try, though. My, my. Behind that shiny brow languishes an intellect starving for education. You have an amazing future, of that you can rest assured. Oh, yes. One small favor I ask in return. I promised your mother, it's in our contract—you are not under any circumstances to take your little life. Now that's in writing, so please, do be careful."

"Careful??!"

"I mention this because in a moment or two, if I'm any judge of character, you shall find yourself overwhelmed with a wave of, shall we say, resentment, frustration, a desire to rebel." He sat himself down again, swiveled his big chair and gave me his profile as he gazed out across the water toward the island on the horizon. "You will feel the need to express yourself in some rebellious way, a show of independence, perhaps fly away for awhile, although where I can't imagine. You may be excused."

Can't imagine indeed. The little monster was more than a good judge of character; he was its creator.

I raced right out of there, down the stairs, across the court to my room, strapped into my wing pack and took off into the sky. I stopped, hovered at about fifty meters, jerked my elbows to turn myself around, and faced the castle. Then, in full view of his window, I hit the release button of my buckle, a good sharp blow, which had I been standing safely on the ground, straps unweighted, would have released me from the harness. As it was I just hung there. I gave it a second blow, a third, several blows. In case he missed the point, I screamed: "It's my life, mine, mine, mine, and I'll take it if I want to," banging my belt buckle over and over until I was quite sure he'd had enough. Then I turned my back on him and flew to the Isle of Catalina, exactly as he intended.

4

I wasn't long on the wing before my mood improved. The significance of the occasion dawned on me after the first two or three passes over the ocean: for the first time in my entire life I was free to fly away from unpleasantness. The right to just lift off and soar wherever and whenever I pleased was mine for the first time, and before many minutes I was giddy with the pleasure of it. Intoxicated.

No doubt my flying reflected it. It took me nine passes, top to bottom, to cross the channel. If I'd been paying attention to what I was doing, I could have done it in five. On a decent wing, one.

As to the mysterious Isle of Catalina, like the man said, better it remain a mystery forever. Scrub mostly, a few goats, frightened of large-winged creatures. It took me most of the afternoon to realize that one cannot approach a goat on the wing and expect a friendly reception. By evening they were all so spooked I couldn't approach them on foot either. So I gave it up and went to the beach, intending to make myself comfortable in the sand and perhaps even spend the night.

I heard a yell. Earlier, flying about, I thought I had heard someone calling. I passed it off as a seagull, but hearing it again, without the rush of wind in my ears, I was certain. A human voice. Female, shrieking, *"hey!"* Scratchy and hoarse. *"Hey!"*

I pulled directly up into the air for a look around and spotted a figure running my way along the hard sand near the water's edge. It was a female person, by no means beautiful even at a distance; naked, running like crazy, flailing her arms, desperate to catch my attention before I flew off. *"Don't go! Come back!"*

I wasn't going anywhere, just up for a look, drifting a little with the offshore breezes. "Hello down there. I see you."

Run run run, like she'd never tire out, very muscular, and as she drew nearer I could see she was a hairy one too. I chose to keep myself aloft for awhile, until we could have a word or two. I felt safer doing that. I lowered to about two meters, just out of reach, but near enough to carry on a conversation without so much shouting. *"Don't go. Wait. Come back."*

"I hear you. I hear you. You don't have to yell." She had a powerful, husky, slightly masculine voice. A loud voice.

"Please, don't go away. I need your help."

"I'm right here," I said, although the breeze had me drifting up the beach at a steady three knots. She had to march right along to keep up with me. The closer she got the less I wanted to come down. She was more muscular than just about any live person I'd ever seen, male or female. She had what might have been called an Athenian frame, flat tummy, sufficient but tight, firm, somewhat high breasts, thin limbs, every joint defined. I preferred the tubular limb, the round belly, what we often referred to as the cylindrical or *smooth* look, with the dents filled and the bulges shaved. Worse than contour, she had hair everywhere, visible all over her body as a thin white halo of peach fuzz illuminated by the sun behind her. Which alone was bad enough, but she also wore the thicker stuff in two patches under her arms and another at the crotch, plus a scraggle of hair on her legs, all the places where I myself glistened tastefully. The only acceptable hair in my opinion was that which hung from her scalp, a long, heavy, thick, straight brown hair reaching clear to the small of her back. Her skin was a good color too, very dark tan, almost Negroid brown, although her face was as European as mine. A handsome face, too chiseled perhaps, too expressive, but pleasing enough, or would have been less the eyebrows and ears.

"Come down, please?" she begged.

"If you don't mind, I'll keep my distance for awhile."

"Promise me you won't fly away. I desperately need your help."

"All right, all right. What's the matter?"

"I'm stranded here. On the island. I need a lift across."

"Oh," I said, "a . . . yeah, okay."

"Will you help me?"

"You got a phone?"

"I've got nothing," she said. I couldn't argue that.

I continued to drift back away from her. She marched right along, keeping pace with me, a bit tuckered but by no means exhausted. The possibility that she might somehow be in cahoots with my weird Uncle Theo didn't entirely escape me. She looked the part, and after all, meeting two total strangers in as many days after nineteen years of no one but the regulars seemed a trifle unlikely. I had my suspicions, but as long as I maintained a safe altitude, no reason to be afraid of her.

"Won't you help me, please?" She was in a conversational rut.

"I . . . I don't know." At that point, I really didn't.

"Won't you at least talk to me?"

"I *am* talking. Aren't I?"

"Come down. I'm so afraid you'll leave me."

"How long have you been stranded here?"

"About sixty days."

"*Sixty days???* With *nothing?*"

"Please, if you won't come down, would you mind holding still? I'm so tired. I've been running after you all day long."

I didn't know how to effect a counterdrift, that is, hover over one point against the wind. It's not such an easy trick. I told her, "This is the best I can do."

"All I need is a ride to the mainland."

"You mean carry you? You want me to carry you?"

"Would you? Please?"

"Oh God. I couldn't." In order to carry her I would have had to touch her.

"Then would you be so kind as to loan me your wings for a short time until I can find myself another pair?"

"What would that leave me?" In a word, stranded. "I just got them yesterday. I don't think I could do that. No."

"I'm entirely at your mercy. Would you please get me another pair of wings then?"

"Well, ah . . ." To admit to her that I had no phone of my own, no credit number, no access to the system of supply would have opened up the deeper issue of my youthful status. Anyone else, anyone else at all, could have ordered up a pair of wings and had them delivered to those coordinates in no time flat. Not me. As heartless as it may have seemed to do so, I had to refuse her even that. Without explanation. "No. I can't. I just can't."

"I see," she said, marching along after me. "If I build a raft, will you tow me across on it?"

"Boy, you're really stuck on this topic. Why don't we talk about something else for a change, okay?"

"I don't think you understand. I'm really very desperate to

leave this island." I continued to drift along. "Won't you at least stop and talk to me? I'm very nearly exhausted."

"You keep up a pretty good pace even so. I know *I* couldn't do that. Especially in the sand. I'm not at all good at walking on uneven surfaces. In fact, if I didn't have wings right now, I'd probably . . . *Ahhh!*"

I hit the cliff. While she kept my attention forward, the wind had carried me not only up the beach but inland, toward the cliff. When I struck I panicked, reached for the up-cord, grabbed the down by mistake, and came down hard in the sand. Immediately, before I could think of what to do, she jumped on top of me and knelt on my chest to keep me from buoying back up. I let myself go completely limp, as I would when wrestling back home, an old trick of mine to make the opponent think I'd given up. She fell for it. She let herself off, and as she did I caught hold of the up-cord. Up I went.

In a desperate attempt to pull me down, she grabbed onto my legs and rose up with me. She shouldn't have done that. I merely took her up a respectable distance, dangerously high for one with no pack, and then eased off on the up-cord to hover, maintaining a good negotiable altitude.

She screamed. She begged me. "Put me down. Put me down."

"I didn't ask you along."

"Please, put me down."

"What's the matter? Afraid you might fall and break your leg?"

"I'm losing my grip," she said. It didn't feel that way. I gave the down-cord a quick tug, just to bounce her, throw a little scare into her. I dropped more suddenly than I had anticipated. She was able to move up on me. She took hold of my leg strap, got a firm grip on that, and with the other hand free to grope, reached right inside my flap and grabbed me by the handle. A perfect stranger, mind you. "Now put me down at once."

"Hey, don't do that! Ouch! That hurts."

"Down!"

"I'm going. I'm going. Don't do that. *Ahhhh.*"

"Not too fast. Be careful."

"Look, *you* be careful, all right?"

I landed her as gently as I could, working one cord against the other. "Easy now, gentle, gentle . . . you're down. Let go."

She held on. I stayed aloft, ready, willing, but unable to fly, as she had me tethered, rather like a balloon on a short stick. An odd situation at best. My choices were limited. Once, when I was little, I spent a day tieing heavy objects to my mid-member, just to see what I could lift that way. Not much. A book or two. She weighed easily as much as our whole library. So I consented to stay, if she wanted that, despite my every instinct to be gone. I settled and stood beside her. Still she held on.

"Please let go. I can't take being touched. Especially there."

"Take off your pack."

"Aww, do I have to . . . *Ahhhh!* Don't do that! Okay. Okay." I popped the buckle and let the pack fall to the ground.

"Now come with me." She led me down the beach, walking on the sand. I reminded her of my difficulty walking on sand; I begged her to slow down. "If you have to pull me along, pull me by the hair. I really don't want to be touched there. You don't know what it does to me." No soap. "Look, ma'am. I really can't take being touched at all, let alone this."

She must have misunderstood my meaning, for all of a sudden she turned to face me, and still holding tight, she said, "Look at me. In case you hadn't noticed, I'm beautiful. The sun is setting, and I'm beautiful. Also naked. And willing."

As she said it she pulled us together and attacked me with her mouth, pushing it over mine and letting loose with a barrage of tongue jabs at my clenched teeth, clutching the back of my neck with her free hand, a fuzzy leg slithering up and down between my own, all the while tongue-ing away between my lips. Never before had flesh entered my mouth, living, dead, raw or cooked, except maybe my own tongue, which I try not to think about. I couldn't bear to touch her, even to push her away. I was totally at her mercy. No matter. What I couldn't do voluntarily my system accomplished all by itself. It sent forth a series of spasms from my stomach, up my esophagus to the back of my throat, along with a spoonful of mustard gunk she may very well have caught the taste of. She pulled back. Let go of my pee-pee. It withdrew from her grasp like a rubber band and shriveled into nothingness. She backed away from me a safe distance while my system threw up the mother lode, a steaming mass of expanded concentrate, all that was left of my morning tab, a single coherent jelly that looked real bad wobbling there on the sand, the end product of our brief romance.

When I was all through retching I collapsed beside my little mess, utterly spent but feeling much better for having it out. She stood there silhouetted against the sunset, looking down at both of us, hands on hips, saying nothing, assessing the situation. In all her experience I seriously doubted that she'd ever come up against a reaction similar to mine. It set her back a notch, I'm sure.

After a long silence, she said, very indignantly, "I came to you naked and willing. I offered myself to you with a full and loving heart, the flesh of my body..."

"*Please!* If you don't mind, let's change the subject. Talk about something else. Anything!"

After another long pause to consider, she said, "Very well. Follow me now, if you will." Cold as ice.

"If you're done with me I'd like to go now," I said, supposing a quickie was all she ever really intended.

"You'll stay with me. We'll leave your wing pack there in the sand. If you attempt to make a run for it, I'll run too. If you beat me to it, it's yours and good riddance. But if I win the race the wings are mine. After all the courtesy you've shown me I wouldn't hesitate to leave you stranded."

"You wouldn't... would you?"

"You were willing enough to leave me."

"Yeah, but, but... you were already here!"

She made me get up off the sand and walk with her down the beach toward where she had come from, retracing her footprints in the sand. It was all I could do to keep up with her, let alone challenge her to a race. What choice did I have?

"Over there," she said, directing me to a tiny cove where she had set up camp. Hardly half a kilometer, but it was as far as I'd ever walked before without plenty of rest stops along the way. When I finally got there I collapsed into a heap (with her permission)—panting and sweating. She stood there looking down at me. I was exhausted, and the current unpleasant reality was something I wanted to escape from. I closed my eyes and went directly to sleep. Just before losing consciousness I heard her say, "Holy Mother of Earth, why am I so desperate?"

5

I went out, stayed out all night long, and woke up in roughly the same position—hot, clammy, hungry, itchy, and in terrible, terrible pain. I made an effort to move and found myself paralyzed from the neck down, the result of so much strenuous exercise the day before. Sometime during the night my cement had set. I tried to move my legs. Solid lumps. My arms, same thing. My back muscles felt like they'd been torn apart; flying uses those muscles. I tried to holler. It hurt me even to inhale. The best I could manage was a meek noise in the shape of the word "water." "Wawa. Wawa." I was thirsty.

No one came to me. I opened my eyes. "Wawa?" No one in the field of view. I tried to sit up. I couldn't budge. "Wawa? Wawa?" I tried to tilt my head. No luck. I thought she'd gone off with my wings and left me alone on the island. I closed my eyes. I tried desperately to go back to sleep. No use. I'd used up all my reserves avoiding the night.

"Help. Wawa. Wawa."

"Good morning."

"Ah . . ." She startled me. "Where are you?"

"Nearby."

"Wawa."

"I beg your pardon?"

"Help me. I can't move. I'm stuck."

"You're stuck?"

"I think I'm paralyzed."

"Oh? Oh, well. Don't worry. I have a cure for paralysis."

"Please, a tab. And a glass of water. I'm in pain. Actual physical pain. I can feel it. All over." I didn't mean anguish. I meant pain. "Give me a tab. Call Medcomp. Help me."

"I think all you need is some food, perhaps. And a little exercise to loosen your sore muscles. Are you hungry?" Her tone of voice didn't convey to me the same urgency I tried to convey to her. Not at all. She was cheerful-sounding. Dreadfully cheerful. "Here," she said. "Eat this. You'll feel better. Then we'll work out the knots."

Something round and hard landed with a thud near my nose and sat there. I looked up as best I could in the direction from which it came. There she was, sitting bare-ass on a flat rock just above me, in what must have been a holy pose: legs crossed, backs of her hands touching ground, palms flat up, chin back, working on that cosmic tan. A pile of garbage next to her.

"What's this?" It looked to me like an apple. I had to cross my eyes to see it right.

"An orange." Same difference.

"An orange?"

"Just what you need to wash away the morning mouth and pep up the system. Go on. It's good for you."

"Please remove it."

"Eat it."

There were some among my mother's friends who would have, but I was not one of those. I told her so. "I do not eat living organisms."

"Oh, go on. You'll like this one."

"That's disgusting. Where'd you get it? Off some tree, no doubt."

"Why, yes. I did."

"Thief."

"It is a gift of nature."

"Thank you. I'll take a tab, if you please."

"Well, I don't please. And if I did please, I don't have tabs or tubes or flavor paste or any of that. I have only what nature in her perfect wisdom has provided."

"Oh, Lord."

"The orange is good in the morning. It wakes the body and refreshes the spirit. I'll peel it for you."

"Oh no, no. Don't bother. I'll take it wrapped."

"Well, if you're not hungry, I am." She selected another orange from her pile. She dug her nails deep into the fleshy skin, causing it to split apart, spattering a clear sticky pus-like substance all over everywhere, and then proceeded to skin it alive, heartlessly ripping and tearing, exposing its insides, which she then divided into parts, setting each of its organs on a flat rock beside her. "Are you sure you won't have one?" She offered me a whitish gland-like thing.

"Oh God."

"Mmmmmmmm." She put it in her mouth. I shut my eyes.

But I could hear her teeth grinding, that horrible, cell-splitting crunch crunch.

"Would you like some berries?"

"Oh God!"

"You know," she said, chewing and talking at the same time, spitting out the little babies, their shells too hard to chew—she knew perfectly well the affect it was having on me—"this paralysis you're experiencing. I have a cure. Works every time. You don't have to do a thing."

"No, don't bother. I'm fine. Actually, paralysis isn't such a bad thing once you're used to it. When you're out of stuff to do, what the heck. No. Really. I'm all right. *No. Nooooo!*"

You hear about folk cures all the time. The cure for total paralysis, for the record: set aside overnight to cool, one cup fresh water. In the morning, lift collar and pour. Follow immediately with threats of more. A moving experience, if I may be forgiven for putting it that way.

It was obvious from the first—I knew it without having to say it or demonstrate it—she was a naturalist, which is anyone who practices naturalism, which is a grubber in any man's dictionary. I love nature, as I've said, to look at, to wander around in. But this monster from Catalina went beyond mere appreciation. She literally *ate* plants. She slept in the open, washed in bodies of water and drank from the same places, sometimes simultaneously. I knew her type well enough from watching TV shows of the nature vs. civilization genre, fairly common in early millennium plots when such decisions were still in the air. But I hasten to point out that unlike her TV counterpart, she did not walk in a stoop, or smell like a dead animal—her teeth and hair were as tight and secure as mine. And she didn't cackle, leer, drool uncontrollably, exude pus from pustules, or sluff skin. She did not, at least in front of me, cram handfuls of live wiggling creatures into her mouth, or anything so gross. Dead fish, an occasional egg, but nothing insectual or wormish. All that sort of thing one can safely assume sprang from the bias of an age when there were still a few holdouts in favor of the hard natural life.

"How do you feel?"

She had me up and moving around despite a pain as intense as any I'd ever felt before, but worse than any before because I felt it everywhere. In the process of flying and walking across the beach the day before I'd strained my entire muscle supply. A tab would have cured me. She had no tabs. This was perhaps the first time in my life that I truly and desperately needed the benefits of that simplest, cheapest, and most abundant of commodities, and for the first time in my life none were available. She smiled and said, "It's always best to let nature take care of these things in her own way, in her own time." That phrase is subject to interpretation. One might suppose it meant to do nothing at all, let nature take its course. That's not what she had in mind. Unfortunately. For the rest of the day I had to be tormented with endless advice, cures, and offers of horrible things to eat.

She led me from the beach camp along a path by a stream, up-canyon a short distance to an area where the stream filled deep ponds and little waterfalls trickled. Very lush. Very grand. Under better circumstances I'd have been pleased to be there.

She sat me in a bed of soft moss beneath a big shade tree and told me to wait for her there. I assured her that I'd be there unless forced to move, hinting how I might die if she didn't get me a tab, even going so far as to point out how it was her responsibility to replace the one she caused me to throw up the night before. She acknowledged her responsibility with a nod and proceeded to do what *she* thought best. She explained to me that what I needed first and most was a substantial meal of protein to replace the damaged tissue in my muscles, along with certain amounts of this and that in such and such proportions—on and on with the lore of nourishment. While she talked to me, since that didn't require much of her attention, she went about performing the most extraordinary and depressing little ritual.

From an assortment of supplies she kept in a sack hanging from a branch nearby she withdrew a few small implements, absolutely terrifying in their simplicity: a jagged pin (bent, but sharp), a thin piece of twine, and a feather. She joined these things together with a knot and made them one. Thus armed, she went to the stream, waded part way in, and proceeded to throw hook and feather out into stiller water. Plop. Now when I throw a rock, it's gone and I have to fetch another. Clever her, she kept hold of the other end of the string, and by pulling on it was able to save her hook and feather for another toss. Plop. And another. Plop. And so on. Plop. Plop. Plop. Until the poor fishes, unable to tolerate that incessant drip drip another minute longer elected some one of them to go up and put a stop to it. What can a fish do without hands or feet? It bit the hook and became attached to her string just like that, and couldn't get unstuck without ripping itself apart, which it even tried to do, flapping down hard against the water, again and again. I couldn't do a thing to help it. The poor creature was in great pain, but she didn't seem the least upset. She held on, kept the string taut until finally the fish was too exhausted to resist any more. At which point she gathered up the string and lifted the fish right out of the water. Now it is a well-known fact that a fish needs water to breathe, and I knew that, so I screamed at her to put it back. But she only laughed at me. She took hold of the fish in one hand, withdrew the pin and string, feathers intact, and threw the half-dead fish up on dry land, leaving it to die. We looked at each other. Its little eyes bugged out. He didn't want to die, but what could I do? I was in as much pain myself. I tried to explain, make its last moments easier by saying, "Poor fish. Poor fish. Oh, poor fish," and the like. Apparently I wasn't very helpful; the little fish died anyway.

She caught another. And another. Each fish had certainly seen the fate of the one before, but they kept on biting. It's a very sensitive creature, I think, that is willing to give up its life to stop a drip. So naturally, when the time came I refused to eat. She said, "Nature in her wisdom will purify you and give you an appetite for her bounty. Sooner than you might think." Shaking a finger. She was right, too.

For most of the rest of the day I was left to sit while she traipsed off into the woods to rob the bushes of their little baby berries, tear down celery stalks, pull onions right out of their nests, as well as carrots and potatoes and all sorts of things that grew wild from the days of cultivation. She'd disappear for an hour or so, reappear with a big sack full of garbage, dump it, go off, return with another and another until she was satisfied she'd need no more. By then it was late afternoon. Sorting time. Fruits in one heap, leafy things in another, and so on, taking great care to name each item and make me repeat the names. Some of them I already knew from my farm days: the pear, for instance, and the potato. Most of what she brought would not have found their place in the sun had not my ancestors cultivated theirs. So, I reasoned, in a manner of speaking they existed solely to be eaten—this as evening got on and my hunger defined itself more clearly as something separate from my general discomfort. "The apple," I said. "Is it all right if I touch it?"

It was quite all right. While she ignited a fire and made preparations to heat water, I fondled a ripe round little apple, caressing its smooth tender skin, touching it to my lips, kissing it. And then while she was down to the water, I ate it all but the core, just as fast as I could, thinking with intense effort about something else so I wouldn't become sick and throw it all right back up. A fitting beginning to a life of sin. It tasted all right, so I had another.

The potato tasted not so good until it was boiled, and then only so-so. After that I was ready to try the peach. Not bad. And at last a segment of orange; not bad either. Another piece. A whole orange, pulp and pith all over my face. I felt like Dracula. Two oranges. Three. Topped with a warm tea made from a plant called mugwort, very bad, but presumably very good for what ailed me. My first meal in the wilds, a balanced meal, that delicate balance between hunger and nausea.

After a while, either as a result of having eaten or spontaneously without cause, I began to feel a little better. The desire to live returned along with thoughts of the immediate future. It was dark again. Her little fire had dwindled to a rosy glow. She retrieved a battered robe from her bag of supplies and made a bed for herself, close, but not too close to me. I wiggled around, smoothed out a few bumps, and prepared to sleep. I was bothered by a question, not certain I dare bring it up, but too curious to let it go unanswered. In the interest of easy sleep, I finally asked her, "Why didn't you take my wing pack and fly away?"

"Would you do that to me?"

"I tried to, didn't I?"

"That was before you knew me. Would you leave me now?" she asked.

"Well . . . you did take care of me today."

"I did."

"But it's your fault I needed taking care of."

"Well?"

"Well what?"

"Would you go off and leave me here now that you know me?"

". . . . . ." I didn't want to be dishonest. On the other hand, about to go to sleep, I didn't want to leave her with the truth to ponder, which was that I certainly would leave her, first opportunity. And furthermore, why not? My hesitation was answer enough, I'm sure.

"What's your name?"

"Mark. What's yours?"

"Synthetica."

"I'm sorry?"

"Synthetica."

"You don't mean Cynthia?" I was hoping I'd heard wrong.

"My name is Synthetica," she insisted. It wasn't open for debate.

I expected maybe Lily, Rose, Peter, or Harry, after some naturally occurring phenomenon. Naturalists, the ones portrayed on TV, would not allow themselves to be called by a "thing" name, any name which smacked of the mechanical. You'd never come across a naturalist on the screen named Jack, for example, or Mike, or John, or Mark, for that matter, which is a unit of currency. Never, never Synthetica.

She was fairly insistent that I get it right. One would have to be, I suppose. She said, "You don't understand about me. People like you never understand. I'm different."

"I *do* understand." Actually, I didn't understand *why* she was different, but there was no doubting the fact that she was.

"You think I'm a Free Marketeer like you, don't you? You think I'm out here on some sort of kick. Well, I'm not. What you see is *me*."

"Who else?"

"My father brought me up in the forest. I've never even seen the Free Market, and I have no desire to. It is full of evil and corruption. My father kept me from all that and made me pure...."

Shit. It was already an hour past sunset. I was tired, sore, and sick to my stomach. The air was hot and muggy and the ground cold and lumpy. Mosquitoes buzzed my ears, and ants crawled into my flying suit when I opened it up to cool myself. I was in no mood. Which didn't stop her. It seemed, judging by the efficiency of her presentation, that her story was one she'd told several times before. It sounded matter of fact. Chronological. Memorized.

"My father raised me outside your world, totally free from all you consider so necessary. I am unlike anyone you have ever met before." She'd make these statements then pause, waiting for me to raise objections. But as I say, I was in no mood. "My father brought me up in the forest to protect me from the wrongs of your world. He taught me to fear the flying objects which so clutter the sky, and to avoid all things of hard and regular shape. As I grew older he gave me reason enough to fear these wretched . . . *things*! He taught me to despise all machines, for they make life too easy, and for this wisdom alone I will love my father forever. But he gave me more. He gave me the knowledge of nature. All that I know of Mother Nature's gifts he taught me. With this knowledge he made me free. I can live anywhere, go anywhere, do anything without fear of starving. How long would you survive alone in the wilderness?"

Curious that she should bring that point to mind. But the fact of the matter, whether I could express it or not, was that I had a much greater knowledge than the art of wilderness survival. I knew enough to avoid the wilderness altogether. But of all the things she said, what struck me most was that she could remember her father and the events of her upbringing so clearly. It's one thing for a young person like myself to have clear recollection of such things, but the average age of everyone else was over nine hundred years, and as yet I had no reason to suppose she might be any younger.

I said, "You can actually remember him?"

"With a fondness you'll never understand."

"What about your mother. Can you remember her too?"

"My mother . . . yes . . . but she . . . you see. . . ." She didn't want to tell me about her mother. Her father was the joy of her life, not so her mother. She went on and on about their idyllic life together; it was Father and I this and Father and I that: *our* foragings in the forest, *our* gardens in the meadow, *our* way of life, the shelter *we* built, *our* education even. Although he taught her the rudiments of natural subsistence from books (no tapes allowed), it didn't take long before they knew more than the books. The books were discarded, and for some unspecified number of years it was "*our* ever-expanding knowledge of the glories of Mother Nature." Her father, I gathered, was a Marketeer convert to naturalism, whereas she had been nature's child from the start. "He made the sacrifice for me," she explained, "so that I wouldn't have to suffer the pains of conversion." Meaning, I knew quite well, the pains I was experiencing that very moment, multiplied by the months and years complete conversion must require. He was more than the beloved parent. He was an entity worthy of worship; according to her, at least.

"It all came to a sudden tragic end the day *she* found us," she said, with contemptuous inflection on the word "she."

"Who?"

"My mother. We'd lived together sixteen years, Father and I. Sixteen years. His life was dedicated to the purpose of freeing me from a world gone mad in the pursuit of petty pleasures, a world. . . ."

"Yeah, yeah. . . ."

"I'm certain now that it was her, although at the time I thought it was . . . my soul."

"Your what?"

"My soul, drifting from my body."

"Oh. Well, sure."

"Father and I were lying in the meadow at the top of the hill. We would often spend that part of the day there to watch the sun set and the stars come out one by one. He was fast asleep. I was neither entirely asleep nor entirely awake, but somewhere in between. This is the time when the soul travels, you know."

"Oh, yes. Yes."

"I looked up, and there above me, descending out of a deep burgundy sky, I saw what seemed to be my very own image reflected in the sky, as if from a pond."

"Your soul."

"No, it wasn't. That's what I thought. You have to understand—until that moment I had never seen another woman in all my life, let alone one suspended in mid-air. And Mark, she was so beautiful. Like a goddess. Like me, actually: same ripe round firm breasts, same sensuous slender thighs, same little bulge of her love nest barely concealed by her gown. I had never seen clothes or any sort of cloth worn over the body before. And I knew nothing of wings. And yet somehow this was what I had always imagined a soul would look like apart from the physical body."

"Well, I imagine so. Yes."

"She called to me in a whisper. She said, 'Synthetica, Synthetica, Synthetica . . .' I rose to my knees and worshiped her, as I would my reflection in a pond. She said, 'Rise, my child,' softly, in a whisper, so as not to awaken my father. We had just finished making love, and it was his habit to sleep for awhile after. She said, 'I have brought you these.' She undressed and gave me the veil of my tears, this gown; and her wings, the wings of my soul. She dressed me in them and without another word sent me into the sky."

"She pulled the up-cord. That's all she did, but Mark, as I rose into the sky I thought I was taking my rightful place among the stars. Mark, so help me, when the sun set and the stars came out, I thought I was a new constellation."

She paused to allow me a chance to object. When I didn't say anything, she said, "Mark, are you awake?"

"Wide. Wide."

"Can you believe that I didn't know it was an ordinary pair of wings that carried me aloft?"

"Sure. Why not?"

"I wouldn't have allowed her to trick me if I'd have known what she was up to or even that she was someone else."

"You think it was a trick?"

"I think she found out where Father had taken me. Sending me away was her idea of revenge. I don't know much about her except what Father told me. I know she wouldn't have allowed him to take me into the forest. He must have stolen me from her when I was a baby and then disappeared, someplace where she couldn't find him. Except somehow ... she *did* find him. And me. So when he woke to find her in my place beside him ... and me gone ... it must have broken his heart, for he loved me more than life itself."

"Did he come after you?"

"How could he? He had no wings. My mother gave me hers. They were stranded on the ground, as I was in the sky. And what did I know of wings? I drifted away from him all night long, completely at ease, never suspecting that I'd been tricked. I even expected Father to join me by and by, that we would live together side by side in the night sky forever more, for all the world to see, a double constellation. Only ... in the morning, when the other stars went away and I didn't...."

"Oh, yeah."

"I didn't know enough about wings to fly, or enough about what the ground looked like from above to know where to fly to even if I could somehow have figured out the mechanism. So I just hung there, drifting farther and farther away from all that I loved, in the clutch of those wings, a machine of the world I hated."

"You can't blame the Free Market just because you didn't know your up-cord from your down. Besides, you must have figured it out or you wouldn't be here now, right?"

"I figured it out. But by then I was so far away, and so confused, and so terrified, I couldn't find my way back."

"How'd you find him? ... You did find him? ... Eventually? No? Yes?"

"No."

"Oh! . . . Well, how long ago did all this happen?"

"Seven years ago. Seven years, one hundred and eighty-two days."

"I thought you said you were sixteen when it happened?"

"I was."

"Wait a minute, now. Sixteen, seventeen, eighteen . . . twenty-three? Uh-uh."

"I am twenty-three."

"No you aren't twenty-three. I'm the only young . . . I mean, no, you aren't twenty-three."

"I am twenty-three years and forty-two days old today."

"Bullshit."

"I beg your pardon?"

"If you were only twenty-three, you'd be famous."

"If I were in the known world, perhaps so. But I'm not in the known world, am I? And I have no desire to be."

"Bullshit. You may be biologically twenty-three, but you're a lot older in actual years." I don't know why I was so ready to accept the rest of her story without comment and not this one particular part of it, unless it stemmed from a desire to hold onto my title as youngest person in the world by the widest possible margin. Without that, what did I have going for me?

"I *am* twenty-three, whether you choose to believe it or not."

"You're not twenty-three, no matter who believes you! You, me, anybody!"

"Suit yourself."

"You bet."

"I am, though."

I said, "You are not," and let it drop.

She said, "I am," and did likewise, apparently satisfied at having the last word. "Go to sleep," she said. "We have a full day ahead of us tomorrow."

Like that, I was gone. Then suddenly I woke right up again: "What do you mean 'we'?"

"You *will* help me, won't you?"

"Help you what?"

"Find him."

"Find who?"

"My father."

"Your father? You want *me* to help you find *your* father?"

"It would be a great help to me."

"I'm sure it would."

"And to you."

"To *me*?"

"Yes. You."

"How so?"

"Your life is empty and shallow now. You could use a good purpose to give it meaning."

"What do you know about my life?"

"I know where you're from."

"What's that supposed to mean?"

"You're a Free Marketeer, aren't you?"

"So's everyone else."

"I'm not."

Curious. That's what she'd been telling me all night long. But it only dawned on me just then. If what she said was true, she would be one of only two living persons who were not members in good standing of the Free Market. I was the other. "All right. All right. Suppose I say I'm interested. How much would you charge for this purpose you're offering me?"

"I'm offering it to you free of any charge."

"Free?"

"Absolutely."

"No deposit?"

"No deposit."

"What's the incentive? What's the risk? What's the reward if there's no deposit to return?"

"Success is the reward."

"Wait a minute. Wait a minute." One or the other of us was not understanding something. "Let's say I buy myself a certificate of purpose on the opportunities exchange, all right? A search, say, for the Holy Grail. Now if I don't put up a deposit, what have I got to lose? Where's the incentive? I mean, risk is the name of the game."

"How about something to win?"

"Well of course, but finding your father isn't my idea of a reward. Now if it were double my deposit, or just a big cash prize . . ."

"If I offered you money? Would you help me?"

"I'd have to see it up front."

"I can't offer you money."

"I thought not. I'm no fool."

"I offer you a reason to wake up in the morning. I offer

you hope each day of success. And if you change your mind about me while we're together, I will be your lover."

"Ah *ha!* So *that's* it. You're trying to seduce me. Well fat chance, let me tell you."

"I simply offer you love, if you want it. Companionship in any case. And a reason to be alive. What do you say? Are you interested?"

"No."

"Then answer me this, Mark. What else do you have to do?"

In those days, belief was never a serious issue with me. The distinction between fiction and reality was of little importance. TV was fiction all through the day. Was I any less entertained? More, I'd say. My life was founded upon fictions. So why should I have gotten petty over a little thing like the truth? Which isn't to say I didn't believe her. I did. The point is, so what?

"It's a search, right?"

"Right."

"Like for the Holy Grail, only it's for your father."

"That's right."

"And you don't know where he is."

"Right again."

It was dark. It was late. I'd had an impossible day. Two in a row. If she'd asked me straight out if I was interested, I'd have said no, but the truth is that without even realizing it, I was very excited by the idea.

"Is he in on it? I mean, does he call up and give you little hints?"

"Certainly not."

"Well, it wouldn't hurt."

"Mark, he has no phone."

"Oh, that's right. That's right. Tell me, do you know where he is? I mean really? You don't have to tell me, but I mean if we get stuck, it would be nice to have some idea."

"Mark, if I knew where he was. . . ."

"Just asking. No harm in asking. Do you know approximately?"

"North America."

"Oh, come on."

"North America."

"*Where* in North America? Utah? Canada?"

"I don't know."

"You mean he could be anywhere at all."

"That's right."

"And he doesn't have a phone."

"That's right." A challenge, no question about it.

"Do you have a search device of some sort?"

"No devices."

"A computer?"

"I said no devices."

"A heat-seeker? A sound probe?"

"Mark. . . ."

"A porta-camera?"

"Mark, I said. . . ."

"An alpha plotter? A shit sniffer? You got to have something, for God's sake."

"I had a pair of wings, but I lost those."

"Ah, now we're getting somewhere. What kind of wings? Racers? Cruisers? Trainers?"

"What difference does it make? I lost them."

I kept at her, going over every detail again and again, probing all the possibilities like a private dick. I came up with nothing, a big fat zero, as they say in the trade. I took her back to the day she was separated from her father. She said she'd drifted for two days on her mother's wings before she realized she could descend. By then she was a long long way from the place where she grew up. Even if she'd known how to fly she wouldn't have found her way back because she'd never seen the land from the sky before; it was all strange and unfamiliar to her. She said she didn't even know what direction she'd come from. She said, "Living in the sky, you probably wouldn't understand that." Quite.

After two days of aimless drifting she figured out the down-cord and descended among the trees. She was careful to look around at the surrounding forest where she settled down, because she knew she would have to begin her search from there. She knew it would take time, but thought that if she kept that place in the center and worked outward in big circles she would find him soon enough. "I gathered some food, made a bed of leaves, and fell asleep, my first sleep since leaving Father. But Mark, when I woke up I was someplace else. Where I made my bed and where I woke up were two entirely different places."

I said, "Well, I mean, you were in the woods, right? A tree is a tree."

"Oh no, that's not true. Each tree is unique and different,

but that's beside the point. I went to sleep in a grove of sugar maples. I woke up in the inner chamber of a ruin."

"Oooo, neat."

"I was so frightened by the sudden change in surroundings that I jumped into the wings and took off."

"I'll bet you were scared." I knew a thing or two about waking up in strange places. But she was all alone. I pressed her for an explanation. No, she didn't walk in her sleep. No, she wasn't mistaken, although she did admit to a confused and terrified state of mind owing to all that had just happened to her. I said, "Ah ha!" and let the matter drop.

She spent the next several weeks adjusting to life alone and learning to fly, accepting instructions on technique and navigation from rare but occasional free flyers she met along the way. She said she was at first very reluctant to speak to strangers, until she learned how "docile and infantile" the people of the Market were, despite their evil ways. I said, "Hey, watch it. I'm a Free Marketeer, you know."

She said, "In every respect. The epitome." I thanked her. She said, "I've been searching ever since, for seven years. Until . . ." I must have been nodding off or she wouldn't have left it dangling.

"What?"

"Sixty days ago I met a man—another free flyer, a stranger. I was alone. I needed . . . well, I needed help. We shared a meal, and we made love. Right here. And when I woke, he was gone. And Mark, he took my wings. He left me stranded."

"No!"

"Yes."

"Who? What's his name? Was he a short skinny guy by any chance?"

"Yes. Yes he was. Do you know him?" she asked, sitting straight up.

"A bald-headed silver-skinned eunuch, right?" Uncle Theo naturally came to mind.

"Long hair, white-skinned, and anything but," she said, sitting back. "Except for that, though, he looked a lot like you."

"Yeah, well, I don't go around stealing people's wings, believe me."

"I can see that you're different. Up close there's no similarity." There was a distinct note of disappointment in her voice. After a short silence she said, "Will you help me find my father?"

"What's his name?"

"Peter Watkins Winter," she said, pronouncing each word like it was something holy.

"Is that his real name or his nature name?"

"It's the name his father gave him."

"Have you checked the listings? You don't have to have a phone to be listed, you know. Or would that be cheating?"

"Mark, how can I get through to you? This isn't a game."

"I know. I know. Just asking."

"Well? Are you interested?"

"That depends. How are we supposed to go about looking for him with no search gear?"

"We'll fly due east, side by side. We'll look for my father's clearing. If by the time we reach the Atlantic Ocean we haven't found it, we'll turn and fly back west. We'll fly back and forth working our way north. That way we're certain to find him. Eventually."

"Eventually? Eventually? Are you crazy? Do you seriously think you can find one little clearing on the whole entire continent just by flapping back and forth on a pair of kiddie wings? It will take a hundred years."

"But with two of us, it will only take fifty."

"Oh no. Uh-uh. No sir. When you said purpose I thought . . . well I mean, no wonder it's free. It's worthless. You'll never find him that way. Never. It's hopeless. Take my advice. *Give up!*"

In a sudden sob she said, "I can't," and began to cry, although it was dark and I couldn't see any tears. It sounded like crying.

I said, "Never say can't. You can give up if you try. I do it all the time."

"No. No. I can't give up. I *have* to find him. I have to," she cried. "Don't ask me why."

"Why? . . . I mean, well, why?"

"You wouldn't understand."

"Try me."

"Because I love him. He's all I care about."

"Oh." She was right. I wouldn't understand.

"Will you help me? Please? I'll take care of you, feed you, be your friend. Please?"

"It's hopeless."

"Does that mean no?"

"Yes."

She cried herself to sleep. I sat there listening to her, thinking over my own rather delicate situation. It was all pretty clear what she was up to. I'd been wondering all along why she didn't just pick up my wings and scram instead of wasting her time fooling around with me all day. She wanted more than wings. She wanted *me*. Obviously. She tried seduction. When that didn't work she dragged me up to her camp and tried to lure me with the promise of a free purpose. Some purpose. So, I thought to myself, she had no options left. If I go to sleep I'll wake up in the morning alone, no wild lady, no wings. Better to stay awake. Better still to get the hell out of there while I still had a chance.

I let some time pass until I heard her breathing deeply and steadily. Then, in spite of my aches and pains, I got myself up, and slowly, quietly, step by step, made my way to the stream, ready if she woke to piss on a tree and let that be my excuse for being up.

I followed the stream down-canyon, careful to place each step quietly on sand or rock until I was far enough away to splash a little without risk of being heard. I moved along the same path she had led me up that morning, the moon lighting the way, taking rest stops every so often, but never allowing sleep to overcome me. Discipline. I had no trouble at all finding my way. The path was easy, the moon was bright, the babbling of the stream gave me an audible clue to the direction, and very soon I had the sound of the surf to guide me. Where the stream emptied into the ocean I turned north toward the place where she had forced me to drop my pack, examining every little clump along the way, hoping desperately to find it.

And find it I did. Exactly true to her word, she had left it where it was. She could have hidden it. She had plenty of opportunity. She said if I got there first, the wings would be mine, fair and square, although at the time she made the deal she imagined two of us in the same race instead of just me. And yet, as I flew back across the ocean, I couldn't help but wonder why she left them sitting there, right in plain sight.

6

I shut off my beacon light before lifting up, which leads me to believe, thinking back on it, that I'd already made up my mind what I was going to do, or else why would I have made the crossing with my light out? And yet it wasn't until I was practically over the castle yard that I realized what I was up to and began seriously, consciously, to consider my options and make plans. My navigation across was fairly simple; I simply flew in the general direction as I remembered it, using the outline of the mountains and the coast as my guide. And then, once over land, I caught a glimpse of a tiny flicker of light among the trees and flew until I was directly over it. I decided the best thing would be to stay high until I was farther inland, then settle to ground-plus for the ride in, since wings make a certain amount of noise in the lufft. I wanted quiet, absolute quiet.

I flew to a position about half a kilometer windward of the castle, descended to the tree tops, hovered on lift power alone, dropped my wings and let the wind sail me over the tops of the trees, back to the castle.

It's amazing how still the air seems in a drift, moving at the exact speed in the exact same direction. Whether the wind is light or strong, the experience is one of dead calm. You get hot even on a cold day, and a little short of breath, but the silence can't be matched, especially in the dead of night when the birds are asleep. Altitude is automatically maintained (a safety feature in most wings), a standard one meter above the highest obstacle in the immediate neighborhood, but one can get turned easily and end up facing sideways or backwards to the direction of travel. For that reason it's a good idea to keep the wings unfolded, out of the pack, available for paddling. There's nothing to it. Competitive drifters use webbed gloves and elaborate ritualized arm motions to keep themselves aligned right, although I've always suspected it was something they did more for show and style than for orientation. If worse comes to worse you can always turn your head to one side and blow real hard or pull your knees up and fart and effect a turn that way, but that was considered a less graceful technique, and it would lose you points.

Mimi Jo's place had a perimeter sensing system that would warn her of the approach of visitors in plenty of time to get me in my room behind locked doors. Uncle Theo's castle might have had such a device too. I considered it and decided not to drift any farther than to the top of the east wall. I kept my hand on the down-cord. As I came up to the wall the automatic put on lift to raise me up and over. I eased down just enough to counter the effect. Doing it that way, without use of wings, I managed to come in without making a sound. I touched the wall, cushioning the gentle impact with one foot, and clung to the rock like a spider. Letting the lift unit handle the bulk of my weight, I crawled up the stones to the ledge and peered over.

There wasn't a whole lot to see in the dark. There were no lights at all except the one I'd seen earlier, which turned out to be the light from my own room, way down at the far end of the colonnade. The door was open. Everything waiting for my return, like a trap baited with a warm, comfortable bed. I was tempted to run in quick, grab a handful of food tabs, and run right out again. I'd been a day without anything decent to eat and I was still aching all over. It was a real temptation, but I knew a thing or two about the self-closing door with the outside lock and decided just that one time to forego comfort in the name of freedom.

The rest of the castle and the yard were vague in the darkness except for the turret, which stood out clearly in the moonlight. That's all I really needed to see. I let myself up onto the top of the wall, put on some weight, and walked along the guardway, ready on the up-cord in any case. Very very cautiously I crept along the wall to the southeast corner and from there straight to the turret, keeping low and light, just enough weight on to make walking possible, but light so that my feet touched softly, soundlessly. But looking back, I doubt that I went undetected, even with all my precautions.

My presence may or may not have been picked up by instruments, but in either case it was assumed. He must have known. It was all too obvious, all too easy. If I set off an alarm, it was a silent one. If my progress was watched, it was judged without comment. He *let* me do it, and what is as likely, planned for it. If ordinarily he kept the place brightly lit—I don't know if that was usual, but if so—that night he shut off all the lights, all but one. And if ordinarily hidden night-seeing cameras kept a watchful eye on the grounds, on that occasion they were instructed to overlook thieves in the night. And if ordinarily the big cast iron lock on his turret room door was kept shut, that night it was left unlocked, and the door ajar. And when I found it open he could trust that I'd say to myself, "Why not? Who does he have to fear alone in the wilderness, halfway around the world from the center of life?" In a word: me. But I didn't think of that. I was no thief. I never stole from anybody.

After waiting by the door many minutes, listening for the sound of someone inside, hearing nothing, I made the decision and slipped in. I stood for awhile just inside, forcing my eyes to see in the dark. The light of a three-quarter moon spilled in through the big glass window behind Uncle Theo's desk, just bright enough to show me what I wanted to see. To the left of his swivel chair, silhouetted against the glass, was a free-standing coat tree. Hanging from the hooks in plain view were not one, but *two* wing packs, one set of Spaulding 880 Racers, a brand I could have spotted in half the light, and another less identifiable pair, small but not doubt as wonderful. I came to steal the one, but did not pass up the opportunity to take the other. It was the obvious thing to do. I was ready for a better wing, but more important than that, why should I have left him the means to chase me?

As to the morality of the deed: it wasn't done without silent apologies and concealed guilt. But I no sooner had my hands on them than I realized how much the son of a bitch deserved it for his part in the plot to put me in school.

But it was too easy. Too obvious. The day he administered the test I saw those wings hanging there. I was a very wing-conscious young man. He knew that. If he was any uncle of mine, he knew that perfectly well. Those wings were put there as bait. But my mind, which always considers those possibilities, was satisfied in that respect by the light across the way. I wouldn't have considered anything so devious as one trap set to take my mind off another.

Heart pounding like something wild in my chest, I quickly attached both packs to my belt strap, walked to the door, peeked outside, ran three steps to the wall and leapt right over the side. I pushed off as I jumped as if I were diving into the pool, and coasted on lift out from the wall. When I ran out of momentum I spread wing, took a couple of short passes downhill, and then, feeling safe, rose to the top limit for a long pass across the water toward the island. It was a clean heist.

Ten passes got me to the island beach. I was slowed somewhat by the two packs dangling from my belt. My plan was to wake her and fly off immediately, just in case sometime during the night Uncle Theo noticed his wings missing, put two and two together, and pursued. But I was unable to do that for the simple reason that I couldn't find her. In the moonlight every little canyon and gully looked exactly like every other little canyon and gully. I needed that one tiny light to guide my final approach. I had no choice but to put down on the beach and wait the remaining hour or two until morning. So I landed, unharnessed, made myself a little bed in the sand, turned up my thermal zipper against the morning chill, propped my head on the softest of the three packs, and went to sleep.

The sun was halfway to noon when I woke. I was hot, groggy, and famished. I examined the sky for signs of Uncle Theo, and when I was satisfied that all was clear I got up, shook off the sand, and put on the Spauldings.

Those who are not wing enthusiasts will never understand how it feels to put on your first pair of 880's, or how disappointing it can be to discover that they don't fit. The harness is tailored. No slip buckles for adjustments. That would add weight and spoil the air flow. Never. It's a snooty brand in some respects. The other pack turned out to be a set of Wilsons. Queens to be exact. The Wilson Queen was a one-time Olympic favorite, but under the circumstances I had no time to get involved in the Queens vs. Spauldings controversy. The Queens fit me; the Spauldings didn't.

I strapped up in the Queens, teased the lift, decided it was in good condition, picked up the Spaulding pack and took off, leaving my Binks to rot in the sand.

I'm very very good at locating myself from the air. I grew up looking down. In the light of day, with a little altitude, I immediately located the canyon where Synthetica had set up camp. As anxious as I was to try out my new wings, I limited myself just then to the briefest pass and settled in among the trees again, very near to where I'd left her sleeping. She didn't see me settle in or hear my feet touch ground. But I heard her. She was crying, heartbroken, in a huddle on the ground, bawling her eyes out. She'd probably been at it awhile, and I figured that if she was anything like me it wouldn't last long. Pretty soon she'd stop crying, dry her eyes, enter into a brief phase of quiet self-pity, then get real mad and maybe throw a tantrum, which I would like to have seen, because besides myself I'd never seen a human being cry before, or throw a tantrum, except on TV. The real thing may not have the same visual impact as a close-up on a wall-sized screen, but it does touch the soul more surely. I watched her from behind a tree until I felt my throat constrict and eyes moisten—those old familiar symptoms—and I knew I'd better act quickly with a cure or run the risk of the full-blown disease.

I pulled up just a few meters and pushed myself from tree to tree like a slow-flying squirrel until I was just about over her head. I loosened the second pack from my belt and let it drop. It landed with a tremendous thud right next to her. She let loose a sudden brief screech, whirled around, saw the pack, and looked up with big wet eyes. I said, "Feed me," pretending not to notice. She understood, turned away, wiped her eyes and proceeded to make breakfast.

I would rather not describe breakfast. Suffice it to say that I endured.

Afterward we discovered that the Spauldings fit her perfectly. As if they were made for her.

7

For a lady professing both youth and the ways of nature she flew rather well. Nothing like Uncle Theo, who'd had centuries to perfect his style, but several orders of magnitude better than I. Hours of absorbtion through the TV screen just didn't do it for me.

She put on her tattered gown, strapped herself into the 880's, tied the rope end of her goodie bag to her belt, took me by the hand, and said, "Let's go." We rose hand in hand to the top, which with racing gear is an automatic two kilometers above ground, which can be thin breathing in the mountains, but not so bad over sea. The average full ascent takes about ten minutes, and if there's any conversation to be had that's the time for it, because during flight the wind drowns out all but the loudest shouting. We didn't say much that first time. She was grateful as hell for my little effort on her behalf. She gave my hand half a dozen little squeezes on the way up, but was kind enough to spare me any verbal gratitude.

When we got to the top I said, "Well?"

She said; "After you."

I said, "I insist."

She was a drop starter, which is the rather old-fashioned but serviceable technique of pulling down with wings tucked, usually head first. That posture is held for a count of three or more (depending on your nerve) or until the terminal velocity is reached, at which point you snap the wings out of the pack. The wings catch the wind, roll you out horizontal, and because of the tremendous speed attained during free fall, lift you right back to your starting altitude less about five percent. You see real old Olympic footage, and that's how they start. Then someone discovered that with a thinner wing you could reach cruising velocity sooner starting full wing, with a loss of only 4.5 percent altitude. From then on the "full extenditure" start was the thing, and remained so to the last Olympiad, fifth century millennium.

Nevertheless, there's something showy in a drop start, and since nature's little girl went off that way it seemed only proper that ace number one, who'd mastered his trainers in a single pass, should do the same. I waited until she leveled out; then I pulled down, assumed a dive, picked up speed, snapped out on the Queens, and immediately assumed proper horizontal flight, just like an old pro but for one thing: my arm bones no longer connected to the shoulder bones quite right.

When the finer racing wing is subjected suddenly to the powerful relative winds of a protracted free fall, it has a tendency to flop back and touch tips, taking the arms back too. It's called a "tip-to-tip wing-back," and the less limber individual is advised against it. It's in the book. It doesn't hurt the wing one little bit. Oh no. A Queen can pass through a tropical storm strapped to a block of cement, sink five kilometers into the Atlantic trench and bob to the surface unscathed, if you believe the commercials; but the flyer himself gets all hurt and sore. His arms come loose at the shoulders and pop in their sockets like little firecrackers, and that puts him right out of the mood to fly any more.

I leveled out, eased up until I came to a stop, pulled my up-cord, rose to the top, and just sort of hung there like a dead guppy. Synthetica glanced back, saw that I wasn't with her, came up beside me.

"Are you all right?"

"My arms."

"What's the matter?"

"They came undone."

"Shoulders?"

"Uh-huh."

"No problem." Not for her. I was all for a tow back. She wasn't for anything of the sort. She'd spent too much time on the island already and was absolutely determined to continue on. Besides, she had a cure, similar in kind to her cure for paralysis. She took hold of me by the wrist, put her foot in my armpit, and yanked my arm out straight, suddenly and hard. The bones popped. I screamed. She turned me half around, took the other arm and did it again. I nearly fainted. "You'll be fine," she said. I thought perhaps, after a couple of years in traction. "Come on. Follow me."

"Don't leave me here. Wait. . . ."

She whirled around and came back with a display of impatience, saying, "Now what?"

"I hurt. Pull me, please?"

"A little pain never hurt anyone."

"Please don't be cute. I'm in serious trouble. I need attention." I needed Medcomp. I couldn't very well return to Uncle Theo's wearing his wings. My fate was entirely in her hands. A tow and a chance to rest—that's all I was asking for. Was it too much? Didn't she owe me at least that for rescuing her?

"Mark, listen to me. I know what it feels like, believe me. It hurts, but there's nothing wrong with you. Pain is just Mother Nature's little way of telling you not to do something again in a way you'll remember."

"I can't move."

"Now, now."

"I'm not getting through to you, am I? I hurt. Very very much. I don't need a lecture. I need surgery. I need. . . ."

"Let me tell you about pain. Pain is when you break your leg in three places, and the bones stick out and there's no one to take care of you and you have to set those broken pieces yourself, reach inside your open wound and push the bones in place with your thumbs. Now that's pain."

"Oh Jesus. How'd you do it?"

"I didn't. But it could happen, and it would make what you feel now seem like nothing at all."

"It would?"

"Well, certainly."

"Then do it. Break my legs. Please?"

"Don't be that way with me, Mark. You're too used to comfort to be any judge of pain. You can fly, believe me you can." But rather than argue the point, she reached out, took hold of my down-cord, plucked it, and sent me on my way. "You can do it," she shouted. I had very little choice, really.

I quickly put out my wings before I got too much speed on, caught the wind, and flew. Painfully. No tricks, no turns, not much speed, zero technique, but I flew. She could see I was new to the art. She pulled overhead and began shouting commands down on me. "Legs up. Arch your back. More. That's better. Now point your toes. Keep those legs up. . . ." She maintained a position above me, shouting strangely worded orders from her own private lexicon of terms and phrases, simple English mostly, like, "Pull in on the grips," instead of "Tuck," or "Bring your wings closer together, pull down, you're sagging," instead of "furl." I was in no position to correct her. Under her guidance I managed to cross the channel in one pass without mishap. She forced me to admit that it wasn't so bad after all. I even confessed to a certain joy at having done it in a single pass. She said, "Good. Let's do one more. Come on, you can do it."

She was going to toughen me up. I could see it coming. A second pass proved possible, and by the end of the third I was eager for a fourth. So what can I say? She was right.

"Are you hungry?" she asked, just as I was about to pull up again.

She had to go and spoil it. "Oh god." I was certainly hungry. I'd never before been so hungry so frequently. One tab used to do me for a whole day.

"Let's stop here and see what we can find." I had no idea where "here" was. We'd lost sight of the ocean. I was a whiz at orientation, but even the best need some major recognizable feature to steer by, a big name mountain, or river, or ruin, because otherwise green is green. "Follow me," she said, pulling up a few meters above the trees. I hovered beside her.

"Look around you. What do you see?" I said nothing. "Don't you see that part in the trees?" She pointed. I didn't. She flew off to show me close up. "We begin by finding a stream," she said. She found one but stayed aloft. "First water, then food. Now look around, especially near the stream. What do you see?" Absolutely nothing at all. But *she* saw a feast. Circling like a hawk above the trees, diving on helpless little plants she spotted, she soon filled her sack with what she called "lunch." I felt like a cannibal, one life form eating another, but that was a better feeling than hunger. Anyway, it was a trade I seemed willing enough to make.

It was a magnificent feeling for the first time in my life to be able to lift off when I pleased, go from place to place as I pleased, flying on the wind. The nearest thing to it in my experience up til then was flying my little cameras on the remote system on those rare occasions when it was allowed. But the pictures they'd send back were only so-so, and without sound. And when all was said and done, where was I? Alone in my room, watching TV. It's a whole different thing being there in person. For freedom, for real honest-to-god freedom, I was willing to endure the pain and the stuff Synthetica called food for almost one full day.

Before taking off again she made me undress and smear a mud and herb concoction over my face and hands, where the sun and wind would do their worst. Another messy ointment on my shoulders, inside my crotch, and around my waist, where the harness straps were wearing me raw. She did the same to herself. The stuff dried like paint. With our clothes off we looked like a couple of primitives. I said, "It's bad enough we have to eat this stuff, but war paint?"

"This time," she said while strapping up, "I want you to fly to my right. I'll set a distance between us, but you'll have to keep it, understand? Stay away from me. There's no sense having two of us searching over the same ground. Remember, we're looking for a small round field with a gentle grassy hill."

"What are you talking about?"

"My father's clearing. We'll fly due east. I'll cover the north, you cover the south. Stay high. Keep an eye on me. If you see something you think might be his clearing, just stay there with your light flashing. Wait for me. You got that?"

"Oh." It had slipped my mind. "Sure, why not?"

"If you get lost, same thing. Stay in one place and blink. I'll find you."

"Roger. But...."

"What?"

"What if *you* get lost?"

"I won't."

"I hope you know where you're going, because I sure don't."

"I do."

"Well...." North America had a reputation for size and desolation. To my knowledge Uncle Theo was its only permanent resident. "All right, if you say so." I wanted to fly, not stand around debating the finer points of navigation. She was just as anxious to begin the search again after three months' delay as I was to exercise my new freedom.

We flew parallel courses, about one full kilometer apart. It was a lot harder flying without her telling me what to do every second, but considerably more enjoyable. The racing wing turned out to be well suited for the job at hand, fast, capable of sustained high-altitude near-level flight. A cruising wing will stay up longer, but the object was to move along fast and cover lots of ground.

We did not find her father's clearing that afternoon, as I suspected we wouldn't. We passed over several breaks in the forest, but nothing resembling the clearing she described. Lakes, mostly. I counted twenty-one, plus two freeway interchanges, a few skyscraper frames sticking up at odd angles from the trees, one truly giant gas station (at least a forty pumper), a refinery, a chemical plant, and one very large U.S. Govt. installation still holding back the forest for no visible reason. No clearing remotely resembling her father's—not on my side, not on hers.

She called it off with a blink of her light about three hours before sunset. Two longs, one short: "Me," short for "meet me." We met halfway between our two courses and spent the remaining hours locating water, a place to camp, and food. The evening search for food was more elaborate than the noontime affair, because she wouldn't settle for the easy stuff. We had to gather cookables for the main course, and that meant more than an aerial survey; it meant getting down on our hands and knees and sniffing around in the dirt. That's grubbing, and I absolutely refused.

She put it this way: "You either help or you can go without. It's your choice."

"The deal was, I help you search, you feed me. That's what you said."

"You see these?" she said, ignoring what she didn't want to hear. We were upstream from a comfortable little spot where she'd decided to camp. "These are onions. I want you to take this stick and dig them up. I'll show you how."

"No. No. No. No. That wasn't the deal."

"It wasn't?"

"You know it wasn't."

"Hum. You're probably right. Ah, well. The deal's off." She proceeded to un-nest the onions, while I stood there trying to figure out what she meant by that.

"Hey, now, you can't back out. It isn't fair. After all I've done for you. You wouldn't even be here if I hadn't gotten you the wings."

"Oh Mark, I think it's wonderful what you did. I really do."

"Yeah, well.... Show some gratitude then."

"Thanks. Now grab a stick and help me dig."

"No. No. I won't. A deal's a deal. You have to feed me. You promised."

"So go back," she said, without so much as a glance my way.

"What??" I couldn't believe it. Even Mimi Jo would keep her end of a bargain.

"You heard me. Go back."

"Oh yeah? Yeah? Just see if I don't." She paused in her gardening, turned her head, saw that I hadn't moved, and continued.

"I'm going."

"......"

"So long."

".........."

"Aren't you even going to say good-bye?"

"Good-bye."

I waited. I had one more thing to say. Then I was going for sure. When she was done with the onions and about to attack some cabbages up the way, I said, "ummm..."

"Yes?"

"Which way's back?"

8

I was born to be diddled with. I passed from one sly hand to the next. There was no escaping it. She had me body, and ... well, according to her, Market people had no souls, so she had my body. Out of disrespect for Free Marketeers in general, she treated me like an animal, a beast of burden, to be cared for, perhaps, but only minimally. Certainly my thoughts and feelings were unimportant. She trained me, told me what to do, and pressed me into service. Oh, there were occasional moments of tenderness, but these were like bits of sugar offered to a horse. Because she rode me, she rode me hard.

She never asked where I got the wings. It probably never occurred to her that I did anything more than put in a request to procurement. I never told her I stole them. I didn't volunteer much about Uncle Theo, school, or anything else that might clue her to the secret of my youth. It turned out she didn't even care enough about me, let alone my pedigree, to inquire about my upbringing. The family secret was kept, not by any great effort on my part, but by virtue of her disinterest. If I'd told her flat out that I was unique among all the Market people, a generation apart, she'd have had me digging turnips just the same.

As to my obvious deficiencies, in her mind all the Market people were so devoid of worth that the difference between one or another of us was insignificant.

Which isn't to say she was entirely wrong either in her attitude toward the Market in general or in her treatment of me in particular. I'm big enough now, I think, at least to entertain the argument that I should have perhaps participated in some small way in our survival effort. One could argue that since we were both in the same boat, for whatever reason, we should share equally in the rowing. That's one argument. Although I maintain that she should have eased me into things more gently. After all, I was totally out of my own element. I was taken out of a world where survival was entirely automatic and put in a position where life itself depended on correct procedure. I'd been raised believing that the aim and purpose of life was to avoid boredom, and most of my talent and accomplishments lay along those lines. Then to find myself with a whole new purpose of life, namely life itself, *survival* no less, was a shattering experience. All of a sudden everything I saw, everything I heard, everything I *did* had to be reassessed, not with the question "will this kill some time," but will this *buy* me some time." Regarding time as a commodity, for the first time in my life I was faced with a seller's market.

On the other hand, maybe I make too much of being stuck in the woods.

I remember how, in the newness of the situation, the simplest things would frighten me almost to death. For example. All that first afternoon I felt very peculiar, a feeling in my gut, familiar and yet strange, not entirely unpleasant, but not knowing what it was, I was afraid. After dinner it got worse. I slept fitfully, as all night long it kept getting worse. And worse. I was almost certain I'd been poisoned by any one or all of those organisms I'd been obliged to consume. In the morning I woke up screaming. I was overcome—*possessed* by a powerful raging feeling, like my insides were about to explode. I jumped up, ran in circles around the remains of the fire, whining and sniveling, tearing at my suit until I had it undone. And then, running around naked, I began to tear at my skin in the same way, until, all at once, I looked up at the trees towering over me and remembered that day long long ago, and I knew. I headed straight into the woods, squat behind a tree, and . . . it was enormous. No resemblance to my usual monthly pellet. It felt like giving birth to a cow. I screamed as it emerged. Screamed again when I saw what I had done. Synthetica woke, jumped up, grabbed a stick, and rushed over to defend me.

I shouted, *"There, there on the ground. Look!!!"* I pointed.

She raised her stick high and brought it down with a thundering thunk, splitting the creature in two. She raised her stick to strike again and sort of woke up to what she was doing. It was no snake at all.

She thought she'd been had. I didn't intend it that way, but I can't say I was overcome by any compassionate urge to ease her embarrassment. She dropped the stick and muttered something like, "You better not do that again."

I explained, "I couldn't help it. It came out that way."

"You know what I mean. You scream like that only when you're in danger."

"To me it looks dangerous."

"Yeah, well. . . ." She walked off to take her morning dip in the stream. I think, I'm not certain, but I think I heard her giggle just a little. Folks overcome with purpose aren't among the worlds great laughers, I'd say. So I give her credit where I can.

She taught me the morning rituals, including the bathing in the icy stream, the rinsing of the hub cap in which the remainder of the evening's stew had caked, and the slaughter of the fish. She knew better than to force that one on me. I learned to get by on leftovers and fruit.

We flew that day, the next and the next a kilometer apart. Over lunch she'd have me report all I'd seen. Again over dinner. If I was the least foggy in my recollection she'd have us backtrack and cover the same ground again. This I think she did to keep me alert, because after awhile straight level flight becomes monotonous and the mind wanders.

We were in the mountains. I was terribly discouraged, not only by my own predicament, but by what seemed to me like a hopeless, pointless waste of effort. I said as much, but got no response from her. I begged her, "Can't you at least remember? You used to live there. I mean were there mountains nearby?" None that she could recall. "Well, then, what are we doing in the mountains anyway, for Christ's sake." She explained that growing up under the trees put her out of view of the local geography. It was a literal case of someone having never seen the forest for the trees. There may have been mountains not far from her clearing, but that was beside the point. The object was to be thorough, cover every inch of land so she would have no doubts whatsoever.

Each day she involved me more in the food gathering. Aside from the digging and the plucking and the snipping, she required me to *name* the plants as she pointed them out. Later on she had me offering a decision as to their nutritional worth. She made me both their judge and their executioner.

I said once, "You cheat. A real grubber wouldn't use wings to hunt down plants the way you do. A real grubber would stick to walking. It's hardly fair. I mean a plant can't exactly run and hide. You might as well use a phone and order real food." It wasn't the best of arguments, because neither of us had a phone. But she *was* depending on wings—another "wretched mechanical contrivance," a product of the Free Market. There was inconsistency in that.

She'd considered that before and had an answer on tap: "It was a wing which took me from my father. A wing shall take me back."

I said, "That's no answer." But it was.

Deep in what was once a lovely desert valley but now because of the unnatural rain supply a thick swampish garden of exotic vegetation, I got to meet Mr. Crenshaw, king of the lopes, and Cousin Honeydew. They were sharing the same patch. Tasty tasty, let me tell you, especially after a couple of days in the high regions eating bitter little nuts and berries. We spent an entire day there restocking the herb supply. She gave me an item by item description of everything she touched. I was taught leaf configuration and coloration, which to eat, which to brew, which to dry, which to grind into ointments, and which to avoid like poison (which could have been all of them as far as I was concerned). Then late in the afternoon, with our appetites at their fullest, we surrounded ourselves with the day's catch. Such a collection of morsels I'd never seen. My mouth watered so much I couldn't swallow fast enough. I drooled with delight. I hadn't been with her a full week and already I was salivating. I'm a fast learner.

At her suggestion we took our clothes off so that we wouldn't get them sticky. With a warm fire, a cozy camp, and a clean pool nearby, we had a feast. We plunged into our victims like a couple of Romans at an orgy, ripping at the melons and the squashes and the fruits, tearing them apart with our bare hands, flipping peels, skins, shells, and pits over our shoulders, squirting each other with grapefruits and oranges and generally making pigs of ourselves. This went on until we were both too stuffed to move. Wet and sticky we laid out on either side of the fire to rest, watching the sky through the trees as day faded into night.

All in all, it turned out to be a fine and pleasant day, and I knew that if we kept the conversation to a minimum it could end that way. We lay there quietly digesting, letting our minds wander where they might. Quite independently (because we didn't say a thing) it seems they settled on the same subject.

In a sickeningly sweet voice that didn't become her, she let on how she thought I'd become much more attractive in the last day or so, *physically* attractive, she insisted, leaving me to suppose that my mind was still just as rotten. The combination of wind, sun, mud, and herb had stripped off the last vestige of my skin shellac. I was as dull to behold and as lusterless as she was, and damned near as hairy. Without cream to keep them in check, my ears had made an appearance and had grown a full finger's width from my head. They gave every indication of continuing. But she liked what she saw, and wanted to touch me. She eyed me from her side of the fire, got that look, and started saying sweet tender things, like: "You got a biggie for me, huh?"

"It's hardly for you. I mean, you know what I mean."

"Who's it for?"

"You wouldn't understand."

She said she would too understand, and wouldn't let up until I explained. I told her what I could about my special preference for the televised image of Emmy Lou, without giving away any of the family secrets. She had me describe Emmy Lou in every delectable detail until I was more than obviously aroused. I was well beyond the point of no return before I realized that she was purposely leading me on.

"Oh no. Uh-uh. Not a chance."

"Are you going to let a thing like that go to waste?"

"Leave me alone."

"Look at me and tell me I'm not more desirable than your . . . cartoon."

"She's *not* a cartoon. Where'd you get that? Don't you ever call her that again. Never!"

"What is it then?"

"It's a *she*, and she's a conceptual entity, pure idea, the essence of perfect beauty."

"A cartoon."

"Oh yeah? You think that just because she isn't real that something's missing. Well, let me tell you. When I want her, she's right there, ready and waiting. Any time. She doesn't have moods, or headaches, and she never never gets bored. She can't possibly refuse me. But look at you . . . hot for my ass and you can't have me because I won't let you. I've got my rights. Show me a cartoon with rights. I mean. . . ."

"Is she really there whenever you need her?"

"Absolutely. Day or night. Channel . . . oh my God. Oh

my God." No phone, no food tabs, and now, no TV. "Ahhhhhhh!"

"What's the matter?"

". . . . . . ." Suddenly I knew how it was with Uncle Alfred and Aunt Caroline and, for that matter, Synthetica. I'd have worked out some kind of a deal, believe me, if any were possible. But I couldn't. She had nothing of worth to negotiate with. My band of acceptance was extremely narrow. It had to be Emmy Lou, on screen or in my mind. Nothing else would do.

If there was an advantage she enjoyed over all others, it was availability. Emmy Lou was there always. As a result I rarely tuned her in. I could take her or leave her. For this reason I was never what you might call an avid sex enthusiast. Then, for the first time since I had acquired the taste, there was no TV to be had, no Emmy Lou. For the first time, sex took on great importance, greater than I'd ever imagined possible.

"Mark, what is it?"

". . . . ." As if she didn't know. She could *see* what was on my mind.

"Mark, watch out. It's going to attack, I swear."

"You shut up. Leave me alone." I rolled over on my side, my back to her and the fire.

"Such a biggie I've never seen."

"Yeah, you come over here and see how long it lasts." She made motions to do just that. I said, *"No you don't!* Leave me alone. I want to be alone." For what purpose she knew perfectly well.

"I won't say a word. I'll be real quiet. Shhhh." She let me get my mind on the subject and my hand into action. I was only seconds away when she said, "What do you see in your imagination? I shouldn't think very much."

I was quite accustomed to being watched. I'd rarely had it any other way. Interruption was something new, though. The folks at home may have been low on scruples, but they would never interrupt another in the act. No greater sin could they imagine. The opportunities for revenge were just too many and too obvious. But she was an uncultured primitive creature, lacking in the moral and ethical standards of the times. She let me establish a rhythm, listened to my breathing, and when most she shouldn't have, she said, "Do you pretend she's touching you, or what? What do you imagine?"

"Aw fer . . . you want to know what I imagine? I imagine you're somewhere else. That's what I imagine."

"Oooo, you got a mean streak."

"Now shut up. That was damned rude of you and you know it."

"Shhhhh. I'll be quiet as a mouse." Another stretch of silence, just time enough, and then she said, "Tell me when you're there, I want to know."

"Well I'll be. . . . Damn it!"

"Oh. I'm sorry. I shouldn't have. I'll be quiet, I promise. My fault." A minute passed, and another. Recovery is always a good deal slower than progress from a clean start. I finally got close again, and she said, "Doesn't it make you feel strange to do that with me watching you?"

"Oh, God damn. I don't believe it. I just can't believe it. What's the matter with you, don't you have any sense of decency? I was just on the verge, you know that? Just on the verge."

"Oh Mark. I *am* sorry. I thought you were done. No, really, I'm sorry. Look, not another word. I promise."

"Never mind. Never mind. I'll go someplace else." I got up, member in hand, and marched angrily away, out of the light of the fire, out of range of her nauseating voice, toward some private place in the woods where I could be alone with my precious delicate imaginings.

She called out, "I hope it's a good one," a touch of indignation in her tone.

I scurried like a rabbit, barefoot along the side of the pond, one hand out to fend off branches in the dark woods, the other to carry the load. Moving along that way, I wasn't quite out of earshot when I stubbed my toe hard on a protruding rock. I hopped on one foot, lost balance, and went head over heels into the water with a loud splash. What had been comfortably cool during the day was cold as ice at night. It took my breath clean away. I let out a shrill cry followed by a series of sharp chirps that echoed back and forth across the valley for minutes after. I scrambled out, shook myself off and just sat there shivering in the dark—limp, meek, and dissatisfied.

When the last echo of my scream had died away and all was quiet again, Synthetica called up to me, with all the sarcasm she could muster, "Gee, I wish mine were like that."

9

Each morning she woke up eager to get a move on. *Frantic* is more the word. I woke up groggy, depressed, and anxious to get back to sleep. When it came time to fly, I would protest. She would ask me if I felt okay. If I said yes, that was it. I flew or was left behind. If I said no, she'd offer me a foul medicine, a tea or some filthy root to chew on, or a painful massage. All threats, every one. It was either fly without complaint or suffer the agonies of acute folk cure. Fly in either case.

The difference between us wasn't strength or health; near the end of the first week I was sufficiently healthy. My muscles no longer ached, and I could reach the end of the day no more exhausted than she. I wasn't the least homesick either. That's a sickness I've yet to experience.

What made it right for her and not for me was purpose. She had it; I didn't. Her purpose didn't work for me. I had absolutely no desire whatsoever to meet the man behind all her anti-Market slander. In my mind there could be nothing more unpleasant than a self-righteous nature buff railing against civilization. Unless it was two self-righteous nature buffs.

Then one morning I woke up with the realization that I too had a purpose, not unlike hers, one that would involve me in a search for something which had been denied me for quite some time, since birth, actually. A phone. It was the simplest idea. It had been on my mind all week how a phone might solve her problems without it ever having occurred to me how completely one would solve mine. I guess up to then I had been content enough to tolerate a situation that was fast becoming intolerable. A phone would get me where I wanted to be, which was *out*. With a phone I would be able to establish my existence with the Credit Bureau and apply for my rightful monthly allotment of Free Marks, not to mention a house from the department of housing, and a flyer from the department of transportation. Because after nineteen years I was, well, nineteen, a legal adult, fully entitled to everything everyone else was. And if all I was suited for was a life of depravities, it would be *my* life and *my* depravities. The one key being contact. A phone would do it. A simple phone. No phone, no dice. Law of the land. Of course, Mimi Jo and company were no dummies. The chance of my finding one just lying about in the wilderness was about equal to that of Synthetica's finding her father. But no matter. I figured if she could wake up each and every morning a trembling fanatic over a million to one shot, then I could muster up enough enthusiasm to get up and wash without being told.

Thereafter there occurred a transformation she was at a loss to understand. I kept the reason for it to myself. There was no need to tell her. My course could follow hers as always, no need to change it. One route was as good as another. But if her method was as thorough as she claimed, so much the better for me.

For this reason I got interested in her navigation. "Trust me" was no longer enough. I pressed her for details. I knew about east and west, and about the sun and all that, but without enough altitude to pick up the important geographical features, or a map, or a compass, or a sextant, or a direction-finder, or a compu-guide, or a satellite grid projector or a hundred and one other fancy gadgets, "How," I asked, "do you know what course to follow?"

She said, "I remember the look of the land and fly north of my previous course."

"Impossible," I said.

"Not if you go over in your head every night what you've seen during the day. It sticks." In other words she was telling me that she used her head. Unheard of. And I didn't believe it until I tried it myself. Difficult at first, easy later. Much later. But I must say it's amazing what even the littlest brain can accomplish when there's something to be had for the effort.

For no other reason but that we were in the same business, I now took a new and lively interest in my food lessons, and learned at twice my previous rate. In no time at all I became an expert on the fruit. Fruits are the easiest. They're found on trees. They are usually some color other than green, and as such easy to spot from the air. No preparations are required—just pick, peel, and eat. And what's more, you can do the tree a service in return by swallowing a few seeds whole and passing them encased in fertilizer on some sunny lawn. That's what nature had in mind, we think.

With my knowledge of fruits alone I might have survived on my own long enough to find my way back. By then I wanted to continue on. In fact, for a few days it was me, not her, wanting to go on for one more pass and one more again, late in the day when it was time to make camp.

She had two advantages I didn't. She knew what she was looking for, and she had me to help her; whereas I hadn't the slightest idea where I'd find a phone or what I should be looking for; nor was she contributing to my half of the search.

I don't know what I expected to see—something civilized, I suppose, something smooth, something shiny. Anything untree like. Except another ruin. We passed over hundreds of broken structures, but nothing I hadn't see the likes of before over Europe with my remote camera. I had no special fascination for surface structures. I was more of a subterranean buff, a reaction to sky life, no doubt.

We passed just to the south of the ruins of Denver. At the time of the Big One, Denver was the largest city west of Detroit, with suburbs in Utah. I wanted to stop. She didn't. She had no taste for ruins. I felt we could spare a couple of hours, just to buzz around the streets and peek into a few shops and offices. I was especially fond of the Denver Subway. I'd been through it end to end by camera, and thought it would be a lovely thing to find some station I'd visited via the screen, if for no other reason than to be there in person and compare the difference. I blinked to stop. She knew what I had in mind and blinked back the big "N.O." She could linger a whole day in the greenery if it suited her, but she had no time to spare me for my particular passions. Just as well. There'd be no phones in Denver.

Our eighth day together. I woke up raring. I got the chores done, the food down, and was standing in the clear waiting for her to get into action. She gave me queer looks like she thought I was making fun of her. Not that she disapproved. Whatever it took, she was all for it. She finished dressing, strapped up, and assumed her position beside me, ready for the first ascent. Then just like that the morning sun winked out. Like an axe, the shadow of Nimbus crossed the land. She said, "Rain."

I said, "We still got a couple of hours, no?"

She said, "We should look for cover."

"A little rain never hurt anyone. Come on."

She knew better, but she let me persuade her rather than risk the end of my delicate new enthusiasm. We rose to the top and found ourselves in sunlight again. But the eastern horizon was obscured by a thin black line growing thicker as it moved toward us.

It was usual in my experience that come rain day, the house would close up, rise the necessary distance, and let the cloud slip by underneath; at night, more often than not, while I slept. So even though the entire weather system was a Free Market institution, I knew less about it than Synthetica—experientially, that is. I knew something of the way it worked.

She took a look at that great wall of dark vapors and flashing blue fire, and said, "Uh-uh."

"Oh come on. It's only electricity."

So we split off, she to the north, me to the south. We turned and resumed our eastward crossing. It wasn't long before we were in its shadow again, and I have to admit, facing it for the first time like that, from a low angle, exposed to it with only a thin flyer's suit and a pair of frail plastic wings, I felt like a fly up against the Great Wall of China.

As much as I might have wanted to, I couldn't call it off. More to save face than out of any big hurry to find a phone I set off toward it. Synthetica, a tiny dot off my left wing tip, did the same, probably for the same reason. Although we were still several kilometers to the west, the advance turbulence caused a terrific amount of buffeting, which made flying extremely difficult. Racers sweep such a wide path through the sky that they never miss a sharp vertical draft or "air pocket" if there are any about. There were plenty in advance of the storm. Still, it was my judgment versus hers, so I continued my pass, searching with extra care for any sort of clearing that might serve as an acceptable excuse to stop short. Unfortunately, we were in among the highest mountains to date, where the chances of coming across a likely clearing couldn't have been worse.

I finished the pass without a tumble, and began my second ascent when I heard the dull roar of thunder. That did it. I put my hand to the grip and was about to flash my light when something to the south caught my eye. A beacon.

I glanced off north. Synthetica was still in parallel position. It wasn't her light. It was the wrong color for a flyer's light and the wrong code. Free flyers flash a high intensity purple.

This was yellow, exceedingly bright, blinking simply on and off; marking a place, but saying nothing about it.

It was no summit marker for the good reason that it was below the peaks, situated on what appeared to be a sheer vertical face. I was naturally curious, and would have been under any circumstances, but especially so now that I was on the lookout for a phone.

I continued my ascent. Out of the corner of my eye I could see purple flashes from Synthetica. She wanted to quit. Right now. I didn't blame her, but this thing looked in easy range, half a pass, no more. Plenty of time, it seemed to me, so I ignored her. She turned herself ninety degrees and focused her beam directly at me, searing me with hot bright signals to meet and descend.

I continued my climb, but stopped short of a full ascent. One wasn't necessary and time was short. I spread wing, pulled down, leveled out forty-five degrees off the old course, and beelined toward the beacon, wings tucked three-quarter for stability. I traded perhaps too much off my glide ratio for a smooth ride, because my pass ended short. I lost some time making another ascent. I looked up at Nimbus, and up, and up. It had gotten huge, literally sky high, 4400 meters from bottom to top, as a matter of fact; fifty kilometers wide and as long as the earth itself, pole to pole, a moving wall, black as death. At my altitude among the peaks it was alive with electric fire and thunder that rattled the ribs. It had always looked like such a pussy from the pool. I'd never imagined.

I turned to look for Synthetica. She was nowhere around. I flashed my light. No response. The western sky was clear and inviting. I decided it was the place to be. I turned and spread wing in that direction. At that very instant control central fired off a bolt of lightning from a nearby generator, so bright it would have blinded me if I'd been facing the other way. Not half a count later I was stunned by a blast of thunder that nearly blew me out of the sky. My wings snapped in of their own accord, and I ended up spinning, feet and arms wide apart, over and over until enough sense was knocked into me to pull up. I spread and flew as hard and as fast as I'd ever flown, due west on a steep dive. I was close in among the peaks. I could see my progress over ground. Facing west, wind shrieking on the struts, I found myself moving slowly, gradually east. Backwards! I was being sucked into the storm.

Big icy drops of rain splattered against my face, the first rain I'd ever felt, and I remember being surprised that it was so cold. The nearest likeness in my experience was the bathroom shower. I wondered to myself how I could be having such thoughts at a time like that, unless in thinking of the bathroom where I grew up I was beginning my life's review in preparation for the end. That thought in turn awakened me to my situation. The brain went click, and all the available alternatives presented themselves for consideration. I couldn't go west because of the powerful eddy pulling me back east. I could pull up on lift, but not higher than the top of Nimbus. Not high enough. I could do only two things: drop, or turn around and face the direction I was going and thereby add a measure of control to my flight. Or a combination of both.

I tucked, dropped, and turned back east. The landscape I faced was hopelessly barren. I could see nothing that might offer me protection. There were no trees anywhere at that altitude, only burned-out stumps and charred logs split by lightning, waiting for me to join them. The yellow light was still there flashing. I reefed, one-quarter tuck, and deadheaded straight toward it, with the clear understanding that I'd have no second chance. If the light turned out to be nothing more than a busted beacon fallen from the peak, I would be spending the duration of the storm at the altitude of the lightning generators, a sure target for electrocution.

As I got closer I could see that the beacon was situated on a small outcropping of rocks in the middle of an otherwise sheer granite cliff that extended hundreds of meters straight up from the rocky rubble below. This was the north face of a medium-high mountain whose south face sloped gently to a plateau region that extended to the next range of mountains many kilometers away. My ground speed was tremendous, the speed of flight plus the speed of the wind. If the summit had stood in front of me instead of to the south, I would have been smacked against it with a force no little lift unit could have countered. I planned my approach carefully. When I was in line with the north face and at the altitude of the light, I turned once again west, subtracting wind velocity with flight velocity, and that way brought myself up alongside the cliff at a reasonable pace. A strong vertical wind drafted me up the side of the cliff. I eased in on my left wing more and more as I came closer, glancing back over my shoulder to gauge my approach. I came in low. I put on lift power, a cheat that would have disqualified me instantly from competition. More suddenly than I expected I was against the rock, hands and feet touching, almost directly below my target. I packed both wings, grabbed onto cracks and crevices, put on more lift, and spidered the rest of the way up. Just as I reached the level of the beacon, a powerful suction swooped me up and over, inside an opening, feet first. A backward sommersault. I ended up stretched out on a dry cement floor, looking out a round opening as Nimbus closed across like a thick black curtain, shutting me inside for the duration.

10

As it turned out, even if I *had* entered the cloud I still wouldn't have died. Far from it. The presence of a sizable foreign body in motion near the perimeter would have been detected, and the local generators would have shut themselves off. A rescue craft would have emerged from one of the weather stations inside the cloud and carried me to safety, entirely automatically. If I'd fainted or been unconscious for any reason, the craft would have scooped me up, dried me off, scanned me for injuries, notified Medcomp, and according to the best medical advice attainable administered whatever cure I required. It would also have put me in voice and visual contact with whomever I desired, plus do whatever else it could to put me in good spirits, free of charge so I wouldn't be inclined to sue the weather company for scaring me half to death. Soft music, the works. But I didn't know about the safety features, and I'm glad, because I would have traded all the cures and comforts in the Market to be where I was at that moment.

There were some back home who would have paid a fortune to be there. I was appreciative. I knew what it was worth the very second I found myself inside, safe and sound. I sat there beaming. I played it over in my mind verbally, imagining the uncles and aunts hanging on every word, green with envy. They would have simply died, every one of them. When I think of the outrageous sums they'd spend on cheap little imitation experiences, it makes me sick. Uncle Michael with his fake farm, a dust bowler where the greatest threat was an overgrowth of crops. Eight hundred fifty Free Marks. Aunt Paula had twenty percent of her monthly income transferred automatically to the Venture Company account so that once every six months or so she could experience a surprise attack on her house, or a kidnapping, or a gang rape by a famous team of specialists that did that sort of thing for a whopping fee. Twenty percent out of every month's deposit! She argued that the rapes were good for her figure. You could lose more weight in one afternoon just avoiding pimentos. Aunt Ruth was every bit as weird. She'd have herself crucified once a year, around Easter, along with several dozen of her friends. Only did they use real nails? Hardly. They gave them little bicycle seats to perch on, and *glued* the backs of their hands to the crosses. By law the Venture Company could incur no injuries. Same with Paula. She had the contractual right to call off her attackers at any stage of the game (although at the forfeiture of her deposit). But what's a gang rape without a little risk? Or the bigger question: what's life without a little living? That wasn't living; that was *acting*. Game playing. They pretended to live as best they knew how, and I give them credit for their ingenuity, but it just wasn't *real*. The threats, the risks, the problems they pretended to face had no ultimate fundamental consequences and therefore left them ultimately, fundamentally dissatisfied. I sat there in that little opening, looking out at the dark and powerful forces I'd faced and conquered, and I said to myself, "My God, it didn't cost a dime. Not one free dime."

After awhile I got to wondering about poor wet Synthetica probably sitting it out under a tree. She'd turned back in time; I wasn't worried about her safety, only her comfort. Actually, I wasn't *too* worried. My greatest concern was what I'd do with myself for the next seven and one-half miserable hours with absolutely nothing to do but sit in my little hole and stare at the dark. I got up, went back inside a short distance to be out of the spray of rain, swept away the dust and gravel from a spot on the floor, and settled down for a nap. I sneezed. I closed my eyes. The echo of my sneeze returned, hollow and muted. I sat right up, blinking. I clapped my hands once sharply. I counted to three before the echo returned. I got up, snapped on my light, and took a long hard look at where I was.

I thought I knew, but I had a powerful superstitious instinct to resist anything too good to be true. Still, the evidence was all one hundred percent in favor—the shape, the size, the spartan decor. It was obviously an ancient cavity. I walked farther back inside. The slope was right too: gentle at first, gradually steepening. It was either the air duct of an economic shelter or my little cameras had been lying to me all those years. I couldn't contain a loud, "Yippie," just one. It returned to me with interest from the end of the shaft, and I let that be a good sign. An economic shelter it certainly was, and me with only seven and one-half hours to explore it.

The thing is, I knew right up front that it just couldn't be. A think like that was impossible. Absurd. Of the over four thousand shelters listed, not one, not a single one was open for personal inspection. No visitors allowed. That was the law. The purpose was to prevent souvenir hunters from stripping them bare, and a good thing too, or people like me would have nothing left from that period but pictures and words, neither one of which can be trusted. On the other hand, it drove the price of antiques right off the boards, effectively killing the market for all but the very wealthy.

Miniature cameras, however, were allowed in through small monitored service ports. There were no limits or restrictions on cameras of any sort, providing they fit through the port and carried no servo-manipulators. It was a known fact, though, that a certain few unscrupulous small artifact collectors owned remote control snitchers designed to look like simple cameras. They'd get caught every so often, put on *Tongue Lash*, cry like babies in front of a prime time audience, beg forgiveness, *get it*, then go right out after the show and steal again. For good reason. There's a case on record of a single unopened bottle of R.C. Cola going for 78,000 Free Marks. Like they used to say, "Money's free," but that was close to fifteen years' accumulation of it. It wasn't *that* free. 78,000 FM. You could buy a house for twelve.

I had no doubt about the reality of my dramatic little brush with death; I mean it *did* happen, and the odds on a thing which has come to pass are one to one. But the existence of an unsealed shelter seemed to me at the time to be quite impossible. Absurdly so. Unless! Grasping for anything likely, I hit upon two possible explanations: one, that it was a genuine antique as it appeared to be, only in the hands of a *private owner*; or two, that it was a refurbished shelter owned by the Venture Company. Private ownership was a thing of the past, although there was always some loose chatter among the aunts and uncles to the effect that a very few wealthy individuals still maintained secret shelters for their own entertainment, but kept them unlisted for the sake of what remained of the market. I ruled out the private ownership theory as unimaginable and went straight for the Venture Company notion. I put it together very quickly in my head: the Venture Company had purchased some stripped derelict way out in the wilderness at a "reasonable" price, and had refurbished it for the delight of a paying clientele who wanted to relive that period of history when people stayed underground. Pure madness, I knew, but for that reason most likely.

I went the way I'd gone by camera dozens of times before in other shelters, using virtually the same technique. I put myself into neutral buoyancy and let the draft suck me inside. Although I'd never put a camera into that particular passage before, they're all so much alike that I was able to make that long-awaited comparison between screen and personal presence. The first and most dramatic difference was the odor, a musty damp sweaty smell that got worse as I moved farther inside. There wasn't much to listen to, but I was able to touch the walls and feel the texture of old cement, which I was never able to do before.

I guessed that I was inside a Coldwell Banker structure (that was the only company to use a left-hand spiral in their ductwork), and in particular a model X/D57, or Midnight Sun, as it was more popularly known. The Midnight Sun was a medium deluxe model common to the seven continents, built during the earliest years of the Big One, when the rich people still had some time to plan and pay attention to detail. All shelters, early or late, had in common many basic features. Cheap lift was still unknown, so they were put deep underground instead of out in orbit, and surrounded by a shell of steel and concrete so thick that they were impervious to all but nuclear explosives. It was assumed that the marauding starving bands of poor people against whom the shelters were built would never be able to afford nuclear devices, an assumption which proved to be correct in ninety-nine percent of the cases. "A" and "H" bombs were just too damned expensive, more expensive than in recent times, despite the added collectors' value.

Every shelter had at least two air ducts with secret, well-disguised, and inaccessible openings, lined from one end to the other with booby traps, everything from a simple but elegant stainless steel grate over the opening to some really clever little tricks farther in to keep out the less well-to-do. The bars in this one, if there ever were any, had been taken off or else they'd rusted out long ago, but deeper down things looked reasonably well-preserved. About 150 meters inside I came across a series of brightly colored pornographic murals on the ceiling of the tunnel (the hallmark of a Midnight Sun, so my guess was correct). These somewhat gross but interesting representations were put there to attract one's attention up and away from the even more interesting fact that there would be no floor for awhile, just a deep pit with an array of self-cleaning spikes at the bottom. Before the age of cheap personal lift, before the positions portrayed on the ceiling became commonplace, that trick deterred a good many intruders from going any farther. I, of course, simply ballooned over the pit with the in-draft, fending off the top and sides, feeling with my very fingertips for the first time what I had only guessed before were mere decals. Same pictures the world over.

Just beyond the pit the tube turned up and ran vertically. Then, at the place where it turned and leveled out again, I found myself confronting the gun bunker, a small square concrete chamber with slots and machine guns pointed every which way, in case somehow someone bridged the pit. A few of those old guns tried their rusty best to nail me in a whimsical sort of way, spitting and sputtering out old corroded bullets which spun around harmlessly on the floor when I crossed the beam. Just in case someone made it past the first and second lines of defense, there was the big ventilator fan itself, milling slowly. In their day those blades were lethal, but now all I had to do was stop it with my foot. Once on the *Tuesday Night Explorer Adventure* the guest star got himself sucked through the fan and chopped up into little thin slices. Rud a dud dud. His friends gathered up all the pieces, slapped them one on top of the other, sprayed the stack with healant, and the poor bastard lived. In the hurry, though, they got the slice with his mouth turned upside down. After that, the others in the party had to stand on their heads to make out what he was saying. Trash, I know, but not without charm.

Beyond the fan was the filter room with its poison gas detectors and what-not, which monitored the air and made it breathable for the shelter's inhabitants. I couldn't fit through the screen mesh, so I went around through the service port at level eight. As a rule, levels seven and eight were nothing but a lot of boring little rooms with a chair and a TV set, the so-called suspension chambers. These rooms were once filled with "Slo-Gas," as it was called, a breathable medication which had the effect of slowing down a person's metabolism and sense of time so that what seemed like half an hour was really anywhere from two to three days. It wasn't quite total time suspension, but it was a whole lot better than time at the usual rate, and it conserved their most precious resources, their TV tapes. A single hour's TV could be stretched to a week. I passed and went downstairs to the lower levels, the "real time" habitation levels.

It was at this point, at level five, actually, that I had to open a door. Ordinarily all doors would have been fixed open for the passage of cameras. The very fact that it wasn't open convinced me all the more that I was on Venture Company turf. It stood to reason that they wouldn't want their corridors swarming with miniature cameras belonging to people too cheap to pay the price of admission. It gave me great pleasure to be able to grasp the handle, lift the bar, and push on the door with my own physical strength, but I'd just as soon have witnessed the remaining 10,000 meters up in the comfort of the screening room. The smell which came through just about knocked me out. It resembled old food of the sort Uncle Flat enjoyed. ("Flat" was short for flatulence, a name he well deserved.) It was the smell of cooking meat with a touch of vegetation, authentic perhaps, but in my opinion extreme, vulgar, and totally unnecessary.

I paused with the door cracked, giving myself a moment to stifle the urge to vomit and think second thoughts about what I was doing. I wanted to go inside, poke around, touch a few objects, maybe take a ride on a golf cart, a pleasure denied me and my little cameras. On the other hand, I knew if I got caught trespassing on Venture Company property with no proof of payment, they'd bring me up on *Tongue Lash*. That alone was risk enough, but with the family secret exposed, I'd have wound up on a pre-empting special devoted to my case and mine alone. Celebrities suffer tragically for even the teensiest little offenses.

On the other hand, I'd killed less than an hour of the seven and a half, and there I was, mere inches from tactile reality. It was hard for me not to just barge in; but luckily I didn't. Lucky for all of us, maybe.

The compromise I hit on was to sneak a peek. Just a quick one. I shut off my light, put my hand against the door, cracked it open just a wee bit more, and put my eye to the crack. At first I saw nothing but darkness, which bothered me some because the Venture Company would have restored power. But I was mistaken. There *was* a light, dim yellow electric light. It took a moment to adjust, but I was satisfied completely regarding the Venture Company. Nothing happened from that point on to change my mind.

I pushed the door open just a tad more, and saw immediately, directly across the corridor, a phenomenon I'd never seen before except on the screen, and there only rarely. It was a human being, made up to look *old*. The person was just coming out of the door labeled "Ladies' Shower," so I took it to be a lady. I hadn't expected that, not quite *that*. I gasped, in spite of the odor. I gasped so suddenly that the suction drew the door shut in my face. I stood there stunned. She was weird—short, misshapen, her skin gray and wrinkled like she'd just come out of a vat of acid.

It was one thing to manufacture an odor like that, but this visual effect carried authenticity well beyond what good taste required. She was either an actress paid to dress the set or a customer paying for the same privilege. I couldn't decide which, but in either case I thought they'd gone too far. I wasn't opposed to accuracy *per se*, far from it. I realized that that was how it once was with people, and that it was just this sort of attention to detail that made Venture Company stock such a hot item on the big board year after year. But detail or not, I was disgusted, nauseated, sickened from the sight of her. I don't know what compelled me to take a second look. I eased the door open and braced myself to keep from sinking, for it wasn't just one, but two, three, four, five . . . *six* in all, coming and going along the wide door-lined corridor, some in golf carts sure enough, but none you'd likely call beautiful. Among just six I saw a fatty, a skinny, a shorty, and an extra tall, each with his or her own idea of posture, skin texture, and facial style, all in all quite an incredible array of pre-millennium aberrations to be represented by so few individuals.

I got goose bumps. The new little hairs all over my body bristled. I shut the door. I leaned against it and slid to the floor. I sat there, my heart pounding. I caught my breath, got up, took another peek, and sat back down. The effect was so deliciously real and at the same time so upsetting that I didn't know how to react. I understood for the first time what it's like to be a critic, because certainly the artistry was superb, the makeup, the lighting—flawless! But I ask you: who needs to be flawlessly, expertly, artistically sickened to death? I for one resented it. A suggestion of age, a hint, okay; but a precise rendition was, in my opinion, not only unnecessary, but scandalous. Just one more quick peek and I shut the door in disgust and went down to level one.

Every shelter had its main corridor, a sort of double corkscrew, one inside the other, connected top and bottom so that a person could take a long "country" drive in a golf cart down the outside spiral and up the inside, back down, round and round, up and down, without ever having to stop (without getting anywhere, either), an avenue known affectionately among many shelter societies as "The Big Screw." This was the corridor I peeked in at on level five. Four flights of stairs got me to the bottom level, the so-called public sector. Here one could expect to find the main lobby, the shops, the restaurants, ballrooms, recreation facilities, convention center, and the like. If there was to be anything of real worth, it would invariably be found in the public sector, even though ninety percent of the habitable space was residential. A residential suite could be anything from lovely to strange, but rarely did one contain more than a bed, a bath, a TV, and a dresser, the most exciting exception being perhaps the giant fiberglass club sandwich found in Shelter #5232 by Maxwell Hardit, first century millennium. There's been some speculation since that he built it himself and put it there hoping to capture recognition in the world of art for his find. For one thing, his "discovery" predated the sealing of the shelters, and furthermore he was a known (if not respected) sculptor of the day with a long record of failures, all of them sandwiches. So one doubts. Nevertheless, he *was* credited with the find, and no one seemed willing to invest what it took to institute revocation proceedings against him.

In any case, one could search a thousand rooms in the upper levels before finding anything of even casual interest to report. The rule is, if one has only a limited amount of time to explore, one would best confine his search to the public sector, where the real character of a shelter would be most evident.

It was typical of Coldwell Banker and the other builders to leave the entire two lower levels unfinished, so that the folks who moved in would immediately find themselves confronted with a massive interior decorating chore. Psychologists had determined that the problems of interior design would totally occupy the mind of the upper-middle class individual of the day, to the complete exclusion of such thoughts and concerns as the condition of those dear friends and family left outside, too poor to buy in, doomed by their poverty to remain above, exposed to the ravages of the Big One. To the everlasting credit of the psychologists of that bygone day, future generations were able to discover and enjoy some simply fabulous interiors, unequal in their opulence to anything built before or since. So whereas each and every shelter ever built was virtually indentical from top to level two, they were unique and special from two down, reflecting the taste, morals, aspirations, religious philosophies and what-have-you of the society trapped within.

It was assumed by one and all during the early days of the Big One that it couldn't last more than twenty years or so, since in all previous history there had never been a depression lasting any longer. Of course it lasted *much* longer, and the later shelters were very Spartan by comparison to the first ones, reflecting the hasty and functional style that took hold as the Big One got even bigger. But the early models, like the *Midnight Suns* and the Walton and Becket *Ships of State* were opulent, well-appointed, tasteful structures, if perhaps not so well stocked with the more mundane items like food and medicine. It is estimated that over eighty percent of all shelter societies perished due to a lack of simple things like food, but it was just those so-called short-sighted ones who built the greatest and most spectacular shelters of them all. I've watched and listened to those smug and wordy "survivalist" types, with all that intellectual crap about how the simple functional shelters were superior to the more luxurious ones, their best arguments being, "look who made it." But put a slide on the screen of the grand ballroom in #37, with its eight and a half ton crystal chandelier, and they shit their pants same as anyone else. Besides, very few of even the most practical shelter builders, with their drab and dreary "functional" algae ponds and hydroponics, ever imagined the Big One dragging on as long as it did. From what I know of it, it was an understandable miscalculation. It seems that everyone back then just took it for granted that with the earth stripped bare and the entire means of production above ground devoted totally to the building and stocking of shelters below ground, that the poor would necessarily vanish for lack of anything to eat. But instead of disappearing all at once when the food ran out like they should have, the miserable creatures dined on one another, and thus died off very slowly, meal by meal. So in my opinion, it isn't fair to argue that societies from ugly functional shelters were in any way better than those that lived in luxury, since the vast majority of both died like rats in their holes anyway when the food ran out. Although I do admit that of the fifty or sixty societies that weathered the storm, very few had interiors worth boasting about.

Every shelter buff has his own pet theory as to why so few of those that went down ever came back up. On the whole, religious groups endured fairly well on the strength of such faith as the one in Jesus Christ, although Hindu groups survived quite nicely. Hindus use less oxygen. But there were a lot of not-so-religious groups in there among the first to come up, including the Market founders from #8258 near Zurich. Some historians feel it was the ones with the smartest and most inventive computers that made it, which may also be true, but what everyone in their theorizing so kindly overlooks is the cold hard fact that the first few societies to come up from under, *our ancestors*, for reasons religious or secular, saw fit to inject a friendly but lethal gas into shelters harboring societies potentially unfriendly to the new economics of the Free Market, which just happened to be anyone without something useful to contribute, like seeds, animals, books, or clever inventions. I'm here because Mimi Jo's great-greats on her mother's side had the good sense to invent a machine that made other machines out of dirt without any human attention (apparently, people were necessary before). I don't pretend to understand. All I know is that they were able to trade their gizmo for a substantial packet of Market bonds and a seat on the exchange. Now I don't see why I can't be thankful for that and at the same time feel sorry for those thousands of people who made it clear through the Big One only to get the gas because they didn't have anything deemed worthy to contribute to the new world. Each new age begins in darkness. I'm not hiding my head in shame, because I wasn't there to do anything about it. Besides, who's to say that I wouldn't have gotten wrapped up in the arguments of the day and gone along with it? I know how I feel now, but how would I have felt then?

One thing we all agreed on, me and the other *aficionados*, few though we may have been: every one of us felt we owed solemn tribute to the hardy souls of yesteryear who were the first to break into the shelters (at terrible personal risk) to remove the bodies and tally up the treasures. I've seen footage of some of the first openings, seen the way the early great ones looked before the flood of tourists decimated them. They were splendiferous. Or, if you prefer, magnificent. Wondrous to behold. The preservationists got them all sealed off eventually, but too late to save the best.

Although I know of one ranking example—about as grand a place as there ever was—that was never sealed.

11

Like all great "discoveries," mine entailed a certain amount of personal risk and danger. Which I don't at all mind describing, not in the least. It's important to remember that at the time I believed I was in a genuine old shelter, real, but one preserved by the Venture Company for the pleasure of their select clientele, those few wealthy individuals who could afford personal involvement adventures of the historical reenactment variety. I needed some kind of logical rationale, and that seemed to be the best. Unfortunately, once a line of thought like that takes hold it's a hard thing to undo. Each new piece of evidence I encountered along the way filled a niche in the prevailing logic and reinforced my first assumption, wrong or right. Someone else might have taken the very same evidence, the unsealed opening, the costumed people, the smell of the place, the general good condition, and used it to support any number of hypotheses contrary to mine. Believing as I did, that I was sneaking through the property of a well-known and respected corporation, made the whole experience considerably less dramatic for me than it might have been had I settled on the notion of, say, private ownership. Imagine, for example, the scare of being caught by some weird wealthy owner desiring to protect his secret at any cost. Who knew where I was? What would have prevented such a one from disappearing me on the spot, to protect his secret sanctuary? Now admittedly, a good scare—in fact, any high power experience—requires at the very least a certain amount of realism and believability. And as I mentioned, the idea of a single owner with that much capital worth seemed a bit too far-fetched to me. So I had to let that one go. If I'd had any imagination at all, though, I could have embellished on the theme and come up with the idea of a collective, a club of wealthy enthusiasts. Now *that* idea would have had all the realism of corporate ownership plus the scare of private retribution.

I refused to consider the least likely notion of all, that the shelter was genuine in every respect, that the people I saw were in reality what they were made up to look like, descendants of the first and original inhabitants, still holding out against the Big One. That idea could have given me deep feelings. Unfortunately, such thoughts were out of my range of acceptance for a number of obvious reasons. For example, how could any supposed shelter person look out on the fertile landscape and not hunger to rush out and be a part of it? Well, actually, that's a bad example, because the local landscape around there was beat to hell by the bi-monthly passing of Nimbus. More important, every society which survived the Big One either joined the Market or was snuffed out by the founders. Although again, a few shelters did escape gassification, but all of those were eventually located during the first century millennium in response to the then booming antique market. In that search, the last ever conducted, only eleven "new" uncharted shelters were discovered, most of them in Argentina, all of them late models with no artistic merit and no survivors. Furthermore, the all-time record, the longest any society managed to stay under and live to tell about it, was 112 years. That was a fluke, a very special case of a fundamentalist sect that believed the voice of God told them to stay below. They escaped gassification that way, but the voice of God turned out to be an unfinished edge in the air duct that gave off a low moan on windy days, or whenever someone dared to open the service port. 112 years is one thing. 1000 is something else entirely. It would take more than an occasional moan to hold a society under for the duration of the millennium. I'd say at the very least a personal appearance, if not several.

So for a simple lack of likelihood, I ruled out the most deliciously exciting of all possibilities without ever really considering it, and thereby denied myself a truly golden opportunity to experience the most profound feelings of mystery, awe, and discovery.

It's a real shame that I let something as insignificant as simple belief rob me of my right to profound experience. I was too new in the world, too uneducated to go about ruling out possibilities just because they seemed far-fetched to *me*. Who was *I* to pass judgments on the general likelihood of things, a mere nineteen-year-old with a TV education, hardly two weeks out of captivity. All that I knew of the world at large, beyond what I'd picked up watching TV, was limited to what a small band of bored perverts chose to have me believe. It has since occurred to me that they may even have gone so far as to have my TV regulated by some override program slipped into the central control monitor. I'm not saying they did, but they could have. Easily. Which means I had no business judging any truth whatsoever, let alone the nature of the shelter I was in.

Nevertheless, being as I was, *what* I was, no matter who determined the elements of my understanding, *there* I was in what I believed to be a Venture Company shelter.

I peeked in on the main corridor at level one and found all the lights off. I figured it was either early morning "episode time" or late evening. I'd noticed a predominance of towels and bathrobes on the "inhabitants," so I assumed naturally that it must be one or the other. In either case, with the lights off in the public sector, I knew I was all alone down there. It was very very dark. I didn't even catch the glimmer of a searchlight from someone's remote camera, which used to mar the experience for me on screen. In other words, it was virgin territory. I don't suppose anyone but a fellow buff would understand the magnetism of a pitch black interior in an unknown shelter. It's real. It begs you to overcome the little doubts and fears about being caught, lessens them to some extent, and puts reason to the task of minimizing what's left of them with jury-rigged rationales. After a few moments standing in the open doorway, listening for traffic, I switched on my beacon at its lowest intensity (bright enough even so to peel the paint), and looked around at nothing much. It was as plain a corridor as any I'd ever seen, cleaner, but just as worn, tire marks on the hard cement floor, scrapes along the sides, doors rusty, every one shut for the night. Run of the mill, as corridors go.

The exciting stuff, I knew, would be found behind closed doors. There were over twenty doors in easy view. Because the corridor was circular, the horizon was vertical. Every step revealed something new around the corner, at the expense of something lost behind. A reasonable trade, I thought, and took a walk.

Now I wasn't so stupid as to forget which door I came out of, or anything like that. I took a good hard look at it, at the ones on either side, memorized my position, and with a throbbing pulse made vows to myself to go no farther than just a few steps away. I certainly knew enough to check the latch and make sure I could open it from the other side. I practiced half a dozen times, until I was certain I had it right. I was cautious, you see. I pretty well knew my way around from so many camera trips, so I wasn't worried about a simple thing like getting lost. Where I missed, if indeed I did miss, was in not having given more thought to the people. Because even if they were just customers of the Venture Company as I supposed, they were *costumed* customers obviously intent on preserving realism at any cost. In their presence I would have been a complete anachronism, an unexplainable event capable of destroying in a single instant the whole carefully crafted effect. Regardless of my low critical opinion of them, I had no business exposing myself to the risk of being seen. My behavior was at the very least selfish, at the most dangerously insane. I even think those who knew me best would have been surprised at my foolishness. Nevertheless, I found myself tippy-toeing right down the middle of the avenue, light on, looking for a fun door to enter, with no more respect for the circumstances than if I were alone in the screening room.

I bounced merrily, in a slightly exuberant high-stepping version of the tiptoe, back and forth across the avenue, checking out the doors. Most told their story without need of an opening: INFIRMARY, and across from that, DIAGNOSTICS, and X-RAY, a whole big medical section. A little farther on, ELECTROSYNTHETICS LAB, PROTEIN SYNTHESIS DEPARTMENT, RECIPES, and CENTER FOR AGRICULTURAL READINESS, which was just an office. Next to it, however, was a room marked, PRACTICE FIELD. I looked in on that—a medium-large room full of dirt, mostly, with a few old-fashioned farm implements lying around: hoes, rakes; no tractors, just little things. Farther down the hall I saw a door marked CENTER FOR CRYOGENIC SUSPENSION, which suggested an advance over Slo-Gas techniques. The door was locked. Business, business, all business. Obviously another "functional" establishment of the kind I had no use for. I found a CHILDREN'S NURSERY

AND CAFETERIA, of all things. The nursery was a delight, full of little tables and chairs alphabetical in nature, and pillows in the shape of numbers. The very notion of a whole room dedicated to the child was beyond my comprehension. I thought of the bathroom where I grew up and my eyes filled with big pitiful tears. I got out of there as fast as I could.

Across the hall was a door marked CHAPEL, no bigger than or different from any of the other doors. So far, of the miscellaneous props, furniture, ornaments, and what-not I'd seen lying about, nothing in particular caught my eye; nothing jumped right up and said "steal me." Bibles, though, could bring a price, especially an original oldie with no third testament. Not that I ever intended to swipe anything. I just wanted for once in my life to touch something of real value, and then be on my way. A tug in the back of my mind said hurry along.

I shut off my light and went in the door marked CHAPEL. I guess I expected a small carpeted room with a lectern and a pew, maybe candelabra. With the door closed behind me and my own light off, as my eyes became accustomed to the dark again, I began to make out what appeared to be a photograph on the far wall, a photograph of a cathedral like the Notre Dame or the Kohlner Dome, taken before they collapsed. It was a dimly lit but very lovely color photo, taken at night with floodlights all around, so that the only thing really visible was the building—no sky, no yard, no city lights behind. I was impressed first with its size and quality, considering that it was supposed to be a period piece. It wasn't until I reached out to touch it that I realized it was three dimensional as well, every bit the equal in quality and resolution of the home TV. I got down on my hands and knees in the dark and began feeling for the edge, inching my way forward, expecting any moment to bump my head on the screen. The room turned out to be bigger than I first imagined. After awhile I got up off my knees and walked, hands poised in front, waiting for the inevitable collision with the screen. I walked. And walked. The image enlarged appropriately, but no collision. I paused to look back at the door, thinking that I must be on some sort of treadmill, but the door was small and distant. I continued on until the image was towering over me. Still no glass, no bottom edge. I began to see detail I'd missed from farther back, small intricate carvings in the stone, the gargoyles and the saints, getting clearer all the time instead of fuzzier as I neared the image.

It was pretty obvious by then that I wasn't going to roll it up and take it home. But I was such a god damn skeptic that I crossed the entire expanse between the door and the cathedral, one slow step at a time with my hands out like a sleepwalker. When at last I touched stone and felt it with my very own fingertips, I thought: "rough glass." But what really distinguishes an image from reality, despite its feel, is its "walk-around-ability." An image doesn't have it. You can't walk up to something on screen and get inside.

It makes me sick to think how I threw away the opportunity to marvel at the grandeur, tremble in awe at the splendor, *feel* something—anything! I walked up the steps, pressed hands against the mammoth door and went right inside. If I'd only stopped to consider the possibility that it was built by hand in the old style, carved tediously from the living rock of the mountain by a society so utterly devout that they would pass away generations in the service of their Holy Master, I mean, what an idea. What a fantastic idea. With my own five senses I perceived that vast creation, that overwhelming tribute of love and devotion. And what did I do about it? I went around examining the stonework for laser marks. I passed the whole thing off, buttress to nave, as a computer-generated replica hacked out of the stone by the hands-off tools of the day, a swarm of servo-cutters guided by an electric brain looking at a picture. You see, the Venture Company could knock out a sizable temple in half a day, a tomb in an hour, a capitol or office building in forty-five minutes. And they *did*, often, to enhance an excavation or give proper background to one of their historical dramas. I thought I saw the characteristic marks of a laser cutter, but what did I know of such things? They could just as well have been chisel marks. Imagine *me* playing expert. At such a terrible cost in experience. I wish I could say more about what it felt like, but I'm afraid it sums up in two words: neat trick.

Everything anyone could expect of a cathedral this one had: fancy statuary, intricately carved gold-plated altar, and so on. Judging it strictly as a find, you could take the multi-ton light fixtures out of #37, the trillion-gallon magic fountain out of #143, toss them in with all the underground golf courses, polo fields, and wild game preserves ever hollowed out from the bowels of the earth, and still not get half the rating that this one single shelter deserved. I gave it a casual okay. I'd like to go back now and wring my neck.

Maybe I'm being a little unfair with myself, because I did

experience one brief moment of surprise, a tiny flutter of the heart, a bead or two of perspiration when I saw my picture hanging above the altar. I didn't quite know what to make of that at first. It was large, well-lit, handsomely framed in gold, with a score of cherubim holding it aloft (cherubim and two strong cables). A gorgeous thing it was, unmistakably the center of attention. I thought first, well, there's a camera somewhere projecting my image. But on closer examination I saw that it was painted in oils, and also that it wasn't me at all, but someone resembling me. A good looking fellow, naturally, long blond hair worn in a flip the way I like mine, same little button nose too, and those sparkling green eyes. His ears, however, were much larger and his face more sharply angled. He wore a beard too, a round fuzzy critter, whereas I myself was just beginning to sprout. His costume came out of no wardrobe of mine. It was an outlandish robe of fiery sequins—just too garish for words. He was dressed and posed like a holy man, obviously, and it wasn't long before I had him worked into the prevailing Venture Company theme that was robbing me of strong experience at every turn. I'd stumbled across a second coming plot in the making. My guess was that the shelter society was about to receive its deliverer, namely the fellow in the photo. For a tidy sum he had bought himself the privilege of leading a select group of fellow players into paradise above ground. I could think of better ways to spend money. Actually, that's a lie. I was out and out envious. I would have killed for the part.

Very foolishly, I spent too much time in the open, exposed to easy discovery. There's no accounting for it. When I finally decided I'd seen enough and was on my way back, just as I was about to open the big doors, I heard voices on the other side. Instantly I ran the other way, as fast as I could down the aisle toward the altar, looking for a place to hide, keeping low, ready to dive should the door open. I paused, scanning the territory for a place to hide. I heard more voices. A congregation was gathering on the steps. In a moment they'd all come flooding in. I dashed across a large carpeted area between the seats and the altar, and jumped behind a stairwell. I flattened myself against the wall, waited and listened. More voices. Then footsteps. They were coming in. I was in a little alcove, shrouded in darkness. I didn't dare use my light. I felt my way around until I came upon a small wooden door. I eased down on the latch, and backed slowly into the next room. I shut the door, turned on my light, and surprised the living shit out of the bishop, who at that moment was putting on his vestments.

My heart was rattling. My face flushed. I was speechless. I didn't know what to do. I stood there with my light glaring, just staring at him. No matter. It was his move, not mine. He fell at once to the floor, knees first, then flat out, prone as a pancake. He said, in a queer and quivering English: "My Lord. I did not expect you so soon."

I put two and two together, realized whom he'd mistaken me for, and said, "Be not afraid. To *you* I make an early appearance. Behold, the time is at hand." Not bad, spur of the moment, not bad at all. My voice trembled as much as his, but I think that enhanced the effect, if anything. He remained face to the floor. I thought that better than to invite him up. I didn't want him to get another look at me. I didn't want him spreading the word either, so I said. "Do not speak of this to anyone." In less than commanding tones. "My time is not quite at hand just yet, okay? I'll let you know when it is." Less convincing than the first. I wanted out of there before the real one came along and gave me away as the imposter. Unfortunately I was in a dressing room. There was more than one door to choose from. I didn't want to risk winding up in his closet. But a lord and savior doesn't ask directions from the clergy. I thought it over and decided that the best thing woud be to buy enough time to find my own way out. "Go!" I commanded. "Go about your business as usual and do your stuff as if I were never even here, okay? I'll come back later, you wait and see." Much much worse. Thank God it was a sellers market. He gladly made allowances. I imagine the old fart was rather flattered, actually. I said, "Go!" one more time, and he got up and went, snap snap. Simple as that. I never saw his face, he never saw mine.

I couldn't hang around for the sermon. It must have been a dilly. With all the folks assembled in church, I figured I'd get no better chance to make a run for it.

The very second the good bishop made his exit I tried a door, and damned if it wasn't a closet. How would that have looked? The next door led me into a long private corridor, which in turn led me to a set of stairs that turned at the top and stopped at another closed door. Unless I was badly turned around, this door would open into the main corridor at level one. I waited with my ear to the door, listened, and then, as I'd been doing all day long, gradually eased it open.

I was badly turned around. I found myself in a little tunnel filled with pipes, some of them hot to the touch. That didn't bother me. I crawled in, made my way to another little door, and another, and so on, checking each one to see if I could discover where I might be. After awhile I realized I was running a course parallel to the main corridor, but underneath. So I decided to stay in with the pipes and the lesser tunnels. For direction, I went by formula one: down. I went by stair, ramp, and ladder through endless pipeways until I plain ran out of down and there was nothing left but up. One more door. A dark hall. Nothing to the left, nothing to the right. Endless. I knew precisely where I was, though. It was the rainbow corridor, a striped tunnel done up with the paint left over from the rest of the place, common to the type. At the upper end of the tunnel would be the shelter, at the other the great outdoors.

I crawled out of the service port, put on a touch of lift and bounced down the hall, kangaroo hops the whole long way down. Very soon I found myself at the other end, standing behind still another set of doors, the doors to the great main entrance chamber. If this were any other shelter I would at that point have come up against a piazo photonic crystal barrier with a hole through it the size of an apple and a sign printed in the four languages of the Market, saying, "CAMERAS ONLY. THE PASSAGE OE ANY OTHER OBJECT OR OBJECTS STRICTLY FORBIDDEN, Section 2606.4 (A) (1) Title 18, Market Administration Code." And beneath the sign, in a heap on the floor, a collection of objects slightly bigger than apples. In this shelter, however, there was no such blockade.

It was my choice whether to make my way all the way back up to level one and from there to my air duct, or simply go boldly out the front door and get it over with. I decided to waste no more time. I pushed open the doors. In doing so I triggered the alarms, a clanging bell, a screaming siren, and I don't know what all. I rushed inside the chamber, ready to fly, only to discover that the mountain hole was shut. The main doors to the outside were still in place. God, I was sick of doors. I decided that wasn't the way out after all. I went back into the corridor, took a look up that long endless tunnel, realized that with the alarms going full tilt my chances of making it undiscovered all the way to the end were terribly slim. I re-decided to go out the main entrance. I turned right around and headed for the switches.

Air ducts, because they were necessarily open to the passage of air, had built into them all those booby traps to keep out the boobies. Passage through the main entrance, however, was blocked, not by cute crafty tricks, but by brute force, in the form of a massive granite slab wedged into the mountainside like a cork, fit so tight that there would be no discernible crack on the outside. Impossible to find, exceedingly difficult to budge in any case.

Inside the chamber were half a dozen giant electric motors and winches bolted to the floor, with cables attached to the inside of the granite wedge, ready, come the day, to pull it out of its hole and let the people free. I'd seen many such chambers before, but never one with the doors shut. I knew that there was no way to operate the motors without setting off all the alarms, but having already accomplished that I had nothing left to do but start the winches turning. Everything looked to be in fine condition: freshly painted, every fitting polished, like a museum. Even the tracks upon which the door rested were polished like mirrors. The switches, located on a big ornate panel front and center, were of shiny brass with white porcelain handles labeled one through six, worth a fortune but apparently screwed down tightly. I closed each one in the recommended order, and accordingly relays down the line closed—thunk, thunk, thunk. The motors wound up to speed. Slowly, very slowly, the winches began taking up slack from the cables.

The door weighed tons, and did not pop right out. I looked for a side entrance. Not a chance. I got terribly antsy, terribly frightened in a delicious sort of way, what with the alarms going like blazes and me having to sit around. After a long while the motors whined down to business, as the last of the slack was taken out of the cables. Work time. Pull that block. Pull, Pull, PULL. I didn't know what to do with myself. I flitted back and forth from cable to cable, pulling on them, adding my feeble strength to the effort. The motors slowed, strained, and groaned to a stop. I panicked. I yelled, "COME ON," and that did it. The stone came unstuck with a loud crack and began moving bit by bit into the chamber, making a dull rumbling grating sound.

Half a minute passed before there was enough room between the wedge and the mountain wall even to see through, but the block was moving. I stood near the crack, waiting for it to widen, ready to push through as soon as possible.

I felt a sudden draft. The alarms grew louder. I turned. There was someone standing at the door. A man in a black suit. And then a woman in pink. And another man and another. Weird ones all, and angry, very angry. To their way of mind this was a terribly bad thing I was doing. I know because one of them was armed with a gun.

I would have been caught except for a very curious piece of good luck. Each one of the people as they entered the room and realized that the door was coming open, instead of behaving in an ordinary defensive manner, seemed compelled by some powerful tradition to shield their eyes from the light of day, which was entering through the crack. Now the light of day was anything but bright, due to the passing of Nimbus, so it couldn't have been that they were simply not used to it. It was evident by the way they held their hands against their eyes that it wasn't really too bright for them in there. What I mean is, they didn't shield their eyes from the glare with a salute, the better to see me. Instead they plastered their hands flat over their eyes to hold them shut, as if against the temptations of seeing something forbidden, such as, I suggest, the light of day. That's how I figured it, and I stayed huddled against the slowly widening crack where no one would dare look, not that I had anywhere else in mind to go. Each one as he came into the chamber plastered a hand over his eyes and then groped blindly with the other; or, in the case of one zealot, fired off rounds of ammunition without aim. Blanks, I thought, although some ricocheted rather convincingly off the walls nearby. I thought it odd that I could find myself worshipped one moment and shot at the next. Nevertheless, my inventive unconscious quickly supplied me with another fine safe theory to account for what was going on—another Venture Company sub-plot, naturally. This one was of the "violation of edict" variety, wherein a player, fed up with subterranean existence, flies in the face of religious tradition and makes a break for the surface, while the other players plead with him for his own good and the good of the holy cause to wait it out down under.

I had two options: one, switch on my beacon light and make like the divine savior again, as I had done so successfully with the bishop; or two, continue waiting until the door opening was wide enough, then slip outside and be gone. The former had tremendous appeal, naturally, but for all I knew, the "real" savior, the player who'd signed on in that position, had already made his entrance. I figured two saviors in the space of an hour wouldn't wash. Besides, it wasn't necessary. The door was already wide enough for me to slip through by the time that the first of them entered the room. It was my pack that held me back.

I pressed myself hard into the opening, such as it was, waiting for the gap to widen a fraction more, when the bishop himself arrived on the scene. Like the others, he felt obliged to cover his eyes against the light of day; so he didn't see that it was his old friend again. He certainly must have wondered, though. When two events of magnitude occur in close proximity, one does get suspicious. I imagine the temptation to peek was rather severe. On the other hand, the occasion of my first holy appearance would have done much to recharge the batteries of faith, and thereby deter a sinner wanting to peek. Perhaps for that reason alone he held true to his beliefs. He may even have viewed the whole proceeding as a test of his faith, in which case he was doubly obliged to do it by the book.

Regardless of the reason, the bishop played by the rules of the game and did not open his eyes. Thank God for that. For had he opened them and seen the messenger of God squeezing out the door like a rat, he'd have been forced by his own good conscience to call a stop to the proceedings, and I'd have had to pay for my transgressions, one way or another.

It was a close one even so. I was struggling at the gap, straining the straps of my pack, when all of a sudden the motors stopped. Someone in his blind groping had found the switches. In the relative silence that followed, the bishop made the following announcement: "Come back. We shall not be divided in our faith. Until the day of the Lord, none shall leave the sanctuary. It is the law of our fathers. None shall disobey it." A short but to the point little monologue, confirming the nature of the plot as I understood it. I thought it would be snazzy to comment, but anything I might have said would have been drowned out by the loud whine of the motors as they suddenly came up to speed again.

I decided the time had come to make my exit. I hit the safety buckle of my pack, let it drop to the floor, and then, taking hold of a grip, pulled it sideways into the narrow opening with me. Now it must be understood that the great main door was anything but the usual tiresome plate of material with hinges and a lock. It was a massive stone several meters thick. Getting myself into the opening between the stone and its cavity, although a significant accomplishment, did not mean freedom. That was just the beginning of a long crawl through a very narrow passageway. It was so narrow, in fact, that I had to enter sideways, and once I got in there was no room to turn my head and look where I was going. I was forced to shuffle, squeezed between two walls, one hand reaching for the opening, the other dragging the pack. The pack slowed me. It was a trifle too wide even sideways. I should have dropped it and scurried to the end of the passage while I had time, while there still *was* a passage. Instead I piddled away precious seconds tugging, squirming, trying to get the damn thing unstuck. I couldn't figure out why, with the motors going, that it wasn't loosening up. It was as though the door had stopped opening. That's certainly what it felt like. In fact, as time ticked, passage became *more* difficult, not less. In fact—it finally dawned on me—the door was definitely closing. On me. It certainly was. I dropped the pack and enjoyed a brief moment of panic. I even let out a scream or two, which nobody heard. That was the most I could muster, though, before better sense reminded me not to worry too much. It was just a silly tactic in a silly game. Instead of falling apart and pleading for my life, I met the challenge and plunged deeper into the opening, content that I could call it off any old time.

They didn't make it easy. I pushed. I shoved. I clawed at the stone. As the walls closed, each step became more difficult. The slippery fabric of my flying suit lubricated the way until it tore, exposing my chest to the cold stone. With my head turned inward, I had no way of gauging my progress except by the feel of fresh air, which only misled me into believing that each shuffle would be the one that set me free. The pressure was greatest on my chest. The more I wanted to breathe, the less I could. I had to make do with rapid little half-breaths. With squeals and chirps thrown in I sounded like an ape in heat. I found it amazing that they'd carry it to such extremes. At one point I was actually stuck with both feet off the floor, held up by the crushing pressure. Another flash of panic. I tried to scream, but couldn't draw enough breath in the space allotted. Frantic, I exhausted every last molecule of air in my lungs and dropped down, two feet on and ground. I shuffled madly, hands and feet slipping on the damp stone, when my right hand finally found the outside corner of the opening.

With a grip on the edge I was able to pull myself out, part by part, my arm first, then my shoulder. By reaching my left hand over my head, I managed to get both hands on the outside edge. With a good tug I freed my head and chest. I turned to look around, only to discover myself situated high up the mountain, staring straight down a vertical cliff.

The gallant floods of Nimbus had carried away the soil from the sill, and all that was left after a thousand years of better-than-average rainfall was a sheer drop. My wings, already crushed between the stones, were completely out of reach.

The door continued grinding shut. I let my right leg out and hugged the corner to keep myself aloft, with just a toehold on the ledge, the wedge squeezing my foot and left arm.

The rain had stopped. Nimbus was to the west. I screamed "SYNTHETICA! SYNTHETICA!" In the after-storm silence my scream echoed around the canyon. "SYNTHETICA!"

Each second the pain increased in my foot and arm. I eased them out bit by bit, terrified that I might lose my hold and drop, at the same time wishing to save all that I could from pulverization. The pressure held me in place, with less and less of me left inside as each moment passed, until I was hanging on fingers and toes. I took to screaming hysterically, nonstop: "SYNTHETICA ... SYNTHETICA ..."

"There you are," she said, sticking her head out of the hole directly above me. She'd found the air duct, and was apparently looking around inside for me.

I shouted desperately, "HELLLLLLP!"

"Sure."

She lowered down on lift, reached both arms around my middle, gave me a big bear hug, propped her feet against the rock and plucked me out like a weed, my fingers and toes sore and bloody, but attached and intact. I hung limp. She carried me on lift directly up to the mountain to the little opening, where she set me down carefully on my hands and knees. I rolled over, straightened out flat on my back, and groaned.

"Close," she said.

I lifted my head, looked into her eyes, and said, "I'm gonna sue. You hear? I'm gonna sue. You saw what they did. You can be my witness, because I'm gonna sue. God damn fuckers. What the hell do they think they're trying to pull anyway? They can't do that. I'm gonna sue their asses. Just get me a phone and see if I don't."

12

It wasn't a complete waste of time experience-wise; I got to swear, didn't I? Poor Synthetica had spent the whole day farther down the mountain, huddled under a tree with nothing but her wings to keep the rain off. When the storm passed she flew back to where she'd last seen me, heading off toward the beacon light. She found the cave, went in, heard me screaming, looked out, and assumed I'd fallen down the cliff. She naturally wanted to know what had happened to my wings. That took some explaining. While I filled her in on the details of my day, she took out her little kit and packed my bleeding parts in an herb mush. She fed me, scooped up water from a puddle nearby, watered me, and did whatever else she could to make me comfortable—a born nurse with shit for medicine. As much as she wanted to camp outside somewhere, she agreed that we might as well spend the night inside where it was dry, considering my condition and all, being careful not to let on that she might enjoy a night indoors herself for a change. She would strictly avoid such luxuries as a rule.

I was eager to describe my day in every detail. It was obvious to her, if not to me, that I'd had a good time. I guess my voice betrayed a certain exuberance I might not have admitted to just yet. Nevertheless, injured toes and fingers aside, it had been a good day.

I never got the chance to tell her the whole story. She wouldn't let me. I got no further than my first mention of the Venture Company when she let out a big *"What?"*

"Huh?" I looked left and right. It wasn't something she saw but something I said.

"You mean to tell me that people will actually pay money for an artificial experience like that?"

"Oh God, not now, okay? Another time."

"Are you telling me that people will actually pay money so that they can pretend to live? Why don't they just live?"

"Look, do you want to hear what I did today or don't you?"

"Is the Market so empty that you people are forced to concoct a life to lead?"

"You're not listening to me, are you? Yoo hoo . . . hey . . ."

"Are you so blind that you can't see what's happened to you? To the world?"

"I can do fish imitations. Wanna hear?"

"The Market is dead."

"Gnnt gnnnt bloop. That's a grouper. Chee chee. That's a bat."

"You're dead."

"Actually a bat isn't a fish. It's a mammal."

"The whole world is dead."

"You know why mammals are called mammals? Because they got mams."

"You all lust for something worth doing. It's right there, and you refuse to see it."

"You're a mammal. You've got mams. All I've got are little taddies. I'm a tadpole. Hey look . . . little hairs between my taddies. Where'd they come from?"

"You're like someone searching for the dark with a light. You're so dazzled you can't see the simple truth."

"Ouch! Damn, they're stuck. I hate little hairs. They're all over me."

"What you mistakenly call living is really suicide."

"It's the plants. They're inside me. They're trying to grow out of me. These aren't hairs. They're roots. Oh God, I'm turning into a turnip."

"Mark, I'm talking to you!"

"At me. You're talking at me."

"Listen to me."

"No. You listen to me. I'm the one with the story."

"You've got nothing to say worth hearing."

"Jesus Christ, a minute ago you were real nice. What happened?"

"Oh Mark, I thought by now you *knew*! That sort of life is wrong—wrong for you, wrong for everybody."

"Look, I didn't buy any adventure, if that's what you mean. I just looked around down there. That's all."

"But you liked it."

"So?"

"I thought by now you understood."

"Understood what?"

"About nature."

"What about nature?"

"These last few days—you've been happy. I've watched you. I've seen you in the morning eager to fly . . ."

"Oh."

"Oh? Oh what?"

"It isn't nature that makes me happy."

"What is it?"

"It's the chance of finding a fucking phone so I can get the fuck out of this God damn forest and buy a house of my own and something decent to eat. I'm sick to death of this stupid search of yours. It's stupid. You'll never find anyone on wings. It's impossible. It can't be done. Now leave me alone. I'm going to sleep. Good night."

"Mark, listen to me. This is very important. It's your whole life we're talking about."

"Maybe tomorrow we have a nice long chat."

"No. Now."

"Good night."

"Mark, listen to me . . . Mark?"

The power of sleep did not leave me in that, my hour of need.

My first dream of substance occurred the next morning, and a frightening little episode it was. I dreamt I was all alone on top of a mountain, high up a sheer cliff with no wings and no rope. That was it. Nothing more. It was enough to wake me up, though, with a pounding heart. I sat straight up, realized I'd had a dream of more than one solid color, my first ever. I congratulated myself. "Hey, Synthetica, I had a dream. Synthetica? Hey, Synthetica? Woo hoo?" No answer. I called again, louder, listening to a series of echoes diminishing in the distance. I called again. "SYNTHETICA." No Synthetica. "Hey, HEY! YOU GOT ME UP HERE. YOU GET ME DOWN. GOD DAMN IT. YOU HEAR ME?"

I got up frantically and looked around. I called again, wondering if she'd fallen in the pit with her wings and left me there to die. I couldn't tell without risking my own life in the dark. I ran out to the opening in a terrible frenzy, peeked outside, called her name, and WHOMP! Something heavy fell to the little ledge next to the beacon, nearly taking my head off. From an indecent height she had let drop a fat heavy bundle of what looked like molding canvas. She lowered and stood on the ledge beside it. "There. Now we're even." She kicked the moldy lump toward me.

"God, it stinks . . . Oh no. If you think I'm going to eat it you've got another think coming. What is it? Never mind. I don't want to know. Get it out of here."

"Mark, don't try me. Just put it on and let's go."

"Put it on? Is that putrid thing a wing pack? Forget it."

"That's the best I can do. Now strap up."

I knelt to take a closer look. It was a wing pack all right, a decaying old pair of Wilson Blue Jays, damp and covered with slime. "You're kidding. You expect me to wear these things?"

"You'll wear them or walk. Take your choice."

"Where'd you get them?"

"You know perfectly well."

"Downstairs? You went downstairs? *You*?"

"Don't be silly."

"Well, where then?"

"You don't know? You really don't know?"

"I haven't the slightest idea. Tell me."

"Can't you even guess?"

"*Tell me!*"

"I thought you knew. Well then . . . Mark. I apologize for last night."

"What are you talking about?"

"Come with me. Seeing is believing."

"I don't even want to touch them."

"They're wet because I washed them. Now put them on and let's get out of here. Now!"

"What'd you wash them in, fish grease?"

"*Mark!*"

"All right, all right." Did I have a choice? Did I ever have a choice? I took a deep breath, held it, peeled the straps loose from the slime, hefted the pack, buckled in, stepped out on the ledge, teased the lift, decided it was okay, pulled up, and breathed again. It wasn't so bad in the downdraft of the ascent. Synthetica kept her distance, I noticed. When I reached the top, she stopped and I kept right on going up. Apparently the altitude limiter had been tampered with. I panicked briefly at the thought of continuing up indefinitely. I let go of the up-cord and pushed out on the grips. To my great relief I dropped, wings spread. The wings themselves were clean and in good condition, if a little stubby for my taste. No sleek racer, perhaps, but a good deal less skitterish and much easier to maneuver. Synthetica yelled, "Follow," and headed due north.

She went one long full pass and held herself at the bottom end of it, waiting for me to catch up. I pulled down beside her. "Look." She raised her arm and pointed in the general direction of the sun.

"What?"

"Do you see?"

"What? Tell me."

"Follow me."

A short pass had us closer to what she wanted me to see, a speck in the sky, a distant dot of no particular distinction, a bird, I supposed. *"What? Just tell me, God damn it."* Not a word. She pointed. "A bird. You want me to eat it. I won't. I don't eat birds."

She flew off again, a short pass, stopping at resting level, one meter above the trees. I came in yelling, "For Christ's sake, what is it? Can't you just tell me?"

"Mark, turn around." She pointed over my shoulder. I paddled once, turned, and saw. We were in the company of another.

My mouth fell open. My face drained of blood and I got dizzy. It was a man, or a woman, impossible to tell which. Its head had dropped off and all that was left was a rotten putrid corpse hanging there adrift at resting level, held aloft by its pack, just a chunk of black meat, really, with stringers and sinews and loose flaps of dry skin hanging down, the whole mess surrounded by a cloud of bees which had made a hive in its abdominal cavity. I'd never seen a dead person, but I knew it was no battery-powered imitation. I squeaked, "He ... it's dead."

"It's more than just a bad cold, I'll grant you that."

"Oh God, oh God. . . ." It smelled more ghastly than it looked. I said, "What'd you have to go and show me a thing like that for?"

"Mark, I want you to thank the man."

". . . . Oh no."

"You're wearing his wings. Or she's the wife and you're wearing her husband's wings. Or else they were lovers. Wouldn't that be sad?"

"Oh no."

"This morning there were two of these here, stuck together. I had to pry them apart with a stick."

"Oh no."

"And then slide the carcass out of your pack. I did it all for you."

"AAAGGGGGHHHHHH!" I could just feel the maggots crawling on me. I kicked. I screamed. I shook myself trying to get free of the thing that held me aloft.

"Mark, is this your very first drifter? I had no idea. I thought you knew. I really did."

"Gigghhhh."

"Listen to me, Mark. They're everywhere. Everywhere," she said, with a wide sweep of her arm. "The Market is dying. The evidence is all around you. Look. There's another. Do you see? Come on, I'll show you."

"Aw naw, hey, Synthetica, no . . ."

Off she flew in the direction of another distant dot on the horizon, leaving me no choice but to follow. I had the smell of slime and death all over me. It was to be a lesson. She had in mind to break me of a bad habit, my appreciation of any and all things Market. She went about it in just the right way too, I give her credit.

She called them drifters, not to be mistaken for participants in the sport of drifting, which were also called drifters. And just like she said, they were everywhere, although not in such concentration elsewhere, perhaps, as around there among the high peaks. A lift unit left running day after day, year after year will eventually lose power and weaken so that it may not have the strength necessary to lift a body over a particularly high range of mountains. For that reason, the corpses she showed me that day were represented in unfair proportion. These were the ones that had run out of *uumph*. The mountains gathered them like a net, and what she showed me was an unusually dense gathering, the accumulation of years.

They were suicides every one. That much I knew without having to hear it from her. I was acquainted with the method. It was a simple thing, very popular during my childhood, relatively pleasurable as such things go. The party wishing to end it all (usually someone with flying experience) would procure a pair of wings or a life belt or some kind of personal lift unit. Next, he or she would then "defunctionalize" the altitude limiter. It was then a simple matter of taking that long last ascent straight up to heaven, where the air is too thin to breathe. Because of the lack of oxygen, a sort of giddy good feeling takes the place of any last-minute fears and doubts, and that final moment is pure joy. So say we who've watched others do it on TV. Then the hand falls limp, the up-cord snaps back, and the body descends to resting level, where the lift unit holds the body aloft, waiting for landing instructions. Years go by.

I knew *that* it was done, and I knew *how*. Until then I'd never realized to what extent. One heard numbers quoted on the evening news. One heard statistics and projections of trends. One saw the stars do it for the camera, but one never knew what it meant until one attended one of their conventions.

The key to enlightenment is a keen eye, and the proper viewing position precisely one meter above the trees—resting level. One simply cannot see them from higher up against a background of trees. The color of a drifter blends too perfectly into the green-black of the forest. They can only be seen silhouetted against the sky, and even then it requires sharp perception and experience to discern that one tiny speck which is a drifter from dozens of others which are birds. Stillness differs the one from the other. Synthetica, it seems, was an expert spotter.

She flew me to a second corpse and introduced me politely. "Mark, I'd like you to meet this gentleman. I do believe it is a gentleman. Bored to tears with a life of perfect leisure. A compatriot of yours. Why don't you shake his hand?"

"What hand? He hasn't got one."

"Oh ... I ... I *am* sorry. Forgive me."

"Is this really necessary?"

"I think so. Yes. Look, another one. See? Over there."

"No."

"Come on."

"Give me a chance to wash, at least. . . ." Off she flew. "Damn it."

The population of drifters was so dense thereabouts that there was always one in sight of another, usually within reach of a single pass. She kept me in a state of high misery all morning long, chasing from one corpse to another. I'd dare to complain and she'd turn from me, raise a limp arm like the Ghost of Christmas Yet to Come, and point out another in the far distant sky. And then we'd fly to meet it face to face. Pass after pass.

You know how it is with a brand new word—you hear it once, and all of a sudden there it is again and again. Well, it's the same thing with drifters. Undoubtedly most had drifted from as far away as Europe. Some had circumnavigated the globe perhaps three or four times, following in the wake of Nimbus. These were the dry bones and empty sacks. Some, however, were quite fresh, almost recognizable. Around noon we parked next to one of these later models, a swollen form of recent vintage, a *she*, and she was the last straw. I wanted no more.

"Now do you understand?" Synthetica asked me. "Does it begin to sink in?"

"Please, can I wash now? Come on, let's take a break. I haven't even . . . eaten. Never mind."

"Oh Mark, how thoughtless of me. Here . . ." She dipped into her goodie bag and brought forth a handful of dried apricots, of all the God damn things.

"I said never mind."

"Oh look. Do you see?"

"Oh no, not another one. Please. I'll never sin again. Honest. I've seen enough."

"Not nearly."

She should have quit while she was ahead. Beyond a certain depth, a point can sink in no further. I knew. I knew. I knew. How could I know any better? But she'd made up her mind to devote the rest of the day to my education. From noon on, however, the effect changed. Instead of suffering more at each new encounter, I developed a resistance that by the end of the day had blossomed into full immunity, a natural immunity, I believe, a right and proper defense.

We chanced upon a blond man, still recognizable as such. She said, "Behold, another of your kind. You would be one of these yourself now, Mark, if I hadn't found you and given your life new meaning. Without purpose your life would have ended like this. Do you realize that? Do you understand?"

"I wonder if it's someone famous."

"Fame, money, what does it all matter?"

"I like the way he does his hair. *Did* his hair. Isn't it odd how the hair stays so neat and clean, compared to the rest of him, I mean?" One of the effects of drifting with the wind is that relatively speaking, there is no wind. Hair and other things which resist decay tend to remain in perfect order— party clothes smooth and unwrinkled, shoes shiny, watches flashing the time, and jewelry winking seductively from across that unbridgeable chasm.

"What do you think it's worth?"

"What?"

"His ring."

"*Mark!*"

"He's a mason. *Was* a mason. Does masonry go with the body or the soul? The body got the ring, I see."

"Look, Mark, there's another one. Do you see it?"

"Where? Oh, yeah. I think I do." I pointed.

"Not that one. Look to the left."

"My gosh, two. Hey, let's go get mine. Come on."

For the first time that day I led the pass. I lost sight of the drifter immediately on pulling up. I flew in the general direction to where I thought it would be, and at the bottom of the pass sighted it again, only a short hop away. I said to Synthetica, "I say it's a man. What do you think?"

"What does it matter?"

"Come on, make a guess. If you're right, you get to lead us to the next one. What do you say?"

Without answering, she led off a short pass the rest of the way. It turned out to be another unidentifiable anyway. "If they didn't smell so bad, I'd collect them, you know? What do you think I could get for one like that?"

"Mark, don't talk like that."

"I could wrap them in plastic maybe, or . . ."

"*Mark!*"

"Or a big jar. Hey . . ."

"*Shut up!*"

"Synthetica, listen to me. We could sell them on the crafts exchange."

"*I said shut up!*"

"What's the matter?"

"Just . . . just . . ."

"Hey, there's another one." I led off another pass and came in on target. It was an immense bloated female, about ready to burst from the looks of it. She was adorned in the most expensive-looking gold brocade negligee that I'd ever seen, absolutely encrusted with jewels, and on top of that, brooches, necklaces, bracelets and anklets, rings on every finger and every toe. She'd apparently decided to take it all with her, and so far was succeeding very nicely. Synthetica looked upon her as the best example of the day. So did I. I said, "God, I wish I had my camera." First words out of my mouth.

"Now do you see what I mean? She has everything in the world and just look at her."

"Yeah. That's a lot of shrapnel there. Boy, when she pops, watch out."

"No, Mark, *you* watch out. It's your life that's in danger. Don't you see? Look at her. She had *everything*." A few loose jewels didn't constitute everything, but I conceded the point with a shrug. "Do you know why so many Market people kill themselves? Do you?"

"Because it's against the law to have someone else do it to you."

"Mark, *why*?"

"It's our God-given right. It's written in the Bill of Guarantees. The board can pass no resolution restricting a person's right to suicide."

"The Market guarantees the right to die, but does it also guarantee a reason to live?"

"Well, ah . . . I think that's something you want to leave up to the individual, you know what I mean?"

"Mark, the Market is bankrupt."

"Blasphemy! There's so much gold in Zurich the earth turns lopsided around it." A Market cliche, but true. The effect, though slight, had been measured.

"Oh God damn it, Mark, will you for once just shut up and listen to me? I'm trying to save your life, don't you understand? You can't go on living the Market way of life. It will kill you. You've got to become involved in your own survival. If you don't then you'll have nothing to live for. It's as simple as that."

"Hey, listen, I know that. Shit."

"Let me finish. In the Free Market, every need is satisfied before you so so much as reach out a hand. There's no risk. Survival is a certainty. Nothing is required of you."

"I know, but . . ."

"Mark, if you are not forced by the necessity of your own survival to face reality each and every day, your mind will atrophy. You will wander off into fantasy and invent bizarre alternatives and strange unhealthy occupations, like the one yesterday. That kind of thing can't satisfy. If you play at life like a game, you'll never know it's true worth, and one day you'll throw it away like—like she did." She pointed to the dead one in our presence. "For your own good you've got to leave the Market and live a different kind of life."

"Mother Nature."

"Exactly."

"You know something?"

"What?"

"You're full of shit."

"Thank you. Thank you, Mark."

"Don't you want to know why?"

"Tell me."

"Because you're gonna die too. Only you don't get to choose the time. Any random germ could kill you. Any time. Or a number. A mere number could kill you, like eighty. Do you think you'll outlive eighty? You survive a whole lifetime in the tulies and what do you get for it? Old. That's nature's way. Personally, I'd rather have the choice."

"If the choice is left to you, you will certainly choose to die. But if you leave life and death to chance, you will fight to live."

"Not so."

"Look around you. What more proof do you need?"

"Synthetica, these people are a *thousand years old*. They've *lived*. Hell, I'm only...."

A tiny voice interrupted me, saying, "Marge? Hello, Marge? Where are you? Please, won't you answer me?"

I looked at Synthetica. She at me. Both of us at our bloated friend.

"Marge, please answer."

Synthetica let out a terrifying shriek, took a breath, and let out another. And a third. She got control of herself, looked the corpse in the eye, and heard it say distinctly, "Where are you? Please answer me." She rose to the top, screaming all the way.

"Hey, wait, Synthetica, it's a phone. She's got a phone."

She knew. It was that very item which sent her off screaming—not the voice of our dead friend, but the presence of a phone. She knew what a phone was and feared it very much. There was something more than a few trite arguments behind her revulsion of the Market and its goods. But that which drove Synthetica away, I wanted with all my heart. I tried to approach the body, reach into her pocket, but I could not do it. I'd adjusted to the sight of her, but the sense of sight had already had considerable training. Touch was another matter altogether. Not to mention the sense of smell. I couldn't bring myself to touch, not even for a phone. So near, and yet so far.

"Marge, we all miss you. You know we do. Please talk to us."

I yelled my lungs out trying to get through to the party at the other end. "HELLO. CAN YOU HEAR ME? CAN YOU HEAR ME?"

"I know you've been unhappy lately, but you'll get over it.

You always do. Remember, we're the weak ones. We look to you. Don't leave us. Please."

"HELLO. HELLO. HELLO. CAN YOU HEAR ME? IF YOU CAN HEAR ME, PLEASE TRANSFER THIS CALL TO PROCUREMENT."

"George is here. He wants to say hello."

"GEORGE, THIS IS MARCUS AURELIUS HORNBLOWER. TRANSFER THIS CALL TO PROCUREMENT AT ONCE."

"I love you, Margie."

"PLEASE CONNECT ME TO PROCUREMENT. MAYDAY. MAYDAY."

"Tell us where you are, won't you please? We miss you so."

"Aw, shit."

"I don't think we'll last much longer without you. We really do need you. Margie, you know we love you very much."

"Oh shut up, God damn it. She's dead."

I ascended, met Synthetica, flew with her to water, and made camp. But I never forgot the lesson she taught me, the meaning behind all those drifters out there. From that day forth I kept in my heart the knowledge that if life ever got too much to bear, too overwhelming for me there in the forest, I could simply don my wings, rise to the resting level, find a drifter, shut my eyes, hold my nose, and pilfer it for a phone. Though the price would be high, it gave me great comfort to know that salvation was always close at hand. In the meantime I could continue the search as before, with a sharp eye out for a better deal.

13

I no sooner touched down than I was all through the storage pocket of my new pack, looking for a phone even before I washed. No phone. Nothing but a beat-up musty old "Outdoorsman Catalogue," with last year's prices.

Synthetica kept in her kit a small quantity of a white greasy substance she called "soap," which she let me use to wash myself, my suit, and above all my pack. We gathered food in the usual manner, prepared it, and ate dinner. Later, by the light of the fire, I read to her from the catalogue about something better than soap and water. "It's called 'Eau du Glas.' You paint it on and it makes you slippery, so dirt won't stick. Not bad, huh? Here's something for bugs called the 'neural realizer.' It's a ray of some kind tuned to bug brains. It says it gives all bugs within a three meter radius a 'heightened sense of aesthetic awareness.' What's 'aesthetic'? It says it raises the consciousness of the insect so that it 'understands what an ugly worthless little creature it truly is, and thus educated, ceases to be of its own accord.' How do you like that? Hey, here's a. . . ."

She got up from her bed of leaves, came to my side of the fire, tore the book right out of my hands and threw it in the flames. "Hey, what the . . ." It flared up and was gone before I could do anything about it.

"Those things are unnatural, Mark. You don't want anything to do with them."

"Can't I even *read* about them?"

"Until you despise all the things of the Market, you cannot be saved."

"That's bullshit and you know it. You mix herbs and plant juices to get rid of bugs: that's chemistry, isn't it? So what's wrong if smarter people do it better and sell it in a catalogue?"

"Mark, didn't you learn anything at all today?"

"Yeah. I learned you got something weird going on inside your head. I mean, who screams at telephones? *That's* weird. If you don't like a phone, fine, don't answer it; but the way you screamed, my God, anyone watching would have thought someone shot you." A bad choice of words.

She sat up like she'd been bitten by a snake. "Who was watching? Who? Did they see me? Who?"

"There you go again."

"Mark, did anyone see me in that thing?"

"Hell no. It was buried in a pocket. How could anyone see you? Hey, what's with you? I've never seen you like this."

"Are you absolutely certain no one saw me?"

"Synthetica, I sat there shouting at it. They didn't even hear me, let alone see me. They certainly didn't see you.

Besides, so what if they did? Synthetica? So what if they did?"

No answer. But there it was, not mere hate, but *fear*. Press her for a reason and she would tell me nothing. The thing is, I don't think she understood it herself. The hate could be worked into a wordy little philosophy, but the fear was totally irrational. On that she was silent.

In the morning we backtracked to where we'd left off the day of the storm, and began again the journey east. Although I hadn't yet guessed the reason why, or even that there might be a reason why, I pretty well understood that Synthetica was set on making me over, diverting my course of development away from the regular sort of fellow I'd almost become toward something more to her liking; which is to say, I knew it was a particular thing she had in mind to do, not just the way things were going. I never wondered why. I was a child. Children expect to be subjected to modifying pressures.

Over the days that followed, as the search continued, she saw to it that I had the opportunity to experience hardships, especially those associated with my feeding. Provisions there were aplenty, all around us, but to see them as such took all my limited powers of concentration. Still, for the longest while I could identify only the most obvious things, namely things of a color not green—fruits, as I've mentioned, and later squash, peppers, pumpkins, and the like. Aside from these, every leafy thing she fed me seemed the same—same shape, same texture, same dreadful planty taste. Nevertheless, with the persistent application of an embarrassingly simple technique, she caused me to learn. During the kill, she'd rattle off the names and describe the powers of this, that, and the other green blessing. Then on the next occasion, it was left to me either to remember, guess, or go hungry. Simple. I actually learned quite a bit that way. It pains me to realize that such a primitive technique could sway me so effectively—no electronics, no special drugs, no brain probing; just learn or go hungry.

Each day I was thrown more and more upon my own. One day she announced that henceforth she would search alone on one side of our chosen pond, creek, or river, and I on the other, all by myself. The day after it was further required that I divide both our heaps into like kinds; the day after that, not only name each item in the pile but also give a little talk on the power of each plant or plant part to satisfy a particular human need. "There are hungers within hungers," she said.

At the end of a big meal she would ask me, "Are you truly content?" Never. "How do you feel? Think about the mustard flower. Does that sound good to you? No? Onion? Garlic? Turnip?" Occasionally she'd hit on something and I'd say, "Hey, now that you mention it I could go for a little . . ." whatever. Within the big hunger for anything edible, there were little hungers for specific things that the system needed in particular. Never did the word "fish" light my eyes, but mention the bean—string, lima, pea, or peanut—and I'd be up half the night, searching with my night light in the tulies, hungry on a full stomach.

The threat each day was not of starvation, actually, but that of eating incorrectly, or eating an item improperly prepared, or just eating the inedible. "If you'd pay attention, you'd know. I've told you. I will not tell you again." Begging for advice when I was already supposed to know didn't work. Tantrums, which until those days had been second nature to me, became embarrassing, even dangerous. All that was left when I couldn't remember was to guess that such and such green thing was okay to eat; then chew it, swallow it, and wait to see which end it came out.

"Mark, can you tell me what this is?"

"It's an almond nut."

"It's a peach pit, stupid. A peach pit. Remember? You just ate the peach, didn't you?"

"Oh, yeah. Peach pit."

"Which do we eat, the almond nut or the peach pit?"

"Ummm . . . I don't remember."

"Well, here. Try it."

"You first."

"I insist."

"All right, but you open it. I always smash my fingers."

A surprising number of small round items, like the cranberry, the unshelled acorn, and the uncooked bean, to name a few, passed through to the right end okay, but came out unaltered, a good sign that I'd done something wrong. Usually this meant I hadn't chewed. It seems I'd never really learned how. I knew well enough how to swallow, and I could do that better than her even, but I couldn't get the hang of chewing. I was more of a biter than a chewer, and in the process of becoming the latter I chewed my tongue beyond recognition.

I had what was known as the "slow-tongue syndrome," common among all us tab-swallowers.

The ruins gave us all the crockery and other utensils we needed, and in such abundance that we never had to carry hard supplies of that sort with us. (*My* contribution to the survival effort, by the way. I knew my way around the ruins much better than she.) Before meeting me she had used an old hubcap for everything—cooking, eating, and washing. I was the one to show her how to loot the ruins. I introduced her to a veritable universe of glass, china, and even occasional metal things which had somehow managed to survive the pre-Big One metals confiscation. I asked her once, after she'd become reliant on scavenged hardware, if she didn't find it repugnant to use those utensils, for as surely as anything from the Free Market, these were manufactured things. But oh, no. That older civilization was good and proper and true and beautiful and everything else because at its best it provided its people with problems in excess of solutions, more wants and needs than means to satisfy them. And in those times, survival was as likely as not, whereas in the Free Market procurement was automatic and survival a certainty.

Eventually I learned to avoid the subject of the Market altogether, at which point talk between us began to decline. I knew the routine. I knew as much of her story as she cared to divulge; she knew as much of mine as she wanted to hear. Nods and glances took the place of words as we got to know what to expect from one another.

Our days got viciously regular. Each day saw me doing repeats of the previous day's routine: morning splash, breakfast, cold ascent, a check for agreement on the day's course marker, the long flight east, the late afternoon hunt for food, the evening chats (which grew shorter and less preachy as I learned how to appear more agreeable), and finally sleep. That's what most of our time together amounted to.

Aside from occasional "likely" clearings, we passed over nothing worth turning back for. Our mission got so dreary that I let a little thing like the Atlantic Ocean very nearly make me shed tears of joy, for the sea meant a complete change to the opposite extreme—flying west instead of east. Ho hum.

When we touched down on the beach, she had me wait a moment to mark the spot while she flew south to a place she remembered from her last trip, where she had set out a big red plastic stop sign. She carried it back to where I was waiting and established it firmly in some rocks as a marker for her next crossing. She said it used to make her very sad to find herself south of her marker after crossing the entire continent, as I imagined it would; she assured me that she had developed the knack pretty well and didn't often do that any more.

Nimbus came upon us again while we were napping in the sand. She had arranged her schedule to meet it on the east and west shore respectively and once again in the mountains. At sea level it was tame and gentle, at least by comparison to what it was like in the mountains. A tent of wings cleverly propped over driftwood provided all the shelter we needed to spend a damp but not wet day. Blue Jays are a broadcloth wing, ideal for that sort of thing.

And then the westward crossing. Sunny morning. Rain in the afternoon. We caught up to Nimbus and flew low for awhile in the rain until the sea salt was rinsed from our hair and the bugs from our wings. Then we stopped, let it pass, and settled into regularity once again.

I had confidence enough in my meager understanding of the grubbing process to set my own course away from hers, but continued on for the same old reason, that I had nowhere else better to go. West was as good as any other direction. In one respect west was better, because I knew I could steal a phone from Uncle Theo at the end of the crossing, if I hadn't yet found one. I desperately hoped to find one sooner. I was nearing the end of my rope with her and her way of life. I'd spot a drifter every so often perched on the horizon, and wonder if it would really be so terrible—one supremely ugly moment in trade for my rightful place in the Market. Dirty hands for a phone. I thought not, but as time passed and no alternative presented itself, I began to have second thoughts about the drifter as a source of phones.

Day after day Synthetica pushed on with inexplicable determination, while day after day mine faded. I suppose that as much as any other factor, the novelty and joy of free flight compensated for the discomforts and indignities of wilderness life. But that faded too, along with any hope of a clean phone. I can pinpoint the precise moment when the balance shifted, the moment when I knew nothing could be worth another day of discomfort.

We were eleven days back from the Atlantic, not yet in sight of the mountains. We'd set up camp along the west shore of a small lake in the plains. It looked like a Nimbus-formed lake, a large marshy puddle dependent on the artificial abundance of rain for its fill. No creek had formed to drain it. Dead trees rose up from the thick green water, evil-looking in the waning light. The entire area swarmed with insects. Not a good campsite. I urged that we push on. No. She'd settled and that was that.

I wanted to wash off the day's encrustation of bug juice and body grease, but the water looked to me like more of the same mixture. I was thirsty, but there was no drinking stuff. She boiled some. It looked the same, only hotter. I declined. The local pickings were nasty little red berries, warm and squooshy, and some herbs Synthetica made into a tea, fouling the already foul water. So after as full a day's flying as any other I neither ate nor drank, and when it came time to sleep I was too miserably hot. I couldn't sleep and I couldn't lie naked to cool off because of the mosquitoes, some as big as wasps (or else there were wasps there too). All in all it was my worst night out, and if I had been experiencing occasional brief moments of contentment with that way of life, that night put me back straight again.

Sometime late in the evening or early in the morning I woke, or more correctly became aware of the fact that I had been awake all along. A sound focused my attention, the not-so-distant hum-buzz of an astronomical population of flies. Without opening my hood to see, I knew that a drifter was settling down into the lake clearing.

We hadn't seen a body in days, and I was glad, for the sight of one would sour Synthetica's mood, and a sour mood would in turn amplify her petty gripes with me. I would suffer. So I suppressed one more time the urge to scream in agony, helped by the knowledge that it would soon pass over.

But it didn't.

The drifter which is not already inhabited by the bee attracts a special breed of fly, a night worker, a large beast which hums a low note. In numbers they sound a little like Aunt Ruth's choir droning chants. Louder. Impossibly loud in the dead of night.

The odor which surrounds a drifter proceeds in front with the wind, for relative to the drifter's motion there is no wind to blow the odor away, and with time its sphere of influence grows to be immense. It hit me and stayed. I drew my hood strings tight and breathed the sweaty urine smell of my own unwashed body (roses by comparison), until the more powerful smell of decay penetrated my suit. I sat up. I pulled open my hood. There, in the light of the full moon, were not one but four drifters, four ripe and full, joined together one to another by their sleeve links, the little eyelets where demonstration flyers would sometimes tie streamers. Four. A suicide pact. They'd come low across the surface of the lake like a line of ghostly ice skaters who'd set out to crack the whip but had died and been carried on by their own momentum. Their ever-loyal altitude sensors, which controlled lift, kept them a proper one meter above the lowest surface, but missed detecting the thin scraggle of branches protruding from the water. The bony foot of the middle flyer caught itself in the upper branches of one of those dead, leafless trees, which stopped all four but did not stop the breeze which carried their odor across to our camp. The middle flyer remained stuck, but those on either side rose up, and for a moment, silhouetted against the moonlit sky, they looked like a necklace of paper cut-out dolls.

Their stay was brief. The combined pull of all four packs freed them and they continued on, up and over the trees to the west and away from me. I breathed again.

Then something caught my eye, some whitish thing in the tree. I knew instantly what it was: a *foot*! As I watched the wretched thing, it fell from the branch into the water with a dull splash, and I had to let out a scream, in the form of the name of my dearly beloved. "SYNTHETICAAAAA!"

She jumped straight up in her usual sort of threatening way, ready to fend off wild bears in a fistfight. Before she had a chance to nail me for calling wolf again, I told her point blank, "I WANT OUT OF HERE RIGHT AWAY NOW!" I quickly explained what I'd just seen, how out there not more than a stone's throw from us was a foot floating in the water, and how it was going to paddle to shore any second and kick me if we didn't get the hell out of there. There was still enough residual stench in the air to verify at least the passing of something dead.

She agreed. Without argument. It was either the tone of my voice or the smell in the air, or the combination, but she got up, put on her wings, and led the ascent. I followed her light one long pass to a wide, easy-to-see river. We settled and made camp. I washed, drank, made a quick bed, and lay down again.

But I couldn't sleep. I wanted more than a better camp. I wanted a proper bath, my cosmetics, and above all a food tab, a simple tab, all in a house of my own.

Morning. Wide awake, having never slept. The moment she stirred I said to her, "I've had it. No more."

She opened her eyes, sat up, rubbed them, looked at me, shrugged, and went about the morning preparations—some last minute gathering, a rinse in the river, what-have-you. I followed her around trying to catch her attention. I said, "I've had it. I'm through. I quit." She avoided noticing me.

I was a mess: hungry with no appetite, sleepy but unable to sleep, and severely bitten. My mosquito bites had joined together to form a general puffiness over the backs of my hands, around my neck, cheeks, and ears. Such ears. They itched the most. For breakfast she handed me another helping of squashed berries. I told her again, "No more. I'm leaving." Another shrug, as if to say, "How can you leave me? Why even suggest it?" But I'd made up my mind. The very next drifter I came across, dry bones or ripe banana, I would dip into it and steal its phone. And if something went wrong, if I were to chase after what turned out to be a phoneless corpse and in so doing lose sight of Synthetica, then so be it. I'd live by myself for awhile until I found one. In my mind I made the break.

14

Which is not to say that Synthetica failed in her attempt to rebuild my psyche. Not at all. Most assuredly I was not converted to Mother Nature's way. Nevertheless, when I left her I took with me a modicum of independence and self-reliance which were never before a part of my character, as well as a tolerance for irregularities and obstacles in the path of life which would have completely blocked my way only a few weeks before. But fundamental to both and a lot more important, I think, was the knowledge that I could exercise my will and accomplish. In other words, *do*. Something. Anything. I had always been able to recognize the need of a thing being done. I got that much from my vicarious upbringing. But that next step, going from awareness into action, was foreign to my character. I was a passive entity with a withered will, a thing acted upon by forces external or innate. I risk making a big deal out of a simple act, but when I turned from her and set my own course, I believe I entered a new phase of existence. I really do. And I have her to thank, for without the benefit of the intense misery she provided I'd have probably gone on living by whatever experience chanced my way, instead of creating by an act of will a misery of my very own.

I say I separated from her, and I *did*. The fact that she turned to follow me doesn't change a thing in my mind. I *would* have gone on without her. For a little while, I thought I had.

We rose same as always, side by side. I paused at resting level long enough to locate the drifter group that had dropped in so unexpectedly during the night. I spotted them a short distance northwest, caught again on some high branches from the looks of it. One of them was definitely losing power. I made a note of the direction and continued on up to the top, where normally we would have stopped briefly to chat on matters of navigation, and to wish each other luck before beginning the day. She waited for me there, but I passed her by without so much as a "see you later." I rose to a point a few meters above her, out of shouting range, then flew in the direction of my unwholesome foursome, making a clean break from her.

That would have been that, I'm sure, but for the prison block peeking up just above the north horizon. It stood about half a pass beyond my drifters. It was a big thing, very big; clean, white, and smooth, easy to spot not only because of its size, but because it was one of the very few objects in the hemisphere that wasn't a tree or a ruin. I'd passed to one side or another of it by house as often as any other place on the ground that lay along the respectable latitudes, so I knew right away what it was. I never used to get particularly excited seeing it from the house. Seeing it from wings, I took it for granted again, out of habit, I suppose. I went about my way.

Not so Synthetica.

I settled in near to my drifters. Indeed, one of the middle two was sagging badly and had gotten itself hooked to a wire stretching between one tottering old phone pole and another, just above the general level of the treetops. I stayed my distance while surveying the chances. One looked as bad as another. No choice, really.

The population of flies was immense, with more breeding all the time. Going at it like that, in a few weeks time there'd be ten billion flies suddenly left with nothing to eat but each other; not unlike the human population of a few years back. Only I don't think flies eat each other; I'm not certain. I wondered if I might not just wait my turn, perhaps come back when the packs were empty. Just a passing thought. I'd made up my mind. I drew my hood up over my head and tied the string tight, leaving just enough of a hole to look through. I began paddling toward the one on the end when I heard Synthetica call my name. I pulled up, relieved actually, undid my hood, and found her hovering a few meters above me.

"You can't stop me," I told her, but she had something else in mind.

"Mark, come up here and look." She pointed toward the cube in the near distance.

"I don't have to. I can see it from here."

"Help me, Mark. I'm frightened."

"You're what?"

"I'm frightened."

"Well, look the other way for God's sake, Synthetica, what the hell." I couldn't imagine anything just then but some sort of ploy to get me back in service.

"Please, Mark, come be near me. I'm so afraid."

"Oh God." How could I refuse such a request? I rose to her level, but kept a safe distance. Apparently such precautions weren't necessary. No tricks intended. She had evidently missed completely my leaving her, and had followed me assuming I was headed toward the big white block. I found her staring, transfixed by the cube. She talked to me but never once took her eyes off it. I said, "It's the prison block. Premillennium. It's full of frozen bodies."

"Mark, I've never been this far north, and yet it's familiar to me."

"It's the only one of its kind, that's for sure. Maybe you saw a picture."

"No. It's like an old memory, something totally forgotten. When I saw it, I just . . . I just . . . I don't know. Something happened to me. Look, I'm all goose bumps. Something's happening to me right now. Mark, I'm scared."

"Oh for . . . if you're going to get spooky, go right ahead. I've got things to do."

"Stay with me. Mark, please."

"If the thing scares you, why don't you leave?"

"That's just it. I can't."

"What do you mean you can't? There's nothing stopping you."

"Mark, please, please don't leave me." She pleaded. *Synthetica* pleaded with *me*.

I said, "Quit that. You're making *me* scared."

"Mark, help me. There's something wrong. I want to go but I can't."

"Well damn it, pull up."

"I can't."

"What do you mean can't?"

"*I can't.*"

"Shit. . . ." I paddled over to her, reached for her upcord, and was about to launch her when she hit my hand away. "No. I've got to go closer. It's as though someone is calling me."

"Not me. I didn't say a word."

"I can hear him calling me. Mark. . . ." She paused as if to listen, then yelped, "It's my father's voice!"

"Oh shit, now I *am* scared."

She flew without further ascension, one short hop, the remaining distance on another. I, of course, did the same, despite my recent bid for independence. Normally I wouldn't have felt any reluctance to approach the cube, assuming I might have any desire to. But she had me spooked. All I could think of were those thousands of Popsicle people tucked away in their little drawers, waiting for the reprieve that never came, and for the first time ever, *that* scared me.

She went straight for the south wall, hovering a few meters back at resting level. I parked next to her. She told me again how scared she was. "You know, for someone who runs away from a mere telephone, you're doing all right." I watched her just hang there and stare, and after awhile asked her what she intended to do next. No answer. "You can't just sit here the rest of your life."

"Mark, I'm frightened to death. I'm shaking."

"Well then, let's go. I'm going. Good-bye."

"Mark, pleeeese."

As with Nimbus, I'd never quite imagined how big the thing was. From the sky it looked like a harmless little cube of sugar. Lower down it looked its size, which was, I believe, an even one hundred meters to a side, a perfect cube. I sat ever so slightly askew, the effect of a dozen or more futile nuclear attacks on the structure by some charitable first century millennium jerk with a guilty conscience. "You can't exactly walk right in, you know. It's been tried."

"Isn't there a door?"

"No doubt several. Do you know the combination?"

"No."

"Neither do I. Come on, let's get out of here."

"Who *does* know?"

"Nobody *does* know. Except maybe Stern, the guy who put all those bodies in there. And he's in there too, stiff as the rest of them."

In the most frighteningly solemn, positively assured voice I'd ever heard her use, she said, "There is a way inside. I know."

"Synthetica, for God's sake. Don't get weird on me, okay? If you want me to stay with you, don't get weird."

"He's calling me."

"Oh damn."

"I can hear his voice. It's like an old memory, things he said long ago, that now all of a sudden I remember, perfectly clear. He's in there, Mark. My father is in that building."

"Not if you're twenty-three he isn't. The people in there are pre-millennium."

"I can hear his voice, crystal clear."

"I can't. Tell him to speak up a little."

"Mark, he wants me to rescue him."

"Oh he does, does he? Does he say how?"

"No."

"Ha. Just when you get to the good part."

"He says I don't have to understand. But I must not leave without him."

"Oh shit. Here we go."

She was going crazy before my very eyes. Her face went pale, her eyes glassy, while her every thought seemed focused on the seamless flawless mirror-white monotonous impenetrable surface. I coaxed her softly, politely, sternly, and with threats. She wouldn't budge. She would neither move nor speak except to say, "Don't leave me."

I said, "What are you trying to do, open the damn thing with mental telepathy? Do you realize how many swami types have parked themselves here with just that in mind? I've never seen you like this. Maybe it's something you ate?" No answer. "Jesus, Synthetica, there are thousands of fathers in there. Mothers too. What makes you think you can have yours if nobody else can? If there were a way in, believe me, there wouldn't be anybody left in there. Besides, if you really are twenty-three, your father's somewhere else. What happened to the clearing? Remember the clearing? Let's go look for the clearing. Come on. Please?" Nothing. "Oh for God's sake, quit it."

"Mark, don't leave me."

"If you say that one more time, I'm leaving, so help me."

"Mark?"

"I'm warning you. . . ."

"Where is the door?"

"You're looking right at it."

"Where?"

"I should think near the ground, wouldn't you?"

"I don't see it."

"You won't either, unless your little voice tells you the combination. Well?"

"No. Nothing."

"Somehow I didn't think it would."

"Mark?"

"Yes?"

"What is a combination?"

"It's a number, or a word, or a picture, or an obscene gesture, for all I know." I knew of one such case.

"If it's a word, where would one speak it?"

"Near the door."

"Which you say is near the ground?"

Somewhere along the line I'd seen that old shot of Stern's farewell. Although my memory of it was hazy, I could vaguely remember seeing him wave good-bye to the cameras, turn around and walk inside the prison vault, closing the door behind him. I was very little at the time. I'm sure the only reason I remember it is Aunt Ruth's insistence that Stern was locking up the devils and keeping guard so that the rest of us could enjoy the millennium without any more ruckus. She encouraged me to pray to him. If Mimi Jo hadn't put a stop to her, Ruth would have had me worshipping Stern as the Lord Jesus come again.

Synthetica and I settled and touched ground, at last. My straps were killing me. I was only glad to get some weight on my feet. The ground air was hot and muggy. The shiny wall reflected the sun so that we had two suns shining on us instead of just one. No shade trees in the immediate area, just rocky barren dirt with a scraggle of shrubs. Synthetica had me direct her to a place near where the door would likely be, and there she sat with her legs crossed, just staring at the blank wall.

I got to thinking about her little act, and it occurred to me that maybe her father *was* one of the prisoners, and unable to bear the loss, she made up the story of a father in the wilderness waiting for his daughter's return. Then, according to some nutty psychology, she convinced herself it was true, instead of just facing up to her loss the way everyone else had to back then. Except for the fact that a thousand years is plenty long enough to face up to any loss, and forget it ten times over. I decided against that in favor of the original notion that she was as she'd always said, a twenty-three-year-old out looking for her lost father, who, I secretly believed, was living it up in the Market, having successfully ditched his child. Just like Mimi Jo. Just a thought, one I never dared to reveal. Until this very moment, that is. I said, "You know what I think? What I truly believe? I believe you're doing this just to keep me from my phone, and you know why you're doing a thing like that?"

"Mark, please."

"Because you're afraid that I'll call him up and prove once and for all that he ditched you. That's right. You heard me. He ditched you. And all this mystery bullshit is an act to keep me from my phone. Well, it won't work. Not any more."

"No Mark, please."

"That's it, isn't it?"

"No."

"It is. And I'm going to prove it. You know how? I'm going to get that phone right now and bring it back here and call him up, and then we'll both know once and for all who's right about your damn father." I got up, stepped clear of the wall, and readied myself for ascent.

She said, "Wait Mark, I can prove it."

"All right!" I walked up to her, stood over her, put my hands on my hips, and gave her my most domineering frown. I said, "This better be a good one." I waited. Nothing. "Well?"

After another stretch of silence she said, "I'm afraid. Please don't leave me."

"Aw, Synthetica, you're so full of shit."

I turned and marched away from her with one hand on my up-cord, when I heard a "ffffff" sound, the sound of rushing air. It was a sound of no particular quality save one; it was a sound neither she nor I could very well imitate. I stopped dead still. I surely did not want to turn around. What I wanted more than anything in the world was to pull up and be on my way without ever looking back. I was scared out of my wits. I wanted to go, but I couldn't. I had to stay, and worse, I had to turn around and see it with my own eyes.

About three meters up from the ground, on that otherwise flawless surface, there had appeared a small black hyphen, a thick line about a meter long. Wisps of white frothy air curled around at the edges. It was an opening, only wide enough to allow the pressures inside and out to equalize. But when the air was still and all was quiet, the opening expanded downward, utterly without a sound, like a shadow projected on the wall. It touched the ground and stopped. It remained open.

"Oh God. Oh God. Now look what you've done. Jesus, shut it. Shut it. Synthetica, do something."

She stood, approached the opening, turned back to me. "Mark, this is where my father is."

"Okay. Yeah. Sure. Anything. Only shut it, please."

"Not until I've rescued him. Mark, help me."

"Oh no. Oh no. Uh-uh. Not a chance. Forget it. Leave me alone. I'm not going in there. You do whatever you want, but leave me alone, you hear? *Leave me alone.*"

"You understand what this thing is. I don't. I need you to guide me."

"I'll tell you everything I know. It's a prison. It's full of people who didn't like the Market and made a lot of trouble, way back when. That's it. See ya."

"The door is open. Why aren't they rushing out?"

"They're frozen."

"Are they dead?"

"Yes. No. Sorta."

"Can they be. . . ."

Resurrected was the word. I answered yes. She suggested we bring her father's frozen form out into the sun. I explained how a slow defrosting would destroy every cell in his body, that it must be done instantaneously by a special machine. She said, "There now, you see what I mean? You understand these things. Mark, help me."

"I won't go in there. I won't. You can't make me."

"You're right. I can't."

"So there. I'm going to get my telephone. Tonight I'll be floating in the pool of my own house with no one to yell at me or tell me what do do."

"You can't leave me."

"A challenge I accept."

"You love me, Mark."

". . . . . oh that's low. That's really low."

"And I love you."

"That's just so low."

"I wanted you to find out for yourself."

"Oh, I mean low."

"But you *do* love me. You don't want to see me hurt. You want to take care of me. Just as I take care of you."

"Low, low, low."

"I'm going in, not because I want to, but because I love someone in there, just as you love me."

"I do *not* love you. I don't love *anybody*. I never *have*, and I never *will*."

"I have to go now, Mark. My father is telling me I must, and I must. Because I love him too, you see."

"It isn't love. You've been hypnotized. You're just his little robot full of pre-recorded instructions. You think I haven't figured it out?"

"Then help me, Mark, because I can't help myself."

". . . .Aw, come on. Come on. We'll fly away. Just like before . . ." She turned. ". . . You and me . . " Faced the opening. ". . . Synthetica? Don't go." And stepped into the dark. "Don't leave me like that. Synthetica?"

No answer.

15

I don't think she invested more than a couple minutes time telling me all that, but she couldn't have done better with a whole month to burn. It's not that she was correct or incorrect regarding my feelings for her. She was speaking not to inform me, but to *suggest*; and thereby create at least the question in my mind: "Do I love her? And if I do, can I leave her when all she asks is my company and a little advice on things I'm much better acquainted with?" She hypnotized me in effect, not with trances or mysterious gestures, but with a word spoken with authority to a born submissive. Nothing like the procedure she must have been subjected to. There was no doubt in my mind as she entered the vault that she was responding to a series of post-hypnotic suggestions triggered by her encounter with the prison vault; not one suggestion, but many, in sequential order. If the entire picture had been revealed to her all at once, I seriously doubt that she would have gone on with it. Dealing with the grisly machinery of resurrection wasn't precisely her cup of tea. Therefore it was given to her in steps, one at a time; each accomplishment triggering the unlocking of a new set of instructions. The precision and detail escaped me, but I knew well enough that she was obeying orders given to her through hypnosis, and having been a subject many times, forced to do ridiculous things in spite of myself, I knew she was helpless to refuse. I felt sorry for her. I admit to that.

I whined and sniveled at the opening like a deserted pup, and then I went in after her. There was never any question. Besides, who was I to be afraid of a dark passage? Years of tradition notwithstanding, the door stood open. So I stepped in.

The faintest click. The faintest whirr. A hiss, then silence. I turned. The door was gone, without a trace. All was crystal. And I thought, "God, haven't I been through this once already?"

She was right there waiting for me. Naturally. "Tonight when I order my house, I'm going to have all the doors removed, so help me. I hope I never see another door as long as I live. You hear me?"

"Mark, need I point out? There are no doors in nature."

"You know? You're right. You're absolutely right. I'm sold. Let's go."

"First, my father."

"I know. I know. But I'd feel a lot better if you'd open it up again. I'm a little edgy, if you know what I mean."

"Ah ... Mark, I can't."

"Oh, now wait a minute. You know the combination."

"No."

"God damn it, the door opened, didn't it? You must have said something."

"If I did then something has made me forget, because I don't remember."

"Oh no. You can't fool me. You know it. You just don't trust me. You think I'll run out. Boy, that's dirty. That's rotten."

"Don't say that. That's unfair."

"Unfair? Who are you to talk about unfair?" And so on. I argued and she argued back, like old times. Both of us were scared out of our wits. We argued with the knowledge that by doing so we were masking a fear neither one of us cared to acknowledge.

Without interrupting the argument we turned to the business at hand. I faced the wall where once had been a door, and pronounced several times each and every word and phrase I had ever heard used to open a door at home or on TV, everything from "Open sesame," to "Honey, I'm home." Meanwhile Synthetica put herself to the task of retrieving the lost combination. No success in either venture.

She insisted right along that we were wasting time, that her father would open the door for us and that we should find him straight away. I thought not. I had more than one reason for wanting it open. Aside from the terrible feeling of being trapped, it was cold in there, and getting colder by the second. The walls, floor, and ceiling were made of a one-way photonic crystal which allowed energy in any radiant form to pass clean through it in one direction but not the other. Whatever spare warmth we brought with us began to filter out, with nothing coming in from outside to replace it. It was a passive substance in that respect, and remained passive unless a physical force was brought to bear against it, in which case it would convert that force into radiant energy, which in turn would pass through to the outside and disappear. I beat on the wall. I kicked it. I threw myself against it, getting for all my effort a few bruises and a bright circle of light which emanated from the point of contact, then slowly faded, leaving us in a dark so dark I couldn't find one hand with the other. We resorted to our pack lights.

The cold was unbelievable. I pulled my hood up, drew the strings, raised my thermal zipper, and balanced on one foot, for the cold cruel floor drained my body's heat right out through my slippers. I traded right foot for the left to give it a chance to warm; then left for right, back and forth, marching in place. I pulled up off the floor on lift power, but found it impossible to hold still. I'd drift toward a surface, reach out, touch the wall with a bare hand and have to peel it free. It was either bounce up and down on the floor or back and forth between the walls for as far into the future as I could imagine. Synthetica was no better off. We both wanted more out of life. I couldn't think what to do, and unfortunately her inner voice was mute regarding small details. Her big voice screamed, loud, each time she touched a surface and felt that electric ice. She'd never encountered anything frozen before and didn't know quite what to make of it. I must admit, had she known the combination I'm sure she would have given up on her father and gone on to better things, right then and there, a situation he had perhaps anticipated.

We were situated between two towering walls, one hundred meters high and extending as far back, but with no more space between them than about three meters, the length of the average drawer when fully extended. The surface of both walls was lined with rectangles, each with a handle, each handle with a tag, each tag with a number on it. We weren't long between the walls before it finally dawned on me that we might just as well bounce deeper inside, with an eye out for a reception room or a turnoff. Though endless in two directions, the corridor was so narrow that we couldn't extend wings to fly, so we hopped unweighted in a delicate fashion down the long long passage until we came at last to a cross-linking corridor perpendicular to the one we were in. We split off left and right.

The main corridor, the one we first entered, turned out to be only one of many like it, each with their hundreds of little rectangles, each with a handle, each with a tag with a number on it. I didn't count. I didn't multiply. But the impression I got was clear: there were more people tucked away in that single cube than alive and free-floating in the Market community. Or if not, the difference was insignificant. At the time of the purges, the Market people far outnumbered the dissidents, but over the years so many capable of suicide went their way, while the population on ice, having little choice in the matter, remained rock steady to the last individual.

Synthetica called from the far end of the cross-link. I turned and bounded her way. She'd come upon a room, a find that made us both very happy. I stepped inside. She followed. A click. A buzz. A whirr. A rush of warm air to greet us, and light. We stood by the register rubbing our hands before surveying our find.

It was a comfortable if not entirely cozy room; steel lined, with steel benches, steel cabinets, steel shelves, even a steel toilet in the corner. Whatever charm the place might have had was utterly destroyed by the apparatus in the center—a steel table about the size of a small bed, equipped with circular metal clamps, two for ankles, two for wrists. Suspended over the table was a large cone-shaped antenna, known as a Martin beam. When activated, it would give birth to a dolop of blue plasma, a cloud of sub-atomic particles which would warble downward and penetrate anything non-metallic in its way, such as a struggling body. After a brief existence, these highly unstable particles would vanish, taking with them out of existence an amount of energy equal to that which formed them. Without energy, there is no motion. No motion, no time. The Martin beam would stay the chemistry of life so suddenly and so completely that not even the teensiest weensiest molecule would be put out of place. Properly insulated, the body would preserve indefinitely, rock solid, invulnerable to the risks and dangers that plague breathers. Quite the opposite of death, it was in fact the very best way to survive. You'd hear it said, and wonder if it wasn't the truth, that those poor souls locked in the vault passing off centuries in an instant were a lot better off than the rest of us, who had to endure time at the slow plodding rate of history.

Synthetica surveyed her surroundings, particularly the machine in the center. Without knowing what to call it she surmised its function. At any rate, she didn't press me with questions, and I wasn't volunteering any unsolicited explanations that day.

A passageway led from that room to another. The second room was little better—another table, another big antenna. One important difference, though. What the rig in the first room did, this undid. It was called a flash heater, and if my memory serves me, it was here that prisoners were unfrozen for brief periods so that they might give names to the inquisitors. In this way, bit by bit, many anti-Market conspiracies were put safely out of the way without the death of a single man or woman. A righteous victory, according to Aunt Ruth.

"Mark, is there something called a terminal?"

"There are lots of things called terminals."

"I'm to find a terminal."

"Little voice again."

"Yes."

"Anything else?"

"No."

"Let's try the next room."

The next room was another de-processing room, and so was the one after that. While Synthetica went on from one room to the next, I crossed the hall to another door and struck gold. "Synthetica, *over here*."

I found the office. It was a single large plain room with at least twenty desks, each with its own microphone and screen. By the time she got there I was already voiced in with the system on, hoping desperately for a tie-line. I gave it my best computer talk: "Bypass identification procedures and key to an outside line. This is a mayday. I repeat, mayday." The machine would hear but not speak. It put its answer in writing on a tiny bright yellow screen that sat in a box half-buried on the desk. I read slowly: "For security reasons no outside lines are available to or from the complex. We regret the inconvenience. For further information please voice . . ." a long list of reference numbers. I expected as much. I tried again anyway, and again, with every opening procedure I'd ever heard used for an outside line, and got nothing. The story of my life.

While I searched for short cuts with long shots, Synthetica, in response to another unlocked memory, sat herself in front of another terminal and got straight to the point: "Where is Peter Watkins Winter?"

She got what she called for without need of a reset or advisory instruction. When I realized what she was up to I switched over to her image and watched on my screen. I came in on the "W's" list, a blur of hundreds of names much too small to read. A thin green line across the top of the screen descended, while another up the side crossed over. They stopped. Where the two lines met the image expanded, bringing into view a shorter list of "Wi's." Another set of lines located the one name on the list that equalled the words Synthetica had spoken, and her long search came to an end. Three blue numbers on a yellow screen: Aisle 38, Column 53, Row 17. All those weeks and all those years before I ever met her spent searching for a grassy oval with a hill and an apple tree. Mother Nature's own. Had she ever imagined. I was ready to share the joy, but apparently the numbers weren't enough for her. No celebration just yet.

Her father's address cued the next commandment. She paused at the terminal with her eyes shut, then turned to me and said, "There's a pallet, something flat. Do you know?"

I did. There was one in each of the de-processing chambers. "It carries the body."

I led her across the hall into one of the steel rooms and located what she was looking for tucked away under the table. It looked like the same make and type of carrier that delivered Mimi Jo's mail, except that the keys would accept only local coordinates.

"I am to give it the numbers."

I showed her how to punch in the numbers, but stopped short of actually doing it. Before continuing, I wanted a serious word with her, for the task ahead was grim to say the least. "You know what this means?" It was obvious that she knew perfectly well, and was anxious to get on with it. I had reservations. "I hope you realize I don't have the slightest idea how to work this thing" (meaning the de-processor). Seeing something done on TV and actually doing it were two different things, a fact I'd only recently discovered. "If something goes wrong, I mean, Synthetica, it's more than just him. It's you and me. He's our only way out of here, from the looks of it." All the more reason to get on with it, she thought. I said, "Look, *I'm* the one who's going to end up working this thing, not you. Synthetica, I've never even touched one before. I don't think you understand about machines. Anything can go wrong."

"The voice tells me to...."

"The voice says '*do*,' it doesn't say *how*."

"Do we have any choice? Mark? Do we?"

"Yes." I didn't want to say what, but the time had come

and she wasn't in a waiting mood. "I think we should practice first. On someone else."

"Oh Mark!" As if to say how could you think of such a thing.

But by the same logic that made my suggestion so abhorrent, she was forced to realize that it was necessary. If a mistake was possible, then the death of a stranger was as wrong from a purely moral point of view as the death of her father. On the other hand, if all went well we would have the joy of two awakenings. All that notwithstanding, from a purely selfish point of view we dare not make any mistake with her father. She debated with me not because she disagreed; because she didn't. She debated merely to establish herself as the opposition, so that in the event of a catastrophe she could shine blameless. But I knew that tactic and tricked her by saying all of a sudden, "You're right. Let's bring him in and try our luck." I took hold of the pallet and punched in two of the three numbers.

She reached out, touched my hand, and eyes cast downward, said, "No. You're right."

Before sending the pallet off I gave the room a brief but thorough examination. It was one of the emptiest rooms I'd ever encountered. The table in the center, a mirror glass partition at one end, some shelves at the other with a few ornaments, and very little else. Behind the glass shield was a button board with an amazingly simple array of controls: two buttons, one labeled ON, and the other OFF. Left to her own devices Synthetica could have figured it out, I'm sure. If there was to be trouble, I knew, it would be with the aging machinery, not with the operator.

"Well?" she said. "Who will it be?"

"I don't see how it makes any difference."

"You do it. . . . Please?" I looked at her. "It was your idea," she said.

"Don't forget, you agreed."

"Please?"

"All right." I approached the pallet, held my hand over the keys, closed my eyes, and punched in three random numbers. The pallet lifted into the air, floated through the door, and vanished down the hall. We weren't five minutes waiting when it returned with the awful truth. Synthetica didn't like what she saw, and turned her head away. It was a woman, shiny as glass, in a swirling white cloud of frosty vapors.

Rather attractive, I thought. The pallet sidled up to the table and attached itself edge to edge. Using its retractable prongs, it pushed the body from one surface to the other. The sub-zero solid sizzled noisily for a moment as it touched the comparatively hot table. Hiding behind the glass shield, Synthetica let out a little yelp, pressed her hands against her ears, and buried herself in the corner. After completing its task the pallet tucked itself away under the table, in preparation for the great awakening.

"Can you think of anything else?" I asked. She shook her head. "Well then, here goes." I pressed the button.

An amber light on the panel said, "System Check." I waited. Nothing. Then a beep tone and the light turned green. "System OK." At that a voice tape told us first in French, then German, then Swedish, finally in English to stand behind the shield, with stern warnings against looking in the direction of the table. Synthetica curled herself into a ball on the floor, head between her knees, the whole package wrapped tightly in her arms. She'd never heard a ceiling talk before. I think that as much as everything else frightened her. After the last of the verbal warnings, to heighten the drama we were given a ten second countdown in beep tones. The entire ceremony from beginning to end took more than two minutes, and by the time it was ready my heart was pounding furiously.

There occurred a brilliant flash and a silent THUMP caused by the sudden expansion of heated air between the antenna and the body on the table. After an all-clear announcement, the system shut itself off automatically. Synthetica got up off the floor and faced the facts.

The woman lay there, warm, damp, and steamy, neither too hot nor too cold. She had nothing to say right off, expressed no fright or fight. A blink of the eyes. I came around the shield, approached the table, leaned over, caught her attention, and said, "You're in the future now. Everything's perfect. Wake up."

She looked into my eyes and smiled. I looked at Synthetica. We both breathed a tremendous sigh of relief. In sudden good spirits, I said to the woman, "Me Zog. Everybody robot now." The woman lost her smile. "Hey, I'm only kidding. Listen, me only Mark, and this is . . . well, a friend." Her expression took on a serious quality, her eyes now darting left and right. Concern. Deep concern. "It's all right," I insisted.

"It's the future. No one's going to hurt you. All that's over. Get up. And don't worry, we'll find you something to wear."

But she was definitely disturbed. No question about it. Much much concern about something. "What? What is it? Say something!" Her mouth formed words. "You want a drink of water? We got water." Desperate pleas for something. "I can't hear a word you're saying. Speak up." She stiffened, then arched her back. Her eyes went up inside her head, showing whites. She stuck out her tongue, a great swollen thing. I said, "Are you mad at me? Look, I'm only trying to help you. Hey, come on." She stuck it out farther, all the way to her chin. I said, "I'm not who you think I am. It's later than you think. It's today. Now. Not then. All that's over with." Then BANG. Her body dropped down hard against the table. She stiffened, arched up again, and BANG. BANG. BANG. BANG. Her eyes turned all the way around back inside her head, then BANG one last time. A few tremors rippled through her limp flesh, a couple of little flops, then nothing. Her head fell to one side and she ceased moving altogether. I said, "There now, that's better. You take it easy." She did.

Synthetica looked at me, at the woman, at me again. She stepped back away and looked at us with disgust, conveying clearly who was to blame. "Oh no you don't. Uh-uh. You got me into this. If I had my way you know where I'd be—sitting in my own house a million miles from here."

"Oh Mark, poor baby, I'm not blaming you. You were right. That could have been my father."

"Oh."

"Now what do we do?"

". . . . ."

"Mark? What now?"

"Try another room, I guess." What else could I suggest? What else could she do but agree?

We left our lady on the table and went to the next room. I got the pallet out and started to punch in another set of numbers. My hand shook so badly I couldn't. I turned to her and said, "It's your turn." For a moment she hated me, then she accepted the responsibility and did as she had seen me do before.

The pallet left, returned with another icy figurine, and put it on the table. I checked and doubled-checked, and when I was quite certain I'd covered everything, I said to her again, "Your turn."

She pressed the button. Everything happened again exactly as before. Everything. The amber light, to green, SYSTEM OK (it definitely said OK), four warnings, the countdown, the flash.

We both ran to our new friend. A gentleman, slightly aged, but fit. Synthetica took his hand and gave it a warm squeeze. He liked that. I told him right off, "Stern is gone. We're here to help," supposing, perhaps, that the woman before hadn't really gotten the message. It occurred to me that she really hadn't understood that the future was now, despite my strong insistence. A moment ago her time, she had been strapped beneath the Martin beam in the other room. I thought that perhaps in flopping up and down she was fighting the restraining straps in an attempt to beat herself to death rather than submit to processing, never once realizing that she'd already been processed and there were no straps whatsoever. This time I yelled the good news in his ear: "IT'S THE FUTURE. EVERYTHING IS PERFECT NOW. EVERYTHING. WE'RE ALL GOOD DECENT PEOPLE. NO WAR, NO CRIME, YOU NAME IT, NOTHING AT ALL." But the gentleman, after a moment's peace, repeated the lady's performance exactly, from the protruding tongue to the flops, eyes up inside, and finally stillness forever more.

I felt that desperate panic well up, that cold sweaty feeling of having gone too deep into wrong. I wanted out of there, out of the vault, out of my own skin. I grabbed Synthetica's hand and ran to the next room. It wasn't a matter of choice. I knew what had to be done and I did it. Another pallet, another random number, another block of ice. Same procedure, same results. There were four de-processing rooms; we tried them all with no success. Synthetica looked at me—*to* me. What could I say? "I don't know. I don't know." We carried our failures into the first room, set them on the floor, and got the hell out of there.

"What'll we do?" was her question again and again.

"I don't know. I don't know. I don't know. Maybe it's the machines. They're old. Nobody's used them since . . ." I got an idea. "Maybe . . ."

"No."

"One more."

"Mark, no."

"Whose turn is it?"

"I won't do it."

"I will." And I did. I was certain I had the answer. Equipment deterioration, namely loss of power. I got another gentleman and buzzed him. Immediately, just after the all-clear, as soon as the panel lights shut off, I buzzed him again. A second press of the button. A second dose to supplement the first. I reasoned that if the first heating could wake him up, the second ought to get him on his feet. While the device cycled in preparation for the next zap, the gentleman on the table smiled. Synthetica started toward him. I held her back. First warning. He began to hurt. I yelled to him, "Stay put. Don't worry. Everything will be all right." Second warning. His back arched. Third warning. Tongue out. Flop, flop. Fourth warning. Countdown. Flash.

I was wrong. The device was in perfect order, just as its little green light insisted. It was set to administer in a fraction of a second just enough heat to warm up the icy body from near absolute zero to normal living temperature. Or a normal warm body to about twice boiling in as little time. The gentleman exploded into a million sticky little pieces which smacked against the floor and ceiling, where they smoldered, filling the room with noxious and greasy black smoke. I had to get out of there for awhile and be sick in the hall. Synthetica too. I was wrong with no one to blame. But she never said a word against me.

16

It's a hard thing to put your faith in a little voice, especially the mundane little voice of a post-hypnotic remembrance. *Especially* when it's someone else's remembrance. A voice from the spirit world is another matter, but even then I would require some identification before I put my life on the line.

Synthetica, with due apologies and sympathy for my feelings, insisted that we should take the next step according to the instructions her father had planted in her brain. I was adamantly opposed to any such thing. I reasoned that since her father was our last hope of getting out, we dare not risk his life until we had perfected our technique. She felt that when the time came, she would "receive" the correct instructions. I said, "What on earth can he tell us that we don't already know?"

"Just that, Mark. He will tell us what we don't know."

"Oh Jesus, Synthetica. I don't want to risk it. We've got to figure this thing out first."

"I won't be part to any more of your murders."

"*My murders?*"

"If you won't help me, I'll bring him here and do it myself."

"*No!*"

"He's *my* father."

"He may be your father, but he's *my* only hope of getting out of here."

"I want out just as bad as you."

"You'll never get out if you kill your father."

"He's dead now. We'll never get out if we don't try to wake him."

"And if we fail?"

"We've already failed. Let's try something else for a change."

"One more test. Just one."

"My father."

"No."

"I'll do it myself." She got up and proceeded to the next room where we had laid out our sacrifices, all but the one on the walls next door. She went straight for the pallet and punched in numbers. I grabbed her hands away. She pulled me out of her way. I lost my balance and fell. I crawled across the floor and tackled her around the knees. She came down screaming, "LET ME ALONE. LET ME ALONE." I turned her over and sat down on her stomach. She reached up and clawed at my face. While I beat her hands away she arched her back and threw me off. Before long she was on top of me. Neither of us knew how to fight worth a damn. For the next few moments we traded places one on top of the other. It ended abruptly when the pallet, which I had missed, returned with the body of Synthetica's father. She quickly forgot about me, jumped right up and rushed over to look at him. While he was being transferred to the table top she leaned over and looked through the layer of ice and frost into his face.

"Is it him? Is it him?" I picked myself up off the floor.

"Yes," she said. "Oh yes." She fell to her knees and wept great heavy sobs, repeating over and over, "Father, I love you. I love you."

I took a look and could see no resemblance. Darker hair, quite a bit taller. It's hard to compare when the sexes are different. It was the same with Mimi Jo and me. Some saw a likeness, others saw none. His face was so stern and businesslike I don't think it could have supported a smile under any conditions. It was a face that said, even in its frozen state, "Step aside, I'm coming through." If a face can say that. I argue it can.

Suddenly Synthetica stopped weeping and looked up. "Mark, the voice. I hear it again."

"You do?"

"Clearly. Mark, I hear it again."

"Oh, Synthetica, I'm sorry. You were right. You were right. I'm sorry. Synthetica..."

"Shhhhh..."

"You bet." For the first time since the doors closed on us I felt encouraged. "What's it say?"

"I am to find a..." she stood, looked around. "I am to find the place to stand. There!" She pointed behind the shield.

"Yeah, yeah, go on."

"I am to see in front of me a, a box."

"Yeah..."

"On the box is something to touch. To press." Looking half inward, half out, as though sleepwalking, she took her position behind the panel and felt it with her fingertips. "I am to press." In so saying, she did. The amber light came on.

"And? And? What else?"

"Nothing else."

"Synthetica, my God. My God. Listen again. There's got to be more."

"No. Nothing."

"Shut it off. Shut it off."

"No." She stood between me and the controls with her arms folded like a punjab. The warning tapes delivered the safety pitch. I tried to reach around her for the off button. She raised her knee and threatened to kick. I accepted the threat and took one hard in the gut. She resisted violently, all out, like a cornered cat. I never got near the button. Very shortly it was too late.

For the second time in minutes, we gave up the fight for the common interest. She ran to the table. I ran with her. There he lay, eyes blinking. She screamed, "FATHER, IT'S ME."

He looked quizically at her, smiled, and tried to speak; but like the others, he could not.

"O my God. Synthetica. Think. Listen. The voice. What's it say to do? Listen again."

She realized the seriousness of the situation. She shut her eyes, put her hand to her head, and listened like she'd never listened before.

"What's it say?" Hurry. Synthetica, my God, we're all going to die. Synthetica, what the hell does it say?"

She opened her eyes, turned to me, and said boldly, "Nothing!"

"Keep listening. Hurry."

"You were right, Mark. You were right."

"Think. Listen. It's got to be there." She closed her eyes again and did her best.

I lost heart. I lost my senses. I panicked completely. I ran behind the screen, back out, back behind again, struggling for an idea. Nothing. Nothing. Just the one. I gave it the briefest consideration, then, for no reason but that I was at the absolute end of my rope, I hit the button again. Amber light, green, the warning in French.

"Synthetica, come back here."

Her father began to exhibit the symptoms we both knew so well. His eyes darted back and forth, looking for help. He saw his daughter with her eyes shut, concentrating. He saw me all the way behind the screen. He mouthed the word "help."

I shrugged a helpless shrug, pleading, "What? Tell me. What?"

Over the speakers the second warning.

His eyes shot up to the ceiling, back to me. He heard. He knew he was about to be exploded. All of a sudden I knew too. I leapt to the board and hit the off button.

It didn't work. I hit it again and again and again. The cycle continued.

I looked at him. He at me. His face grew stern. He knew it was his game if it was anybody's. He carefully mouthed words he could not utter. He was definitely saying something. I shouted to Synthetica. "What's he saying? What's he saying?"

Eyes shut, she answered, "Nothing. Nothing. Oh you were right, why didn't I listen to you?"

"No, Synthetica, open your eyes. He's saying something. LOOK AT HIM!"

Over the speakers, the third warning.

She opened her eyes, saw her father, and put her face close to his.

"It's too late. Synthetica. Get back here. It's going to fire again. I can't stop it."

She paid no attention to me at all. She was prepared to die with her father if that was to be his fate.

I could not make out his words from behind the shield. I didn't dare leave my place of protection. But Synthetica seemed to understand him. At one point she looked up and scanned the room. Eyes to her father, back to the room. He wanted her to get something. What? She had few choices. Sitting on a shelf out of range of the antenna were two suction cup things made of brass. She grabbed one off the shelf, brought it to her father, and showed it to him. He approved. No. Yes. Something else.

The fourth warning began: ALL PERSONNEL TAKE WARNING . . . I got up on the top of the control box and came down hard on the off button. It would not work.

"Synthetica, it's too late. Come back here."

"Mark, he wants something. What does he want? What is it?"

"Synthetica . . ." All of a sudden I knew what it was. The shockers. "The other one. Get the other one."

". . . DO NOT LOOK IN THE DIRECTION OF THE TABLE . . ."

She dropped the one she had and ran to fetch the other. She returned with it to her father's side for instructions. By now, though, she had lost touch with him. His back arched up and he came down hard on the table.

I screamed, *"No. No. Both of them. Get both of them."*

". . . IF YOU ARE NOT WEARING PROTECTIVE CLOTHING, STAND BEHIND THE SCREEN AT ONCE. TIME TO FIRING TEN SECONDS FROM THE TONE. BEEP."

She picked up the one she'd let drop. She held them both up for me to see, tears streaming down her face, ready to serve if she only knew how. She hadn't the slightest idea.

BEEP.

"Touch them to his chest. *His chest.*"

BEEP.

"Damn it. *His chest.*" I hollered from the safety of the shield. She did as I said. Nothing.

BEEP.

"The buttons. Press the buttons."

BEEP.

She didn't understand. I raced out from behind the shield.

BEEP.

Tore the shockers from her grip.

BEEP.

Applied pressure against her father's chest with the two shockers, one on either side of his heart. Pressed the buttons.

BEEP.

The body lurched up violently from the combined effect of the death throes and the electricity from the shockers. At the same instant I pushed him off the table onto the floor.

BEEP.

I yanked the pallet out over him. In the same motion I drove Synthetica down under the shelves, and lay down on top of her.

BEEP.

FLASH.

And the old boy lived. She did too. And me? I got the most beautiful tan you'd ever want to see. On one half of my face.

17

Resurrection requires not only the restoration of normal molecular activity, but a re-establishment of, what did he say, lost inertia, I believe. Anyway, the shocker provided the finishing touch. I'd seen them used in TV dramas often enough, but it never registered as anything significant; mere ritual, like the sprinkling of holy water. I did remember, though, just in time, and Synthetica, with her long-lost not two steps away, took time to thank me. She grabbed hold of my head, held it firmly so I couldn't shy away, and said, "Mark, I love you very much. I'll never forget this as long as I live. Mark, open your eyes. I love you."

"I, a . . . a . . ." I couldn't say it back.

"It doesn't matter. Come meet my father."

Peter Watkins Winter entered the world out of breath and weak of heart. He got up on his hands and knees, raised his head, beheld the unseemly accumulation of limp nudes on the floor, looked back at me, and said, "Are you on the staff here?" His first words in a thousand years, wasted on a rhetorical question.

Synthetica ran to help him up, crying, "Father, Father," and so on, with her usual tendency to repeat. He stood up. She threw her arms around him and buried her face in his chest. Peter stroked the back of her head and said, "There, there. I'm here to protect you now. You're tired. You're very tired. Very sleepy. Very, very sleepy."

"Yes father."

"Rest. Relax. Go to sleep."

"Yes father."

"Nice and easy, sound asleep."

"Yes fa . . ."

She collapsed unconscious in his arms, breaking all records I'd ever set for such a thing. Peter looked at me and said, "She's been through a lot, I can see that. She must be quite exhausted." He was hoping to hide from me the fact that he'd hypnotized her.

I said, "You might at least have said hello first."

He lifted her head and was about to set it on the table when he thought better of it and set her instead on the pallet. To my relief. "We'll let her sleep, and then when she's rested we'll have a proper reunion." Done with her, he turned his attention to me. "I suppose you already know perfectly well who I am, however you have me at something of a disadvantage . . ." I was given a chance to speak my name. I missed his meaning. "You are a friend of my daughter, a close friend perhaps?"

"We've been flying together."

"You both wear packs, I see, ah, I'm sorry . . ."

"That's all right." I missed again.

"What is your name?"

"Mark."

"Just Mark?"

"Sure."

"How do you do, Mark? You look exhausted too. If you care to rest, please feel free. I could use a little sleep myself. I've been up several days now without sleep . . . several days plus how many years?"

"I don't know."

"What is the exact day and year?" Very soon he would learn not to speak to me indirectly with implied meanings and subtle intentions.

"Oh, a . . ." I had to think. The year was easy, but I'd lost count of the days. It was the year that interested him, though. He begged my pardon. I forgave him. He rephrased. I repeated the year and watched to see if he'd count up on his fingers and toes the way I did. He did not, but he was thoroughly impressed. And a bit concerned. He looked at me, the room, the figures on the floor, and back to me. "Who else knows about this?"

"Just about everybody. Maybe not the exact month, but we're all pretty certain about the year."

"Yes. What I mean is, who besides you knows of your present whereabouts inside the vault?"

"She does, you do, they . . . did." I nodded toward the others. "For a moment or two, anyway."

"No one else? No one outside?"

"Oh God, I only wish. We've been stuck in here for ages."

"How did you get in?" I assumed he knew. I'm sure now he *did*. But he played ignorant of everything until he could get a better feel for the climate of the times. He managed to avoid anything about himself or his circumstances prior to his awakening. As carefully as he must have prepared himself for the instantaneous arrival of the distant future, he was still immersed in the dangers and suspicions of the distant past.

"She had the combination. Then all of a sudden she lost it."

"She lost it?"

"I think she was hypnotized and told to forget it when the door opened. Oh, hey, you must know it. Of course you do. You gave it to her, didn't you?"

"I'm afraid not."

"Huh? But she said . . . the suggestions? The hypnosis?"

"You know about that, do you? Unfortunately, I wasn't the one who gave her the suggestions."

"Who did?"

"I don't have any idea." A lie. An out-and-out lie. One I didn't suspect, however.

"Oh God, we're still stuck? Oh no!"

"Stuck? Certainly not. We'll get out, don't you worry."

"How? *I* don't know the combination."

"From the inside, it is a simple matter. One delves into the control circuitry and rewires it if necessary."

"You can do that?"

"Why of course I can."

"Jesus Christ!"

"Is there something odd? If so I don't understand."

"I didn't know *anybody* could do that."

"Oh. Yes. I see. Well, it just so happens I can. So you can rest assured."

Bit by bit, through lack of wit and perception, I gave away truths I might have better kept to myself, such as the lack of any sort of technical talent in the world outside. Once out of the bag, he quizzed me relentlessly on that very subject. When a thing breaks, I explained in answer to a specific question, we throw it away and order a new one. Who makes the new one? A plant in Zurich. Who operates the plant in Zurich? A big computer. Is the name of that computer Zee Three by any chance? Yes. Who tends to Z^3 nowadays? Zee Four, I told him, and that was about as far as I understood where things came from.

I was still uneasy and restless about being locked in the vault. He didn't want me uneasy or restless either one. He assured me again and again that without a doubt he would be able to open the door. It would take him some time, perhaps. I didn't think it out of place or presumptuous to ask him to get on with it. He understood completely, and began digging into the panels and mechanisms of the room we were in, offering as an excuse that he needed first to locate the source of power.

Before my very eyes he exposed bare wires and circuits and other electronic innards. He'd reach right inside and fiddle with those disgusting sinews, and it was all I could do to keep from getting sick. When he realized the affect it was having on me, he suggested I might take the opportunity to rest, relax, sleep. In that order. I must be very tired, he thought. Indeed, but not a chance. Whatever the instinct, I didn't trust him. Actually it was no instinct at all, just good common sense. In the next room was the means of putting me back where *he* came from. Not that he had any reason to, especially, I simply thought it prudent to stay awake.

"How long do you think it'll take before we're out of here?"

"Oh, about thirty hours, I'd say."

"Thirty hours?"

"Less if you know anything about conceptual mechanics. We could bypass the entire power network and go straight to the computer, leaving everything intact and inserting a combination of our own."

"Thirty hours?"

"These things take time," he said. "That's the motto of bureaucracy. I don't suppose you know what a bureaucracy is?"

"It's where you put underwear."

"Z^4 you say. In my day it was people in charge. Thousands of people, and Z^4 was something on the drawing boards. Hardly a dream."

"Ah, I don't dream much."

"But you are sleepy?"

"Huh? Oh no. A little hungry, maybe. Hey, she's got some food in her sack here." I approached Synthetica, who was still asleep on the pallet. She was lying on the goodie bag. I started to roll her over, but was interrupted.

"Please, let her sleep. She needs it."

"Yeah. I guess I can wait. Thirty hours?"

He wanted me asleep. Worse, after the ordeal I'd just gone through, *I* wanted me asleep. I just didn't dare. He kept at me with questions, never once interrupting his work with the wires, not needing full concentration to follow my answers.

"Just you and the girl, you say? No one else?"

"Thass right. Just her and me, me and her."

"And you say the door opened, and then what?"

"She forgot the combination."

"You didn't hear it? When she spoke it?"

"I think she whispered it."

"Why do you suppose she forgot?"

"I said."

"What did you say?"

"Hypnosis."

"Oh, yes."

"Hey! Do you think you could hypnotize her and make her remember it again?"

"Certainly, but then why interrupt her sleep with all that bother?"

"But you could do it?"

"Yes, yes."

"Boy, that's a relief. I mean, I'm sure you know what you're doing and all."

"There's nothing to worry about. Why don't you stretch out on one of those empty shelves and get some rest? We'll have a busy day tomorrow."

"Busy, busy." I took his advice, lay myself out on the table, but absolutely refused to shut my eyes except to blink, and I held that to a minimum.

He glanced up every so often from his work to check on me and Synthetica, who by now was breathing very deeply, very peacefully. At one point he caught me looking sorrowfully at the poor souls who didn't make it. "It's obvious they did not recognize the possibility of future inadequacies and prepare their thoughts and actions accordingly. I'll take care of them. It's nothing you need be embarrassed about." "Embarrassed," mind you, not guilty or sorry. "Under the circumstances I'd say you did remarkably well." A horrid thing to say. Nevertheless, it put my mind at ease another notch.

He kept me busy with questions, hoping to tire me out. Sometimes he'd forget whom he was speaking to and slip back into his natural tongue, which was English of another kind. "Earlier you used the phrase 'News drought,' a phrase which compares to and therefore presupposes a richer season. When last was there a time of worthy and interesting occurrences?"

"When, ah, what was that?"

"Tell me about the most exciting news event you can remember."

"The great ebb tide of ninety-four. I didn't see it, actually, but I saw the footage."

"An ebb tide, you say."

"And how. They showed the beach before and after, you know? And there was like three meters difference."

"Nothing more exciting than that?"

"Well, it depends on what you call exciting. Personally I don't watch the stuff. Nobody in their right mind does."

"What sort of employment is available?"

"Jobs?"

"Jobs."

"Only the very rich can afford a job nowadays. And they're mostly mineral."

"Menial?"

"Menial, right."

"Tell me, Mark, are you rich enough to be employed?"

"Oh, no. No. You have no idea what it costs."

"What do you do?"

"Do?"

"Day to day."

"Lately I've been flying with her."

"So you said."

"Before that I related mostly."

"Related?"

"To things, people, the environment. You know."

"Oh indeed yes. Tell me, do you know someone who *is* employed?"

"Aunt Ruth sings in the heavenly chorus. She's not in heaven, that's just the name of her group."

"I see. And is she paid for this job?"

"Sorta. They put on wings and hover around people's porches singing. People are supposed to throw money, but they throw a lot of garbage mostly. You've got to have 25,000 Free Marks to join that choir. That's assuming there's an opening, which there usually isn't."

"Anyone else?"

"Uncle Benny plays crash victims for the news services. He puts on fake guts and wounds and poses in old wrecks. Stuff like that."

"How does one become rich now?"

"One accumulates."

"How is this done?"

"By sitting around, mostly, and not doing much. Why? How was it done in your day?"

"Exactly the same."

"Some things never change."

"You might say that. I certainly would."

He was naturally curious about the times, of course, but I think he also wanted to find out just how well I represented them—if I was typical. He may have guessed my age. To him nineteen would have been nothing to get alarmed about. He never brought it to question. I don't know if I would have told him the truth on that matter or not. Over the recent weeks the secret of my age had taken on an air of great unimportance to me. Even so, if he mistook me for typical, then his impression of society at large may have been biased unfairly toward the decline—not so much as to make any difference, however.

"How you doing in there? Making any progress?" By this time he'd completely removed a section of wall and was deep inside a particularly stringy compartment with multi-colored wires in bundles running every which way. He got right inside with all that.

"So so. How about you?"

"I'm awfully tired. Boy. I've been in this place so long now I don't know if it's day or night out. I got this little tattoo thing that's supposed to tell the time. Have you ever seen one of these?" I presented my wrist for inspection. "It works on body chemistry."

He peeked out of his hole in the wall. "Tri-amino consumption rate."

"Oh. Well, I've been eating such weird stuff lately it's running backwards."

"Have you ever had any sort of education at all?" he asked, resuming his work inside.

"Hell no! I don't see why I should spend the next half of forever forcing myself to learn a bunch of stuff just so I can have more to forget when I'm older and can't remember anything anyway."

"I touched a nerve, I see."

"Did it open the door?"

"Not yet."

"How long?"

"I'd say another twenty-nine hours yet."

"You're kidding."

"If you'd like, I'll fix your watch. Then you can keep track of the time for both of us."

"Never mind. I intend to get a new one just as soon as you get me out of here."

"Tell me, what's the status of the legal system?"

"What?"

"Who makes the laws?"

"Nobody. They're all made."

"Who enforces them?"

"Channel forty-seven."

"I beg your pardon?"

"You go right ahead and beg." My eyes closed.

He crawled out from his hole in the wall, saw that I was nodding, and said, "I'm terribly sorry. I won't consider it a discourtesy if you sleep."

"No, no. I'm fine." I caught myself. "I'm okay." He went back to work. I nodded and caught myself again. "I'm fine. Okay. Anyway, where was I? Wake me when I'm through, all right?"

18

I woke halfway, enough to realize I'd nodded, which in turn caused me to wake the rest of the way with a start. I sat up straight and banged my head against the shelf above me with a loud crash. Thirty heads spun around. "Ah . . . ah . . . excuse me." I sat there shaking the cobwebs, hoping to make them vanish. They were naked, a mixture of sexes, some considerably aged, all huddled near the hot air register. A sudden burst of bright light penetrated through the door from the next room. They turned from me. Peter Winter appeared in the next instant nodding his head, giving them the okay sign. Very shortly there was another at his side, a gentleman looking a little confused, but pleased to see all the others. The newcomer entered the room and was greeted with handshakes and hugs and whispered congratulations. Peter Winter, about to return to the next room, caught a glimpse of me wide-eyed and awake. He made his way quickly through the assembly and took a position next to me. "Friends and colleagues, may I have your attention. It seems the child of the age has awakened. As most of you know, his name is Mark. Mark, why don't you say hello to the nice people?"

"Ah, you know, I don't think . . ."

"I know, but the others may need convincing."

"Hey," I said, getting down off the shelf. "Ah . . ." Unaccustomed as I was to public speaking. "Look, I don't think this is quite right, you know?"

"Whatever your opinion of this fellow, I'd like you all to remember we owe Mark our gratitude. He was the prime mover in this sequence of events."

"Yeah, me and . . ." Synthetica. Where was Synthetica? "Hey, where. . . ."

Peter Winter turned his back to the others, affecting a casual pose. He said, sternly, so that I would understand without question, "Be quiet about her. I don't want the others to know."

"But where is she?"

"I'll explain later. In the meantime, not a word." Not giving me a chance to reply, he addressed the others again. "Now that he is awake, I think we can all speak in a normal tone of voice. If you are among the most recent arrivals, Dr. Janson will fill you in. I know you have a lot of questions, but let's wait until we're all revived so that I don't have to keep repeating myself."

"Dr. Winter, just one thing, please."

"Yes Dr. Freeman."

"Is it safe to speak out loud?"

"If you are referring to listening devices, I've checked. If there is a means of detection I have been unable to find it. I have removed all panels and inspected both rooms very carefully, and the rest of the vault superficially. I believe we are safe. You are certainly free to satisfy yourself on that matter. I encourage you to do so."

"Dr. Winter, if, as you suggest, so much time has passed, how do we know what sort of device to look for? Their technology must be staggering."

"On the contrary, I am led to believe that there has been little advancement since our own time. Our children have survived on the momentum of our own creations. So in this respect, we begin again where we left off yesterday, though a millennium has passed."

"Dr. Winter." Again, another body asked for attention. So polite. Everyone acknowledged Peter Winter as the rightful chairman of the occasion.

"Please, if at all possible, I would like to postpone questioning until later."

"Dr. Winter, this pertains to what we are about to do."

"Very well, Dr. Hanley. By the way, it's good to see you looking so well. We all mourned your departure."

"I'm very happy to find myself well, as you can imagine. I was revived three times in what seems like the last half hour and tortured for names. Mildly. I gave them two names, of course, just as we agreed. It must be so with the others here, for I look about me and see quite an assembly. So we are all here, or about to be. But that's what concerns me. With so many of our eggheads in one basket, suppose you are wrong. We are taking a terrible risk, it seems. You speak of the passage of a thousand years. I would love to believe you, but how do we really know? We might very well be right here in our own time."

"To the point as usual, Dr. Hanley. May I direct your attention to the source of all my knowledge of the present, this fellow rubbing his eyes. You've all looked him over. Perhaps now that he is awake, you might question him as I have. Physically he looks to be about twenty. His face does not support a full beard, although it tries." Without so much as a "may I please," he rubbed my cheek with the back of his hand. "One has no way of knowing his true years, but I can't imagine how it matters. What *is* important is this: intellectually he is barely human. *But*, since he shows none of the physical characteristics we normally associate with retardation, I conclude that he is a product of the age. Our children have degenerated into imbeciles. We have nothing to fear."

"Hey, that's not nice, after what I did for you?" I spoke so the others wouldn't hear, but they did, and a murmur of chuckles passed among them.

"As I indicated to some of you earlier, he will answer questions put simply and directly as best he can. I believe you will find as I did, that the general picture is available. I have questioned him at length and have formed an opinion as to what awaits us outside these walls. You question him. Later we will compare notes and evaluate our chances."

"Dr. Winter?" Another body was recognized by the one so clearly in command. "Is this all you have to go by? This one sample?"

"Question him. You will be satisfied. Not by his answers, perhaps, but by the consistency of background presupposed by them. It is too much for me to imagine that one such as this could fabricate both a personality and a consistent substructure of current events."

"Dr. Winter, I protest. You trust him, I do not. I'll grant you, his presentation may be air tight. I'll take your word for that. But that proves only that he lies well. How do we know he is not a plant, or an agent working for Stern sent here to ferret out our little group? If so, he has succeeded, for here we are together as a group for the first time, about to revive the others."

Nobody liked hearing that. I know *I* didn't. The whole gist of the accusation seemed so preposterous to me, that I of all people would be associated with a name from ancient history. But the very nature of the argument precluded the possibility of my protesting. Not that I was the least capable. Fortunately, for his own reasons Peter Winter took up my case. Every eye was on me. The mood was grim.

"If you have doubts, then I guess we must take a moment to consider them before continuing with the de-processing. I ask you, how could Stern be better satisfied than to have us in permanent suspension? What possible reason could he have to wake us?"

"Information."

"Hear hear."

"But what can we reveal that he doesn't already know, presuming that he has gotten us this far?"

"Phase two, and the names of those not yet revived."

"Yes, you're right. But phase two has begun. This is it. It can only unfold one way. If Stern is behind it, then I'm afraid he already knows. Which is my point. If he knows, why bother to revive us? We have nothing left to do but continue."

"Or postpone, return to storage, and wait until we can be surer," someone suggested.

"Well, now, really, Dr. Lapin, one can never achieve total certainty in any endeavor."

"Dr. Winter, with all of eternity before us, no risk is necessary. Others like Mark will certainly happen along. . . ." All at once everyone in the room was hit by an idea, something important judging by the urgent show of hands.

"Dr. Winter!"

"Dr. Winter!"

"Dr. Winter!"

"Yes. Yes. Please, one at a time. Paul."

"This fellow couldn't have just happened along. One does not 'happen' one's way into a sealed crystal vault. I suggest to you that Stern allowed him to enter."

"Dr. Winter, I *do* protest."

"And I."

"And I."

"My certainty is based on reasons other than those I have revealed so far. There are secrets within secrets which must be kept, even from you. I am asking you all to trust me. I have more than just Mark's performance to go by. I'm sorry, I can say no more. Subject closed."

"Dr. Winter, how are we to be certain that *you* aren't Stern's man?"

An immediate protesting response arose from one individual: "I can vouch for Dr. Winter, if you please."

"Yes, Fredrich, but who will vouch for you?"

It seems that Eileen would. And there was someone to

vouch for her, and so it went around the room until someone put a stop to it, saying, "Dr. Winter, this is meaningless. Of course we each know two other people, and can vouch for them; that is our system. But now we are all together for the first time. The time for secrecy has ended, for good or ill. Unlike Fredrich here, I do not know you personally. I need more than his word on the matter of your loyalty."

"You are all too relentless. And thorough. You have advanced the arguments very quickly to the crux of the matter, something I am most reluctant to reveal. Nevertheless, to enlist your cooperation, I will tell you."

The mood was less than pleasant. If Peter Winter wanted to continue on as number one, he knew he would have to come up with some sort of story or step down. He let a silence elapse to signify his reluctance, then began.

"There were two combinations put into the lock monitor, Stern's and one of his own. We have Dr. Tanaka to thank for that."

"Tanaka was Stern's man," someone said, protesting immediately.

Peter Winter shot back, "With first loyalties to us." A murmur of surprise passed among them, and he continued: "It saddens me to have to tell you that Dr. Tanaka's suicide was committed in the line of duty, to keep the secret of the second combination from Stern's inquisitors. I hesitate to reveal now the secret this man gave his life to secure." He glanced from face to face to see if any among them would settle with that and let the matter drop. None would. "So be it. There were others besides Tanaka who knew about the combination. I was one, but in that I was not in Stern's employ, I was safe with it for a number of years. I had twenty years to somehow make use of that knowledge, until the probing network tightened around me and I was obliged to be done with my work. Rather than submit to a probe, I came to this place of my own free will and confessed, as it were, to a lesser crime. I was frozen without interrogation, along with my secret. It was that way with the others."

"Dr. Winter, if everyone who knew the combination was either dead or frozen here in the vault, who opened the door?"

Suddenly there were two of us in the room who knew something special. I tried unsuccessfully to hide any sign of understanding from my face, but unfortunately my eyebrows bob of their own accord. Peter Winter was watching, and he knew that I knew. Thereafter and forevermore I became wedded to their little conspiracy, for better or for worse. They would keep me close at hand until the day they could all see for themselves that the world I gave hint to was actual—that there was no harm waiting for them outside. With all their hesitations and doubts, that could take a long long time. Hopes for my own house in the sky began to fade, not only for the near future, but forever. I had to consider the very real possibility that they might put an end to the Free Market as I knew it. The people of the Market would be like sitting ducks to them. The Marketeers' first and last line of defense was the threat of verbal abuse on world-wide television. These, our ancestors, so far removed from our own ways and customs, might simply refuse to acknowledge a summons to appear. Then what?

Whatever their shortcomings, and they were many, the people of the Free Market were incapable of committing violence, even in their own defense. They were, in the words of Randolph Stern, a "clean generation," safe from violence by virtue of the fact that there were none among them capable of it. Those that were violent by nature had been weeded out from among them by Stern's probing networks and isolated in the vault. Every man, woman and child alive in Stern's day was tested for that trait that sometimes turns anger into injury. Those with the least trace, no matter how latent, were sealed off from the living in the crystal vault.

The uncles and aunts understood the purpose of the vault, but took it for granted. I would have known very little about it had it not been for Aunt Ruth's convictions, along with her obsession to convert me. The vault was there when we passed over, as were the pyramids and half a dozen other odd tombs of no particular interest. A curious aside, though: I was one of very few people outside of it that had not passed Stern's little test. I was not a part of the clean generation. I was my own generation. Given the chance, it's possible that I might have qualified for a place in the vault and been a bona fide member of Peter Winter's conspiracy, instead of its mascot.

"Mark did not open the door, if that's what you're thinking. He came here with another, someone I can personally vouch for, more certainly than any of you can vouch for one another."

"Who?"

"My daughter."

"You trust your own daughter? I wouldn't trust mine."

Peter Winter raised his hand to silence a round of "hear hear's." "The question you should be asking is, 'how did I succeed in putting someone outside with enough information to unlock the vault and still be able to pass undetected through Stern's all-pervasive probe?'" A hush descended unlike the others before. Here was a question everyone there had considered unsolvable. And yet there I was, a throwback from a degenerate age, with the answer already clear in my head.

"I am here now, awake and well, as you are, because I was able to put someone on the outside, someone highly motivated to perform the necessary task, someone with all the information necessary to perform that task, and yet totally unaware of either our conspiracy or my involvement in it, and therefore safe under any probe. That someone was my daughter."

"Dr. Winter, certainly *your* daughter would be subject to the closest scrutiny . . . what am I saying??"

"Yes, Fredrich?"

"You don't *have* a daughter."

"Precisely."

"I beg your pardon?"

"Kathryn, ah, Dr. Rousseau here can fill you in on that."

The woman indicated separated herself from the others to accept her moment of glory. I nearly choked. She was the mirror image of Synthetica, plus one or two degrees of maturation, slightly thicker all around, deeper textured skin. I gaped. Peter Winter watched my reaction with some interest. Before Kathryn had a chance to speak, he began again. "The question on everyone's mind should be, 'how was this done? How did we succeed in placing someone on the outside without running the risk of her capture and interrogation?'

"First: we did not look for volunteers or recruit someone from our ranks. That would have been too great a risk. Instead we created our own human being specifically for the task. We did this in isolation in the North American wilderness. I might add, we did this without the use of any tanking apparatus. Kathryn bore the child in her own womb. So there is no record whatsoever of my daughter's existence, no unaccounted for name on Stern's list."

Kathryn soon realized that her part in it was over and silently slipped back among the others without due recognition.

"Secondly: I raised my daughter alone, completely outside

the Market system. I taught her basic self-sufficiency. I instilled in her both a love for natural subsistence and a hatred for technical aids, so that she would willfully avoid all unnecessary contact and thus the dangers of detection, without her ever having to know why. Which brings us to the third precaution: *her* knowledge. On the chance that she might nevertheless be discovered, I could not give her knowledge of her purpose or her role as an agent, let alone any details of our conspiracy. Because of the probes, I could give her no specific instructions. Instead, as a part of her upbringing, I nurtured in her an overwhelming desire to be with me at all times. I conditioned her. Details another time. At the age of sixteen, an age of emotional vulnerability, having lived her entire life with me, she became separated from me. Dr. Rousseau and I staged the separation in such a way that my daughter believed she had become lost from me. It was therefore perfectly natural that she should set out to find me, and being created intelligent, taught to be resourceful, guided from detection by a basic distrust of technology, it was only a matter of time until she succeeded. I might add, she did not even know consciously that it was the vault she was looking for. The final goal was given her in the form of post-hypnotic suggestions."

"Dr. Winter, I admire your genius. I always have. But even a child born in the wilderness with all the love in the world will either give up or be discovered eventually. We're speaking of a span of a thousand years here, I believe."

"You're quite right. I did not set my daughter free to begin her search at once. On the second night of her separation, during her sleep, I froze her with a portable Martin beam and vaulted her in a small crystal vault concealed in a ruin. I left the exact time of her resurrection to the discretion of a J 5000 S conceptual analyzer, which monitored the general transmission bands for signs of intellectual and institutional decay in the Free Market. Her revival was entirely automatic, triggered by a weak moment in history. Judging by our captive sample, I'd say weak indeed."

"A full thousand years?"

"A much longer time than I expected, true. But are we any the worse for it?"

"Dr. Winter, this is all quite incredible, of course. I can understand how your daughter might retain a motivation to obey without knowing specifically what she was doing. The principle is well established. But how could she both *know* and *not know* something as specific and precise as a combination sequence?"

"I'll answer this one last question. Then I really must insist that we get on with our business. Is that agreed?" No one disagreed, so agreement was assumed. "Very well. My daughter knew the combination without knowing it *was* a combination. It was therefore not addressable information. In a probing session, even under hypnosis, had she been asked, 'Do you know any combination whatsoever?' she would have answered, 'I do not,' and registered perfect truth on even the most sensitive instruments."

"It was not a post-hypnotic suggestion."

"That is correct. That would have been too obvious."

"And yet she knew it nonetheless."

"Yes."

"A word combination?"

"Yes."

"It had to be spoken in the presence of the door, I presume."

"Correct."

"Dr. Winter, God damn it, I hate riddles with a passion."

"Think. It had to be a word known to her, but not as a combination, nevertheless a word likely to be spoken in the presence of the door, but unique in its structure; that is, unlikely to be spoken at random by anyone else, a good word for a lock monitor, four distinct syllables . . ."

"Dr. Winter, please."

"Why it's so simple, I wager even Mark here knows the answer."

"Synthetica," I said, with no particular pride.

"Louder, please, so everyone can hear."

"SYNTHETICA!"

"Dr. Winter, *will you explain!*"

"I'm sorry, did I fail to mention? Synthetica is my daughter's name. It is also, thanks to Dr. Tanaka, the combination to the vault door."

The applause was spontaneous, no doubt well deserved too. I'm certain that even Dr. Tanaka would have joined in. Peter Winter absorbed all the credit, of course. Before the cheers died down, while I had a chance to speak to him without the others hearing, I said, "Where is she?"

"Where do you suppose?"

"The secret's out. Can we get her back now?"

"Her part is done. Be content that you are still of some use to us."

With as few words as that, he shut me up and made a behaver out of me.

19

"You will be our native guide, an honorable and important position, right next to me. In the meantime, I would appreciate it if you would cooperate in answering questions the others might have, especially regarding your authenticity. Does that suit you?"

It suited me a whole lot better than being processed and vaulted, but not so much as the freedom to go my own way. I was kept within the confines of the heated rooms, but otherwise allowed to wander freely from one to another, examine what they were doing, even ask questions of my own. I gathered from the snips and snatches of conversations I overheard that someone had already been sent outside to examine the surroundings. So in addition to my personal testimony, they had a trustworthy eyewitness account from one of their own, to the effect that the local terrain had undergone vast changes. Furthermore, they had found Stern's name on the register, located his drawer, and examined his body. All of this they had done before I woke up. I couldn't understand how, with so much evidence in support of my contention, there'd be any room left for doubt. But those in the habit of doubting will always find a way. As to the changes outside, I overheard one of them saying that these could be accounted for two ways: either by the passage of time, as "the lad's" presentation suggests, or by the relocation of the entire vault, a simple trick. Stern's body? Likely as not someone else, a double, put there solely to verify the lad's story. Would they resurrect him for questioning? Perhaps later, but not yet, on the chance that it was the actual Randolph Stern.

Many felt I should be subjected to lie detection testing. They had all the equipment they needed left over from

Stern's day to gauge my deepest thoughts. It was pointed out, however, that the best results would be inconclusive if I were another "innocent," like Dr. Winter's Synthetica, impervious to lie detection, unaware of my part in the cause against them.

Despite Dr. Winter's arguments on my behalf, they had their doubts about *the lad*. The lad was left with nothing he could say about himself or his world that could not be taken two ways: as the truth, or as a clever lie intended to lull them into a false sense of security. They would have dearly loved to believe that the world at large contained a majority like me. But they didn't dare. It is the nature of evidence *per se* as much as any paranoia of theirs that created my predicament, for any piece of evidence can be made to serve the pro as well as the con if the mind that considers it is the least bit inventive. Acceptance of even the most fundamentally obvious truth rests ultimately on faith. Fresh from the world of purges and plots, their faith was shaken, and my truth remained nothing more than one of several available hypotheses, not necessarily everyone's first choice.

Unlike the others, Dr. Winter had a reliable second witness, one he could be certain of even if no one else could. I can only guess what words he might have had with her prior to her vaulting, but under hypnotically induced guidance from a father she loved and trusted, she must have explained my presence satisfactorily; without Peter Winter's support I would have been frozen and vaulted just as she was. He wanted me awake and available to the others, for aside from any other reasons, I was truly the only other person in the vault, awake or otherwise, who knew anything at all about the present state of the Market. But aside from Dr. Winter, no one bothered to avail themselves of my expertise.

I was disappointed, because I had such a collection of silly answers on tap with which to confuse them. I was prepared to do my part to stem the tide. I felt obliged to intrude on their little work groups of twos and threes with my suggestions. While they went about the business of resurrecting the rest and dismantling equipment, I did my best to inform them of some of the amazing new developments and dramatic achievements of civilization that they might have missed during their forced retirement. Like the atomic finger. "See this finger?"

Very few noticed. Those that did more often than not ignored me. Occasionally I would get some response, usually in the third person. I was third personed to death. "His language, even his gestures are remarkably like our own. I ask you, George, how can that be after a thousand years?"

"It's not a finger, really. It only looks like a finger. It's really a tiny atom bomb."

"Don't underestimate the power of recorded media to arrest the development of language, both verbal and non-verbal."

"It even wiggles like a finger, but see this hangnail? One bite and it's all over."

"You really shouldn't expect much difference in language, or life style either. It always amazes me when I consider how similar the ancient Greeks were to us, and yet we are a hundred generations removed from them. Despite the span of centuries, only one, at the most two generations separate us from this fellow."

"Booooom. Just like that," I said, making explosion noises and a spray of spit.

"I should say at least two to account for him."

"Booooom! Everybody in the whole vault. Except me . . . ah . . . Actually it doesn't go boom exactly, it sorta shoots out the end."

Bit by bit, despite my warnings, they dismantled every piece of equipment they weren't using, including me. I was forced to relinquish my wing pack, flying suit, and slippers. The wing pack they kept, adding it to their arsenal of gizmos and doodads they'd scavenged from the walls of the rooms. My suit and slippers were given a thorough examination for some sign of technological advancement, pronounced unextraordinary, and left lying on the floor. No one would be so impolite as to wear my warm things while others went naked, so after awhile, when no one was looking, I walked over and got dressed again. Without wings, though, I felt as naked as they looked.

New members appeared at the rate of one every fifteen minutes. Each resurrectee gave two names upon request, forming an unbroken chain, with each new arrival naming the next to come. One of the two names was rushed by courier across the hall to the computer room for slot number identification. The other belonged to the one previously awakened, and served as verification of the newcomer's claim to membership. Of the thousands Stern had pronounced unfit for the millennium, only those belonging to Peter Winter's conspiracy would be awakened at present. And of these, over half were returned immediately after giving up two names. Only those with a talent that could be applied to one of the tasks at hand were allowed to continue on. Not a one of those forced to give themselves back to the Martin beam resisted, or even raised a fuss. Some went smiling. All in all, it was a staggering display of ethics.

They divided chores among themselves without a bicker or a squabble. Those assigned to corridor duty returned to the heated sector with bare feet visibly blue. I'd have been relieved of my slippers again if just one among them had worn a size junior petite. I offered the suggestion that they might wrap towels around their feet, or use the pallets to scoot across the crystal floor. The pallets were being used for more important things, I was informed, and the towels were there for the purpose of drying off the new arrivals. All bullshit. They wanted to hurt. They enjoyed their pain. Which was fine by me, but I could see in their eyes Aunt Ruth's compulsion to have others experience the same inner joy.

Throughout the day (or night, whichever it had gotten to be), I explained to anyone who'd listen how I'd lied before, that I was an agent and that everything I saw or heard was being transmitted outside to headquarters via a tiny radio in my brain. Most took the news pretty much in stride, although one turned to his work partner and said, matter of fact, "There now, the lad confesses. Tell us, Mark, why did you lie before?"

"Just to see if you'd believe me."

"Oh well, in that case, no harm done. You say you're an agent?"

"The army sent me. They need food. You're it. They're hiding in the bushes outside. Boy, are they hungry too."

"The army, you say? I didn't know there was an army."

"You should see it. There's six million of us in my seargeant alone."

"You mean platoon, don't you?"

"Which is smaller?"

"Seargeant."

"That's what I mean."

"Have you told Dr. Winter this?"

"No. Do you think I should?"

"Perhaps not just yet. He's awfully busy."

"Did I show you my finger? It's real modern."

Those not directly involved with the resurrection process spent their time dismantling equipment. They took one of the

Martin beams down from the ceiling and reassembled it on a push pallet. Then they took the whole thing out in the hall for a test firing. It worked, giving them basic artillery of a sort to add to their collection of makeshift devices. I was amazed at their capabilities, but at the same time alarmed at the prospect of an armed conflict with Martin beams and flash heaters against insults and water balloons. I went around telling everybody I'd lied earlier, that there really was no army and no atomic finger. But the buildup of weapons continued without interruption.

My time to contribute to the cause finally arrived. Peter Winter, interrupted from his duties in the resurrection chamber by a dark-haired large-breasted abundant woman, glanced toward me and said, "Mark, come over here." Hippity hop. "Mark, this is Dr. Weiss. I want you to accompany her to the computer room and answer any questions she asks. No monkey business, there's a good boy."

Dr. Weiss led me into the corridor, where the air was cool but decidedly warmer than before. Apparently, the outside door had been opened to let warm air in. Not that she didn't have some trouble crossing the crystal floor. She led me to the office, through the door, and while she continued on briskly I stopped to take in the scene and get nauseated, for all but two of the twenty desk-top terminals had either been removed or ruthlessly slaughtered where they stood, their innards ripped out and spread mercilessly all over the floor. Utter barbarism. All she had to say for herself (apparently it was her work) was, "Watch your step." I was unable to do that. I shut my eyes and began to reel. Rather than deal with me she came up, took my hand, and dragged me into the far corner. She faced me the other way and sat me in front of what she called a television receiver, a ghoulish monstrosity she'd assembled like Frankenstein from the corpses of the disemboweled terminals. "Please pay attention. We have an antenna outside leading in here. I am able to pick up images, but so far no audio. We're working on that, but in the meantime I'd like your help in deciphering some of these visuals. Now this first one here . . ." She massaged a tiny organ inside a box of wires until a picture formed. "What is that? None of us can identify it. Can you?"

The image was flat, fuzzy, and upside down. But any idiot could see it was Channel Thirty-one. I said as much. She said she was well aware of the band, but the image itself confused her. "I can discern a rhythmical movement of two amorphous shapes, but the identity remains a mystery to us all."

"Oh well, you probably wouldn't recognize them. That's *Max und Gerta*."

"Max und . . ."

"Gerta. The fuckers from Bavaria."

"I . . . I'm sorry, what was that again?"

"Forget it. You don't want to watch *Max und Gerta*. Nobody watches *Max und Gerta*."

"Oh? What do I want?"

"Try Twenty-eight. Oh yeah. Please."

"Very well," she said, switching over. The image popped on clear and in good color. "My God, what on earth. . . ." It took her by surprise. No less me. We were both horrified, for separate reasons, perhaps. "What is it?" she said, in a tone that raised eyebrows clear across the room. She backed away from the screen as though it might ooze out on her.

I cried my usual, "Oh God, oh my God, oh God," adding every so often the question, "What has she done to herself? What has she done?"

"She?" Dr. Weiss pointed to the image on the screen. "That's a she?"

"Emmy Lou. Oh Jesus. Emmy Lou, you shouldn't have. Not without me." I was shaken to the core. My poor Emmy Lou had deformed beyond recognition from the lovely ravishing ultra-female beauty I'd left only weeks ago into a gross misshapen pulsing blob with twelve breasts, two long skinny arms, and two long skinny legs as thin as rope twined around the bedpost, labial folds extended halfway up her middle between two rows of tits, and no head whatsoever. Not even a bump.

"You . . . you know this poor creature?" Dr. Weiss asked. I wasn't immediately available for comment. I was in tears, head in hands, sobbing uncontrollably. She repeated her question two or three more times before I was able to answer.

Between sobs I said, "Yes. I know her. We were in love."

"Oh you poor poor dear. Was she in an accident?"

"When I left . . . when . . . when I left her. . . ."

"There, there," she said, patting me on the head. "She'll get better. I'm sure she will." But I don't think she was sure at all.

"When I left she only had six."

"There, there . . . six? Six what?"

"Breasts. And her arms and legs wouldn't wrap around like

that, and she still had a neck. Oh Jesus, she went on without me. I'll never catch up. Never."

"When did you last see her?"

"A couple of months ago."

"Dr. Ennis, come over here. I think you should see this."

The doctor across the room looked up from his work at one of the intact terminals, saw the urgent look on Dr. Weiss' face, and came right over. Dr. Ennis was impressed. He said he'd never seen such a case in his entire medical career, and he assured us he'd seen some doozies. Dr. Weiss explained that two months prior there had been only six where now there was twelve. That worked out to be three a month, a rate of progress which astounded Dr. Ennis. I explained how they used to come and go, which brought his hand to his forehead. He was willing to suggest that it was no ordinary tumor, and perhaps we ought to investigate it carefully before allowing anyone to exit the vault, on the chance that it might be contagious. Word was shot across the hall, and others came to see me and my Emmy Lou.

"The lad knows her, apparently," Dr. Weiss explained. "You can see he is very much taken with her condition." Indeed I was.

Since it was a medical matter now and not just a bad picture, Dr. Ennis took over the explaining. He addressed the gathering crowd: "It seems the lad has not seen her in two months, during which time her condition has deteriorated considerably. Where you now see twelve breasts . . ." everybody crowded the screen to see as Dr. Ennis pointed, "there were only six two months ago. Apparently the head and neck are entirely eaten away. So, for the most part, are the limbs, althought they are greatly extended. It's much too early to make a statement at this time, but as you can see, the female primary and secondary sexual characteristics have greatly enlarged, apparently at the expense of everything else. I think we can safely say it's a runaway glandular condition of some sort. We dare not even guess at the cause. It's evidently quite painful, as you can see by the way she is writhing. The very fact that they have seen fit to secure her to the bed suggests that she has lost control of her. . . ." The doctor interrupted his lecture in mid-sentence. Something caught his eye. He put his nose to the glass, turned to the audience and proclaimed, "That's incredible. Not five minutes ago, the lower two breasts had barely formed, and yet now they are twice the size of the top two. You'd better get Dr. Winter in here. I don't like the looks of this one bit."

Neither did I. But listening to him describe her with my eyes shut I was reminded of the way she used to be before I was so rudely removed from her presence several ages ago.

Dr. Winter stormed angrily into the room, complaining about all the interruptions, but when he saw what was on the screen he apologized and called for an immediate suspension of resurrection activities. Dr. Weiss filled Dr. Winter in. "It's apparently got the whole Free Market alarmed. Her monitor is patched into Channel Twenty-eight, which is a general broadcast band. I've yet to see a doctor or nurse try to do anything about it. Perhaps they don't know what to do."

Dr. Ennis reminded Dr. Winter about the dangers of a new disease. "In our isolation we have developed no new antibodies, no new immunities. We are therefore particularly susceptible to any new disease that may have developed during our confinement."

"Do you think we should shut the outside ports?"

"So far Dr. Nash has found no airborne diseases. I believe we are safe."

"Nevertheless, I think you should join forces with Nash and perhaps bring Paxton in on it. Make that top priority. We don't want to end up looking like that thing. I suggest you begin by questioning our friend here to see if he can help shed some light on it. It's worth a try." Peter Winter came close to me, put his arm around me, and said, "Now Mark, this is important. I can see how overcome you are, but certain questions must be asked. Dr. Ennis?"

Thus consoled, I was turned over to Dr. Ennis, whose first question was, "Mark, how long have you known Emmy Lou?"

"I've known her since she first came on the air."

"How long has that been?"

"Oh, five, six years. Maybe more. I'd have to count."

"Was she all right when you first met her?"

"Oh . . . so so. Kind of plain. But I guess I thought she was gorgeous. I've got snapshots of me and her, and . . . well, you can see I must have thought she was pretty special."

"I know how painful this must be, but could you describe her? The way she used to be?"

"She looked like . . . like Dr. Weiss almost. A little thinner in some places." My eyes lingered on Dr. Weiss as an old memory crossed my mind.

"In other words she was perfectly normal five or six years ago."

"Mundane even."

"I'm sorry to have to ask you this, but can you tell me what happened to her?"

"Yes. Yes, I think I can."

"Take your time."

I dried my eyes with my fists, blew my nose on the floor, and said, "She evolved too far is all. It never used to matter if I missed a day or two because I could always play the tape, but I'll never catch up now. It's all over with. We're through." I began to sob all over again, and those kind people understood. The same ones who'd been cold to me all day long were dabbing their eyes and consoling me with kind words. Dr. Weiss drew my head to her hot plump tummy and began stroking my hair. Something down under tingled and tightened. Suddenly the loss didn't seem so tragic.

"Mark, please tell us as carefully as you can what happened to make her this way. It's very important. You said she evolved too far. How? What made her evolve? Do you know?"

"Yes."

"Tell me."

"The computer." The assembly, which had grown to include everyone awake so far, gasped in unison as the thought of Z^4 run rampant on some grisly experiment crossed their mind.

"Oh my God. Some God damn idiot has patched into the genetics section. It was only a matter of time. How'd it happen? How in the hell did it happen?"

"I . . . I think people just got tired of looking at the same girl day after day. I know I certainly do. So they programmed the image to change, you know, get kind of sexier, bit by bit, faster than boredom, but not so fast that you'd notice." I discovered to my great surprise that my hand had risen from my side, traveled around up behind Dr. Weiss' bare behind and was scanning for a landing site when I caught it, pulled it back, and sat on it to give it a good scolding. Dr. Weiss kept my head against her, and that felt nice. With both hands tucked under my butt I began to rock slowly back and forth on my stool, then faster and faster.

"Mark, tell me, how does the computer change her?"

"How does it *make* her? *I* don't know. If I did I'd back it up where I left off . . . hey, you don't suppose that maybe one of you guys could do it?" I looked up and noticed for the first time all of them staring at me. I stopped rocking. Dr. Weiss let go and backed away. I was surrounded by people staring at me.

"Then the image we see is . . ."

"She's *not* a cartoon. She's not. She's . . ."

"Am I to understand that this deformed creature we see on the screen is someone's erotic fantasy?"

"Not mine. Not any more. She's gone to pot."

"Oh my Lord."

"You think *she's* bad, I'll bet Mr. Big is worse. Can you get Mr. Big on this thing? Huh?"

I looked at Dr. Weiss. She was backing away from me like I'd farted, as were all of those who'd jammed in so close just seconds before. They looked at me the way they'd looked at Emmy Lou when they first saw her. Full from the ranks of the untouchables to something several notches lower. I was an un-step-on-able, getting worse by the second. They began to filter out of the office one by one. A surprising number made it all the way out walking backwards. Dr. Winter paused at the door and said to the remaining few, "Behold the opposition."

Dr. Weiss apologized for the interruption. Dr. Winter assured her she'd done the right thing. When asked what he thought now of their chances outside, he looked me in the eye, winked, and said, "I think it's a piece of cake, Dr. Weiss. How about you?"

20

"Your attention everybody. Attention. Our number stands at fifty-eight. Our nearest supply depot is buried five kilometers away. Assuming the seals are still intact, we will have at best food and clothes for only fifty. Eight of you will therefore have to be reprocess."

"Dr. Winter, would it be possible for those eight to wait in the vault? Awake, that is?"

"No. Because of the tremendous changes that have taken place outside we expect to experience considerable difficulty locating the other depots. Our return here may be delayed. Anyone left behind, awake, runs the risk of going too long without food. That risk isn't necessary. The next few days will be spent hunting and digging. Those of you perhaps a little less physical than most might be better off in the vault. I leave it to you."

Dr. Kathryn Rousseau saw herself as one of the "less physical." She stood first in line at the processing room door, and others queued up behind her. Extraordinarily enough, the line grew to contain more volunteers than were necessary, which put Peter Winter in the position he'd tried to avoid, that of having to decide who should stay and who should be refrozen. He viewed the line like a general, pointing, "You, you, you and you. Come with me." He did not choose Kathryn. She was the first to be returned. I watched her go. He did not even pause from his duties to say good-bye to her. Nor did she beg for the special favor. At the very last moment, as she was frozen, her eyes were on him. That was all. The pallet took her body back.

The number soon dropped to fifty; fifty-one counting me, which they did not. I was equipment, along with four pallet-loads of junk.

"If I may have everyone's attention again, please. The sooner we move the sooner we eat, so let's make this brief. Dr. Weiss assures me that there has been no mention of any sort of emergency on any of the television signals she's been able to monitor. Dr. Burgner has sampled computer activity—nothing there either. So as yet it appears we are undetected.

"Now I know many of you still have doubts. I respect them, but I must overrule them. I am satisfied that the Market is at the end of a long decline, utterly incapable of stopping us from returning to our rightful place as the legitimate heirs of our own creation. If we wait another century or two, as some suggest, there will be nothing left to inherit. I don't know how many of us are really suited for farming life.

"So the time has come at last. I don't know about you, but I will feel a little strange entering the world naked again, although it didn't seem to bother me much the first time. We'll have our historians make something poetic out of that.

"Are we ready?

"Mark, I want you up here. Paxton, you follow with the Martin beam. Equipment first. Single file. We have warm air in the corridors, but the floors are cold. Move fast and keep hopping.

"Ready? Let's go."

On any other occasion fifty prancing nudes would have evoked a chuckle. I bounced right along with the rest of them, keeping the same rhythm so as not to look conspicuously comfortable. Peter Winter might have preserved his feet and his dignity better if he'd hitched a ride on the pallet carrying the Martin beam, as some others did, but he was a better leader than that and chose to suffer right along with the troops. A tactical blunder.

The processional moved right along at a good fast clip. Peter Winter apologized to me for not spending more time with me earlier, and promised to make it up. He began with a list of duties I would be expected to perform. I would supply voice, name, and face identification for any Market transaction requiring these. On the off chance of personal encounter, I would do the talking in my usual manner, and so spare them the risk of an odd or anachronistic phrase that might give them away. Above all I was to explain the unexplainable, a task of which I had already proved myself both worthy and capable. Dr. Winter apologized for the cool treatment I'd received from the others, and said that when I saw my name in the history books beside his own all bad feelings would vanish. He wanted to thank me for everything so far, and was about to shake my hand when we reached the door.

The door was already one-quarter open. Our leader stepped up to a small box next to the opening, and whispered the word "Synthetica." The hole widened for passage. "Quickly, quickly."

But I was already out the door and running. Peter Winter lunged at me and missed. I bounded over the field, leaping over rocks, crashing through the shrubs, which tore at my pants and lacerated my ankles. But I ran on as hard as I'd ever run, without any thought to the pain. He yelled for me to stop. When that didn't work he ran after me, but that's where I had the critical advantage. I had shoes. His feet were still too cold. He could barely stand, let alone gallop over rough terrain. He tried anyway and collapsed in a heap. He threatened to fire the Martin beam, but by the time they got the big thing out the door and aimed my way I was safe behind the trees. They fired just the same. A big blue jelly bean drifted across the grassy clearing, caught on the first obstacle in its path, and went no farther. A baby sapling met an early winter. They couldn't use their flash heater without risking a forest fire, which in turn would have signaled the world.

I ran until I was too out of breath to continue. By then I was deep among the trees. I could hear Peter Winter's voice shouting good logical reasons why it was foolish for me to continue—my lack of food, transportation, and communication. "How long can you survive in the wilderness? Mark, come back. Now. We can't wait for you. We've got to keep moving. You'll get hungry. You won't be able to find us. It's now or never. Mark, come back."

I didn't know whether he actually believed it or was saying it to frighten me, but he was wrong on all three points. Thanks to Synthetica, food would be no problem. As to the other two, I had just spent the last thirty hours with very little else to do but think about such things.

With good concealment, I watched the rest of them file out the door one by one. I counted on my fingers—five sets of ten and that was that. The door closed. I lingered and watched as they massaged their cold feet, organized into groups, and hobbled awkwardly across the clearing and into the woods. In a few minutes they were gone, all fifty, to find their supplies before they starved, caught pneumonia, or simply fell from exhaustion. The thousand-year rest did not count for sleep, not even a second's worth. So they were tired at the very outset. For these reasons they neither pursued nor waited for me. They couldn't afford to.

I watched for a long time after the last of them departed, one eye to the forest for food. I would eat much sooner than any of them. And sleep.

I woke in the late afternoon, in time to see the long shadows vanish and the west wall of the vault glow cherry red. Then night.

I waited, watching and listening. The thin crescent moon set early, leaving me in a fine darkness suited to my next good deed.

I took my flying suit off, turned it dark side out, and put it back on. I smeared dirt on my face and hands. I walked, placing each step quietly, to the edge of the woods. I lay down and crawled across the clearing through the bushes and grass, making my way to the south wall. While still far enough back to see it all, left edge to right, I gauged the center and made my way there.

A word to the door and I was in. It closed again automatically after I passed through. I didn't really need any light to find my way, but I was supplied with faint flashes from the crystal floor at the point of impact of each step I took; not bright, but bright enough with night eyes so that I didn't have to feel my way along the icy wall.

Finding the one operating deprocessor again was no problem. The light came up, hot hair poured in, all as before. I headed straight for the pallet and punched in the numbers 38/53/17, with little doubts that she'd be anywhere else. At the time of her processing Peter Winter knew of only one open slot, his own. He might have frozen her and put her in the hall along with my poor unfortunates, but he did not. The pallet returned with Synthetica.

The rest was easy. I'd done it before, once correctly, and seen it done many times since. Not five seconds after the flash I had her sitting on the edge of the table, alive and well—physically, at least.

Her first words were the last of the last she had spoken to her father. A "No," and another "No," followed by a "Please, Father, please, no, no, oh Father, don't make me do it. . . ." The one problem I'd anticipated dissolved away. If she'd been put away content that all was well between her and him, I'd have had some explaining to do. As it went, she saw me alone and cried on my shoulder. There was nothing to say worth saying that she didn't already know. Without need of argument, she accompanied me.

She knew where to find her flying suit; it was hidden away under the counter. She put it on, and began looking around for her wings. I explained our wing situation. She expected as much, but didn't care. She had nothing to fly for any more.

I drew the pallet out from under the table one more time and proudly proclaimed it mine for the duration. Unfortunately I couldn't get it out the door. It was assigned to that room and stubbornly refused to exit without a slot number or minor surgery. We were forced to hop in the usual undignified manner all the way.

At the door I asked her, "Do you know?"

"Yes. I do now."

"And?"

"My name."

"Say it."

In minutes she was home again among the trees, ready to spend the rest of her life there. Alone, if necessary.

I'd like to think I pulled one over on Peter Winter, but I don't suppose that would be quite fair. He'd banked on winning me over with a job offer and a few kind words. I was not worth the investment of any more effort. What they needed me for was minor and presupposed cooperation. As a belligerent I was of no use to them. Nor much of a threat, trapped in the wilderness. With no communication and no effective way to move around I could do him no harm.

It stood to reason that he would have grilled Synthetica throughly with all the hypnotic power he could muster to find out everything there was to know about our communications with the outside world. I had to assume at least that much. However, if he had asked her, "Do you have, or does your friend have any means of contacting anyone else?" or more to the point, "Does either of you have a phone?" she would have had to say in all innocence, "No, Father. No." He would expect no other answer.

But the drifter was more than he could have imagined, let alone anticipated—not just my group of four, but drifters in general. The whole idea of a society killing itself off in vast numbers couldn't have formed in his mind, not a society of Free Marketeers in paradise above. But even supposing he'd picked up a statistic from Dr. Weiss, he could not have envisioned the decade's most fashionable technique, let alone what that might yield in the way of phones and wings. Peter Winter did not ask me (nor did I think it necessary to tell him) about my four drifters stuck in the wires a few kilometers south; insofar as he went off ignorant of that, I had pulled a fast one.

Synthetica and I spent the night wide awake, just waiting for the day. Both of us had slept recently. Both of us had thoughts to mull over. She ran through as many alternative interpretations of what had transpired as she could concoct, reaching dead ends with every one. By morning she was ready to accept that she'd been used her whole life long by the one she loved. And still loved nonetheless.

First light of morning, first chirp, I turned to her and said, "I think your father and his friends are going to take the Free Market away from everybody else and keep it for themselves; the homes, shops, and everything. They're going to trade places—a home for a slot in the vault."

"I think so too."

"If they do, they'll probably fix it up and keep it working for at least another thousand years. They built it. It was theirs in the first place. Did you know that?"

"He told me."

"So if I have any feelings for the Free Market. I should probably just sit here and let them take it back. I'm sure they'll take better care of it than anyone I know."

"Is that what you're going to do?"

"No."

"Why not?"

"Because I hate the son of a bitch with all my heart. I want to stomp on his head."

We spent much of the morning scrounging for food and water just like old times, glad to be free from the vault, but sad in that we both knew it would very likely be our last morning together in the wilds. When I was clean again and less hungry, I climbed a pine, not the first tree in my career, just the first without lift to assist me or catch me if I fell. From the top I located my old friends about where I expected to see them, not more than a pass length away, ten minutes by wing, most of the day trudging through trees.

I climbed down prepared for the unhappy good-bye, for I had no reason to expect her to join me in this venture. But there she was—goodie bag in hand, ready to march.

We didn't talk much. She knew well enough what I had in mind to do. I tried to keep the pace up. She didn't hinder me, but she was never quite beside me either. She was the one calling for rest stops all day long, not me. When she simply had to stop I'd climb a tree and double check our course so there'd be no time wasted.

Much sooner than I had any right to expect I found myself within easy sight of my goal. Of the original four, only one was left. Sometime after our last get-together the other three had broken free and gone on their way, leaving their friend dangling all by himself on the telegraph wire that had snared him, midway between two ancient poles. I took a careful sighting on the poles and clambered down the tree in a big hurry, very excited and nervous about any last-minute obstacles that might pop up now that I was so close. I headed us off west, perpendicular to our original course, which had roughly paralleled a slow stagnant creek. We came upon a black crumbly path, which I knew to be an ancient roadway, alongside which ran the wire, from pole to pole according to custom. Following that path, we were there in no time, directly underneath the drifter, looking up at a great big round ball of flies.

Here's when I could have used the pallet, for it was quite a ways off the ground, well out of reach of any stick around. Another pine tree nearby seemed the best answer; climb that, *then* reach with a stick, and I'd have it.

I was looking about for a stick when I noticed that Synthetica had already found one. I reached out to accept it and she drew back. I reached again and she drew back again. She had a funny look on her face that begged the question, "What's the matter with you?"

"I can't let you stop him."

"Synthetica, for crying out loud."

"No, Mark. Please, no. For my sake, no."

"Are you crazy all of a sudden? Give me the stick."

"NO!"

"All right, I'll find another one."

"Please, Mark, don't."

"It's no big deal. They're all over. Here's one."

"Mark, no."

"Aw come on, look, I'm going to miss you too, but there're more important things going on."

Then, speaking as though she were telling me something she'd rather not have to discuss, as a last resort, she said, "The wings you gave me had a name written inside the cover. My father was very upset by it."

"What, Spaulding? God damn, he's a Wilson man. I knew it."

"He can make me do anything he wants me to do. I can't help myself." I took one step toward my tree. She raised her stick and widened her stance.

"Hey, you're getting weird again, aren't you?"

"I don't want to hurt you. Please don't let it come to that."

"Synthetica, what the hell's gotten into you?"

"I know everything. He told me everything. Mark, *everything*." She said it like I really should know what she meant by "everything."

"What are you taking about?"

"The man who put my father in that place is the same man who sent you to me."

"Nobody sent me anywhere. Come on now. This is dumb. All I want to do is climb the damn tree. Jesus, I've been climbing trees all day, what the hell's the matter with you all of a sudden?"

"I can't let you. . . ." She got serious with her stick as I took another step.

"Hey!"

"The name inside my wings was Randolph Stern. My father went all through it and found it written deep inside. He showed it to me. I saw it. Mark, you gave me those wings."

"Hey, wait a minute now. I swiped . . . borrowed those wings from an . . . an uncle. Where he got them I don't know. But if you think for one minute I have any connection with a character out of history . . . Christ, Synthetica, I've got to tell you, I'm only nineteen years old."

"And I'm twenty-three."

"Twenty-three plus one thousand, or did he forget to tell you that?"

"Mark, I know everything. Everything."

"Stop saying everything like that and get out of my way."

"You were sent by Stern to stop my father."

"Aw, did he tell you that? He's a liar."

"It's true."

"If he thought for one second I had anything to do with Stern, I'd be solid ice and so would you."

"He says you don't know it. And as long as you don't tell anybody, you can't hurt him."

"Believe me, if he thought for one minute I had any connection with Stern, conscious or otherwise, he'd never have let me get this far. You can be dead sure of that."

"He's stopping you, Mark. He's stopping you right now."

"Whaaa. . . . ??" I had to give that a moment to sink in. And another moment. I started to speak, and had to think again. "Why that son of a bitch. He *knew* I'd go back for you. What'd he do, hypnotize you again? Is that why you're acting so weird?"

"Mark, I can't help myself. I love you. I don't want to hurt you. But my father is my life. I can't go against him. No matter what."

"He *did*, didn't he? He hypnotized you and set you up again. That son of a bitch. That dirty motherfucker."

"Watch it."

"Oh for God sake, put that thing down. You could no

more hit me with it than I could you." I took steps toward her.

"Mark, no. Please don't."

"God, you look dumb." I kept coming and she backed away. "You look like a God damned baseball player, so help me." I stopped under the lowest branch my tree had to offer, jumped, and caught hold.

"Please, Mark, please..."

I was just about to swing my legs up when she clubbed me hard in the belly. A serious case of poor judgment on my part. I fell to the ground and crumpled, wheezing and gasping for air, completely disabled.

She collapsed on top of me, threw her arms around me, and began kissing and hugging and crying and begging for forgiveness. I was unable to give it even if I'd been so inclined, which I was not. Her punch had landed in the solar plexus, and although not too pleasant, the symptoms of a hit there or thereabouts are out of all proportion to the damage done. I couldn't draw breath for awhile. My eyes must have stuck halfway out of their sockets. My tongue went out searching for air. I probably turned a few funny shades of red and purple too, the whole thing adding up to a fair imitation of the folks we'd sacrificed in the vault. I'm certain she thought she'd killed me. For a few minutes I wasn't so sure she hadn't.

The injury was minor, though, and it wasn't long before I was breathing okay again. However! I'd never been hit before. By anyone. By accident or anger. I didn't know how to take it in stride. It made me mad. The logic and justice and moral considerations, such as whose fault it really was, hers or her father's, just turned to crap.

Another thing. I was a boy and she was a girl. One can argue endlessly about how things might better be, but in the end, boys are stronger. At least in this life. I stood up. She stood back. I picked up my stick. She took off. I ran after her with my stick in the air. She screamed. I swung straight down, hard, striking her shoulder. She whirled and fell to the ground in tremendous pain. While she was down, I raised my stick high and brought it down as fast and as hard as I could on her leg. There was a loud crack. I looked at the stick. It was undamaged.

"There now, nature girl, let's see you patch that up with your God damned herbs and spices."

Her face turned ashen, her eyes turned up, and the pain in her leg drove awareness right out of her brain.

If anyone thinks I felt bad, think again. It doesn't work that way. Later, yes—right now, even. But I'm talking about then. And then, it was the only thing to do. It quelled my rage and made the next step in the operation a bit more feasible. Oh yes, one more thing. Of the very few things Peter Winter could not have foreseen, high on the list of importance is this: I was not a member of the clean generation, which is to say, I could be violent.

Without pausing even a few seconds to fuss around with her, I went for my tree. I stormed right to the top without stopping to rest, taking my trusty stick along with me. And there, at long last, was my benefactor, hitched to the line, patiently waiting my return.

It was apparent that his three friends had not gotten away without a struggle. His sleeves which had attached him to the others had been torn clean off. And the wire which prevented him from accompanying them any farther had been pulled straight through his abdomen clear to the spine. They'd been gone awhile, long enough for the abdominal mass to re-form, flow together, and in effect heal, for the wire which severed him completely appeared merely to have been threaded through him with a needle, in one side and out the other.

I didn't want him. Or his wings. Or his phone. Not for a house of my own, not for nineteen years accumulated back income. I wanted both, plus the satisfaction of putting Peter Winter back a notch. That alone would have turned the trick.

My tree did not bring me quite face to face with the drifter. But with a good leg grip around the two very top branches, I was able to lean me and my treetop out far enough so that I could hook him with my stick and slide him along the wire toward me. Once I had him nearer, I was able to reach through the cloud of flies, hook the barbed end of the stick behind his down-cord, and give a tug.

He lowered, but not far, because of the wire imbedded in his rib cage. When I slacked off he rose up again to where he started, but no higher.

I'd planned on doing the whole job with the stick for separation's sake, but its smell was so intense even a stick length away that I figured it wouldn't matter if I brought it closer. I was wrong about that. Odor increases by the square of the distance. On top of that, pulling it up closer put me within the orbit of the big blowflies that swarmed like electrons around the corpse, pelting my hands and face and eyes and lips.

As fast as I could, to get it over with once and forevermore, I shut my eyes, held my breath, reached out with my bare hands and managed to grab the wings. I peeled off the straps, taking huge gobs of putrid flesh as I did. I shook off that miserable goo and somehow got the wings on just as the odor became overpowering. I began to fade. I gave the down-cord a pull and settled gently through the trees to the ground.

I needed help. Fast. Synthetica was unconscious and helpless. I was about to join her. I knew it. I untangled myself from the slimy pack, tore open the storage pocket, desperately hoping, praying . . . and there, at last, after weeks and weeks of dreaming, was a real honest to God working blinking beeping minature portable pocket telephone, complete with camera and screen.

Fading fast, fighting for conscious seconds, I put my thumb to the button and squeaked, "Medcomp, mayday, see for yourself." With that I dropped off. And I'll say this for myself: if I'd had the whole dictionary in front of me, I couldn't have chosen a better thing to say.

21

The word "Medcomp" had the programmed power to cut through identification formalities and patch me directly through to the emergency standby network of the great search, rescue, and repair system known by that name. "Mayday" put me past a barrage of chickenshit inquiries designed to discourage hypochondriacs and lonelies, such as "Where does it hurt? When did you first notice . . ." and the like. It got me straight to the central processor, with the certainty of a fine should I be even honestly mistaken. As I fell to the ground, I aimed the lens of my phone toward the compound fracture case across the way, and nothing more was necessary.

It took coordinates off my phone and dispatched out of parking orbit one of its many hundreds of medical orbiters. Within minutes it came crackling down through the branches, belly red from re-entry. It hovered a few meters up to cool and survey the situation. After a brief conference with Medcomp back in Zurich, it set about the business of restoring health, beginning first with the most needy case, the one it assessed as having the most serious medical difficulty, which was my scattered friend the drifter. It laid a fine mist of sweet-smelling vapor over the ground, a germicide, I believe, with perhaps a touch of loveliness to encourage a cooperative attitude in the patients should surgery be required.

Very shortly a second craft descended out of orbit into our midst, paused, cooled, went to Synthetica and laid a haze of medication over her so thick it ran down her like syrup. She woke licking her lips, a smile on her face, only to discover that she was about to be torn apart by this winking blinking beeping chromium cigar with half a dozen insectual manipulators prodding and poking at her wounds and otherwise making free with her body. She recognized and understood. She knew by all that was sacred to her that she should get up and flee, or make a good show of effort for the sake of her conscience. But by then she was fully bother-proofed, and even as the device cut into her leg, spread open her wounds and tidied up inside, she only giggled and made woo-woo sounds.

It was that way with me too a little. I only caught the merest whiff off the edge of a slender tentacle that drifted my way, but for a few seconds there I couldn't have been more pleased with my situation. Still slimy with gore and reeking, I thought, "How satisfactory that rotten flesh smells like this. How else would I have it smell? No other way."

In a matter of minutes Synthetica's attendant had her leg encased in a hard plastic sheath that would dissolve away gradually in the hours to come, as the bone healed. For her shoulder, a dab of healant and she was done.

A third unit arrived, came directly to me, looked me over and decided all I needed was a scrub. It directed me with a few sharp words to stand up, strip, and hold still, which I did. Whereupon it sprayed me down good with a mild alcohol and left me there dripping. Then it joined the other two machines in the search for missing bones.

Synthetica noticed me across the way licking myself dry, and blew a kiss. She didn't quite realize yet that she was free to get up and walk about, or for that matter that there might ever again be any reason to. I didn't tell her otherwise. I made straight for my phone, picked it up, and was about to place a call when an incoming call took command of the little screen.

A tiny female face on the screen, no one I recognized, said, "Who is this, please? Identify yourself." Curt, matter of fact, as though she owned the airwaves.

I thought at first it was a friend of the departed, so I was perhaps a little more polite than absolutely necessary. "I'm sorry. I borrowed this phone, you see, and . . ."

"If this conversation between us is to continue I must have positive identification and a sworn statement from you giving us all rights to do whatever we please with your image and anything else you may wish to tell us."

"I didn't steal it, I just borrowed it. I'll give it back."

"Perhaps I should explain who I am, since you obviously don't recognize me. I am Pecan Regent of Consolidated News Services. Now then, to whom am I speaking?"

"Oh. OH! I was just going to call you."

"Name, please."

"Ah . . . yeah. Listen. Will you hold the line a sec? I'll be right back. Don't go away."

"I beg your pardon?" she said, in wide-eyed disbelief. Pecan Regent was one of the better-known news scouts, very wealthy of course, and probably unused to being put on hold, especially by a complete unknown.

"I'll get right back to you. I've got to . . ." She blanked out in the middle of my sentence, beating me to the punch with her own hold button. She didn't hang up. Line one stayed lit. The news was in desperate straits. A three-alarm medical alert was already bigger news than anything they'd run in months, without my having to say a single word about the really big news. And besides, I had a handsome, wholesome (if a bit woodsy) look about me that demanded media attention.

I punched line two and pronounced the words "Michael and Mimi Jo Hornblower, please." A few preliminary flashes and there they were, Michael in his flannels, sitting at the foot of the bed, Mimi Jo bundled up in blankets, peeking through the folds, both too stunned by the face on the screen to say hello. "Hey! Uncle Michael. It's me . . . my gosh, it's been so long."

"Ah . . . ah . . . why yes, ah, Mr., ah, I'm sorry, what was the name?"

"Mommy? Is that you under there? I see you."

"You jerk got some wrong number." She leapt across the bed to the screen to cut me off. Michael stayed her hand.

"Are you alone, Mr., ah, old man?"

They weren't going to betray themselves with a show of parental authority nor give any sign of recognition whatsoever until they were sure I was alone. Last they knew I was in school, locked up with their precious secret intact and secure. Suddenly, in the middle of an ordinary night, their big screen woke them with the hard truth. Somehow, God forbid, Mimi's child had gotten hold of a phone.

"Yeah, I'm alone." For all it mattered, I *was* alone.

"All right then you listen to me and you listen good. I don't know how in the hell you got that thing, but I want you to disconnect this instant and destroy it. NOW! DO YOU HEAR ME??!!"

"Aw, come on, Michael, Mimi Jo. We haven't seen each other in two whole months."

"Get the fuck off the air before someone sees you. Smash that phone. NOW!"

I have to admit, I was hurt. They'd spent a portion of their lives and all of mine keeping me out of reach of a phone, so I guess I had no right to expect anything better, but I was hurt just the same.

"MARK, GOD DAMN YOU, DISCONNECT. I'M TELLING YOU . . ."

"All right, sure. Okay. But first, guess what?"

"NO. WHEN I SAY NOW I MEAN NOW. NOW!"

"Not until you guess what."

"MARK . . . All right. What?"

"I got Pecan Regent on the other line."

". . . . ."

One thing I'll say about Michael. He knew where he was every second of the day. Mimi Jo fought hard to pretend me away, closing her eyes, shaking her head, but I continued to be. Michael never doubted. He carefully considered all his options and said to me, "I want to apologize for the way we left you. It was your Uncle Theo's idea, the school, the wings, everything. We had nothing to do with it. We never even heard of school until he called us up and suggested it. It seemed like such a good idea at the time, but honestly, Mark, we've had second thoughts. Now I know how much you've wanted a house of your own, so Mimi's going to move in with me and give this one to you." Mimi had never considered any such gift, judging by the look she gave Michael, but she had sense enough to smile at the lens. "We'll throw in the flyers, but Mark, please, not a word. Okay?"

I had interrupted my call to Pecan with nothing but kindness in my heart, for such as they were, they were my family. I simply wanted to say hello and see them once again while I still had a chance, maybe for the last time before the world flipped over. And then Michael had to go and say a thing like that. It served only to remind me of all those dreadful years spent in the misery of their company for lack of a simple bargaining position. In a few moments Mimi Jo's all-consuming fear of discovery would be reduced to the most inconsequential trivia, of no concern to anyone. The age of small matters was soon to end, or at the very least suffer a postponement. It occurred to me all of a sudden that if I were ever to even the score with her, I'd have to act fast. So rather than waste time with sentimentalities, I said, "What is the current market value of the place?"

"I tell you what, you stay there and we'll come pick you up."

"The house. You offered it. I want to know what it's worth."

"We'll discuss that when. . . ."

"Quarter million? Wouldn't you say? Thereabouts?"

"Ah . . . I . . . ah . . . I would say so."

"Don't go away." I put them on hold, winked back at Synthetica, shooed a wayward orbiter, and put a call through on line three to the Legal Services computer. After a brief back and forth, it agreed to record and notarize any transactions I might enter into in the next few minutes. I had an idea how I might have my house, get even with Mimi Jo, and do my duty all in the twinkling of an eye.

With line three open I went back to the news lady. "Pecan? Still there?"

"With whom am I speaking?"

"I've, ah, I've. . . ."

"Waiting."

"Well, I've got an offer."

"You? You have an offer? My dear fellow . . ."

"Yeah, well ah, I have a news story, right? Which I'll sell to you for, oh, . . . half a million Free Marks? Sounds okay, huh?" My voice barely managed to squeak the figure, but I didn't back down.

"Don't be absurd."

"Wait. I'll tell you the story for free."

"Well, I should think so."

"But then you can't use it without paying my price."

"That's fair. I'm listening."

"By the way, I've got Legal Services on the line."

"You what? Just a moment." She blanked the screen, no doubt to consult privately with the other big stockholders and board members, then came back, saying, "State your terms, please."

"I will describe an event. You can't report that event without putting aside five hundred thousand Free Marks made payable to me." I took my language from the computer on line three.

"We still don't know with whom we are dealing. We cannot come to a binding agreement without a verbal signature."

"Yes, ah . . . one moment." I punched her off and brought back Michael and Mimi Jo. In my absence Mimi had managed to scrounge up her old Buddha suit and was just poking her head through when I came on the line. Michael had on his blue gorilla. "Listen," I said. "I've got an offer of five hundred thousand from News, against your two fifty. They'll need my signature, and I guess you know what that means." Mimi Jo made some hurried adjustments with her mask, and began reciting haiku. Michael growled and bared his fangs. "Waiting," I said, with Pecan's look of impatience.

Through no planning of mine, their position was beautifully restricted. Because of the great distance between us they could not order me to my room or recapture me in any reasonable time. To hang up would have been tantamount to default. They could not appeal to family ties without admitting to same. I had them both by the balls.

"Still waiting. Five hundred thousand. Going once, going twice . . ."

"No. Wait. We can talk to Benny."

" I don't have time for that."

"Mark, baby." Mimi blinked her big sad eyes from behind her mask. "Have a heart."

"I've got all the heart you ever gave me."

"Aw, Markie, sugar pie. I hardly recognize you you looken

so goot." She talked to me like I was one of her lovers. On me it worked the other way.

"Pecan's waiting."

"All right. Five hundred thousand," Michael said.

"No. I've changed my mind. I've already got that. Let's hear seven fifty. And remember, Legal Services is listening."

"Seven fifty? Where would we ever get seven fifty?"

"Sell the closet."

"NEVER!"

"All right." I reached toward the buttons, letting my fingers play across the big wall screen.

"*No. Wait . . .*"

"Yes?"

"You got it. Seven fifty."

"Hold the line." I switched back to Pecan, flashed a wheeler-dealer smile, and said, "Pecan, listen. I hate to do this, but I've got to raise that figure to a full million. I'm terribly sorry, but I can't see my way out of it at this time. It will have to be a million."

"Remember, as the price goes up, the chance of our using your story goes down."

"I know. I know. One million, agreed?"

"It will have to be exceptional."

I grinned a knowing grin and clicked back to line two. Mimi Jo and Michael were embracing one another when I came on—very upset, naturally. I listened unnoticed for a moment or two. I could hear muffled sobs from behind her smiling Buddha face. Michael consoled her with the reminder that whereas he had stood by her all these years, he was not technically responsible. Need he remind her—he placed his hand underneath his furry flap—"Marbles. They clink."

I let them know I was there again with a gentle "Ahem."

"Mark, you realize what you're doing. We'll have to sell both wardrobes. And the flyers, everything. There won't be anything left."

"I've got one million from Pecan Regent."

"One million?" He made as though it choked him to say it. "Have pity."

"One million once."

"Mark, no. We don't have it."

"One million twice."

"Wait—we'll save. We'll sign over future income. We'll. . . ."

"*Sold* to Consolidated News!"

"You can't do this to us."

"I just did. Toodle." I cut them off cold and disconnected. Glad to do it. They never had a chance.

I punched in line one and said, "Pecan, one million, agreed?"

"Yes," she said, "although I warn you again, it is very unlikely we will ever air anything for that price."

"And another thing, ah . . . can I sort of not say who I am?"

"Who would we send the money to?"

"Ah . . . right. I checked briefly with Legal Services for any loophole beyond its capacity to plug. It gave me the okay. I felt I could trust the legal machinery to do right by me. It had a reputation for protecting the little guy in cases like these. I knew of several instances where without any qualms it declared whole important stories untrue and had them stricken from the airwaves because it was later found out that they were illegally obtained, more often than not at the expense of some poor wretch like me who couldn't put his words right.

So I said to Pecan, "My name is Marcus Aurelius Hornblower. I am registered with Medcomp and Z^4 if you can't find me anyplace else." Once and for all that particular cat was out of the bag, and the bag burned. "Now listen. A few hours ago, the doors to the Crystal Vault were opened. Fifty prisoners were brought to life. They are at this very moment collecting supplies and weapons, which they will use to take control of the Free Market. What do you say to that?"

Pecan Regent did not get to be Pecan Regent by just sitting around dumb. She was an icy pro. With a million at stake, she wasn't going to crack that famous poker face and betray an enthusiasm she might later wish to deny. Still, she knew that I knew that the story was very very good. So without the slightest trace of excitement in her voice, she said, "Frankly, Mr. Hornblower, I have never heard a more powerful story. My congratulations to you."

"Thank you."

"It's timely. It's easy to understand. It doesn't require a lot of background material; we all know what happens if anyone escapes the vault. It signals the end of the world as we know it."

"Yes, I think so too."

"It's an absolutely splendid story."

"It's true too. I'll tell you how to check it out."

"We're not concerned with the truth here. We merely quote. If the story turns out to be false, you, not we, must pay the fine. Is that clear?"

"Oh yes. Very clear."

"Very well. Would you pronounce your name one more time for signature verification?"

"Marcus Aurelius Hornblower."

She glanced off camera to one of her terminal screens. "All right, I have a Hornblower, M.A. here—just a moment. . . ." Something caught her eye. "Just a moment. . . ." She stood up, leaned across her desk so that all I had to look at on my screen was an out of focus hip. I could hear other voices in the background, excited voices, some live, some on other lines, but I couldn't quite make out what they were saying. Pecan returned to the screen, a look of absolute amazement on her face and excitement in her voice, which, I have to admit, I fell for. She sat down, positioned her face for my screen, and said, "I hereby claim all rights to the following story and related details. Nineteen years two months ago, a *child* was born to Mimi Jo Hornblower, *You*, Mr. Hornblower, are that child. I have it right here."

"Yeah, well, check again and you'll see I'm a legal entity with full rights under the law to enter into binding contracts."

"Mr. Hornblower, of *course* you're a legal entity. Of course. Don't worry. You will receive your money, every bit, according to our agreement, when and *if* we use your story."

"Yeah, well . . . If? What do you mean if?"

"Young Mark. May I call you that? I'm not certain the world is ready for a doomsday spot at this particular time. Not now. Not with a story like this one. I do mean to tell you, Mr. Hornblower, a new child is *news!*"

"Oh come on, who's going to care about that with the world about to end?"

"Don't get me wrong. That's a great story, yes. But by no means perfect. You must admit, it's a little offbeat. And dubious. Oh, I'm not saying it isn't true, mind you, it's just that it doesn't have that ring of truth we here at News like in a story. And you can't deny that it's a negative story, can you?"

"Well, now, look . . . negative, positive, I mean shit."

"And furthermore, it doesn't really have anything people can relate to, no human interest factors, nothing that touches the heart the way a new child does, if you know what I mean. And of course, need I tell you, it's a very very expensive story by comparison."

"Hey now, come on. We don't have time to mess around. This thing's happening right now."

"Young Mark, excuse me, but would you hold your camera still? That's much better. Give us a big smile and tell us in your own words what it's like being, well, born, as it were, thrust into existence, one moment nothing, the next everything."

"Are you crazy all of a sudden?"

"Perhaps you aren't yet aware, but when you get to be as old as most of us you simply don't remember being born, Or being young, for that matter."

"Okay. Okay. I can take a hint. Two hundred fifty thousand. Is that better?"

"In fact, a growing number of people claim never to have been born at all. They say that all these notions of babies, childhood, youth, and development are so much superstition. Mortalist fabrications. Young Mark, what do you say to that?"

"One hundred thousand. Is that asking too much?"

"All right then, let me ask you this: who is your favorite TV star?"

"TV star? You know God damn well nobody's going to give a shit about my TV favorites with an army of ancestors out there about to clobber them. Don't be ridiculous."

"Mark, you're about to be famous. People will want to know these things."

"Famous?"

"TV star."

"Holy Moley from the *Goosey Goose and Gander Show*."

"Live star as opposed to cartoon."

"Pietra DiAngelo from *Oh Too Solid Wall*."

"Favorite supporting actor in half hour weekly series."

"Wait a minute . . . you can't possibly be serious . . . I mean . . . oh, come on . . . All right! *All right*! Ten thousand Free Marks. That's all I'm asking. Ten thousand and it's yours. Come on, what do you say?"

"Do you have a favorite song?"

"Aw come on. What's ten thousand to you guys anyway?"

"We're all going to want to know. It will be an overnight hit."

"You want to know? You really want to know? 'Hard Hearted Hannah!' "

"Would you raise your camera and bring it in closer? Nice big closeup. Hold it. Now Mark, sing 'Hard Hearted Hannah' for us."

"You're kidding."

"Do you need a start?"

"*I know it.* Jesus. It's *my* song."

"Very well. Sing it."

"Let's see. 'Hard hearted Hannah, swamp in Alabama . . .' All right. Okay. Look, I'll pay *you*. How's that? Does that suit you? Did you hear me? I said *I'll pay you!*"

"What with? I've checked your account. You don't have one."

"I'll *get* one. Along with nineteen years back income and a house allotment. So there."

"How much is that?"

"I don't know. Fifty, sixty thousand."

"*Sold!*"

"*Ha!* I knew it. Didn't I know it? Favorite TV star. Shit."

"Now tell me, this is important: when did the breakout occur? How many in the party? I need names . . ."

"Yeah, I'll bet you do."

"Where are they now? You mentioned weapons. What kind? How many?"

"Wouldn't you like to know."

"Very well, Mr. Hornblower. You win after all. Answer my questions, and you can have your inheritance."

"Well *now* you're talking."

"Agreed?"

"Agreed."

"Good. We're going on the air in sixty seconds with this. I want to know first, who is the leader of the escape?"

"Yes. The leader is a man named. . . ."

THUNK. A rock cut me off. A simple rock. Not another word got through. According to a binding agreement, I was out one inheritance.

22

I had made too easy a target of my phone, perching it so delicately between my thumb and middle finger for the sake of an easy closeup. With one clean shot she reduced it to its component smithereens. In the next instant, before I could wake up to what was happening, she launched the drifter's empty wing pack into the sky.

My first practical impulse was to tackle an orbiter and hold it hostage until Medcomp agreed to deliver me another phone. Unfortunately all the orbiters were gone, their work done, the drifter's bones polished and set in skeletal order in a shallow pit, leaving *me* the task of the last rites. So once again we were stranded, no phone, no wings, no more drifters hanging conveniently about, and no inheritace to entice me into the future. It seemed I had no option but to pick up the stick once again and this time beat Synthetica to death with it. Proper justice, no doubt, but I didn't have the heart for it.

Besides, as it turned out, she was too late. The lack of details and substantiating data did not stop the news from airing. The word went out. I saw proof within a few minutes, in the form of flyers shooting across the sky toward the vault. These were the lucky ones who happened to be near when the news broke. I knew exactly what that meant. It was the way of people to chase after excitement, especially during times of scarcity. In my day I had seen the entire Free Market break formation, take flight, and reassemble over the locations of such astounding and newsworthy events as the wreck of the garbage scow Merit (a small pilotless trash barge that ran out of power just short of its chute and made a stink for awhile), and the more recent formation around the house of Laura Serena Kennedy, who came out of obscurity one day to announce the great gypsy moth invasion of ninety-five. We'd all been angrily scraping our windows for weeks, so it wasn't exactly fresh news. She was merely the first to put plainly into words what we all knew in our hearts. Her reward was fame, guest shots on several TV shows, a slew of ghosted books listing her cute observations on life's funny ways, and center position in every Market formation thereafter. Compare news of a prison break by an army of our ancestors preparing to capture the world to news of an increase in bug impactions and what you get is a brand new formation tightly packed around a brand new center (and perhaps, given the time, one more book by L.S. Kennedy on her rejection of fame and her desperate attempts to withdraw into seclusion). She would never have admitted to a one-upping by an unknown the likes of me.

I counted maybe fifteen flyers zipping across just that tiny portion of sky visible to me, all heading toward the vault. I knew that I'd achieved my place in history, despite Synthetica's efforts to stop me. I'd just decided to head off that way myself in hopes of a pick-up when a big white windowless Liston came crashing through the trees and settled down directly on top of the remains of my phone, apparently having taken coordinates from my last transmission. It looked to me like Uncle Benny's machine; he had a Liston of the same shade of orange, same turtle feet landers, same in every respect. I couldn't have been more pleased. I approached it and waited by the side door. Synthetica hobbled up beside me, cautious and unsure what to make of it. I assured her there was nothing to worry about, that Ben was a harmless twerp. Just then I was feeling that way about all the uncles and aunts.

After a few seconds cooling, the okay-to-touch light winked and the door opened. I shouted, "Uncle Benny?" and waited politely for his invitation to board. "Hey, yoo hoo, Uncle Ben?"

It wasn't Uncle Ben, although it could have been his flyer. I don't know. In the fraction of a second before he appeared it popped into my head who it must be. The words were forming as he stepped out the door. "Uncle Theo?"

"Delightfully yours," he said, bowing. "And the young lady's, to be sure." Of all the uncles he was the closest (geographically, that is), and therefore the most likely first arrival. As he stepped into the light of day I had to ask again, "You *are* Uncle Theo, aren't you?" Although he'd maintained the thin birdlike hollow-boned posture of the professional wing man, he'd lost his sun repellent coating and was no longer bald.

"Oh yes, it's me of course. Why? Whom did you expect?"

Now Synthetica, who might not have recognized him as the little chrome eunuch of my school days recognized him instantly in his (I presume) more natural form. She greeted him with an emphatic, *"You!"*

To which he replied. "I'd be hard-pressed to deny it. But then who could?"

It didn't make sense to me that the two should know each other. In fact, I found it alarming. So far, unexpected connections hadn't done me much good. I looked confused and worried enough for Theo to offer me an explanation. "I'm afraid I am the one who left her stranded on the island where you met her."

"You?" I said, in a burst of indignation. *"You* stole her wings?"

"You're in no position to get self-righteous on such matters as the theft of wings, my dear boy." He shook a bony finger at me. "I forgive you, though. The question is, will she forgive me?" As easily as that he had me on his side, looking pleadingly at Synthetica. Poor Theo hovered near the door of his craft, afraid to step too far into her domain without permission. "Synthetica, my dear child, I meant you no harm and no harm has come to you. But I had a young boy in desperate need of companionship and a new way of life such as you might provide for him. Unfortunately, at the time of our first encounter he was six weeks short of legal age, and there you were about to discover the vault on your next crossing. If I had let you continue on uninterrupted, well, you would have found your father all right, but poor Mark here would still be as miserable and selfish and useless as he ever was. How you must have loathed him! Ah, but look at him now: strong, alert, ready, full of youthful enthusiasm, a rare and priceless personality. I have you to thank for his improvements, and myself of course for being so clever. By the simple act of taking your wings, I purchased this young boy's education. So what harm is done, I ask you?"

Synthetica's eyes darted back and forth between us like the numbers on a calculator. She had thoughts, but none faster than mine. In confessing to his little crime, Theo had left himself open to a much more significant accusation. While speaking to her, he kept his eye hard on me to see what my face might reveal in the way of understanding. It didn't disappoint him. Synthetica had the words ready and was about to protest when I beat her to the punch. "How did you know about her father?" I said, wide-eyed and accusative. "*She* didn't even know." To say nothing of what *I* didn't know.

"Ah, there's the bright lad who chose 'D' the very first time. You might have asked any number of good questions, but you went straight for the fundamental and that is good in the eyes of your Uncle Theo."

"Well?"

Synthetica had that pre-attack look to her that I'd been too slow to recognize twice already that day. Theo's sense of priority, if not self-preservation, drew his attention to the immediate problem of her defusing. What I might have done with a stick and with pleasure, he accomplished with a few swift words aimed directly at the crux of her distrust and alarm. "You think I am Stern," he said, "but I am not." She drew breath on that. He'd anticipated her deepest suspicion. "Stern is in the vault where he should be." He didn't even give her a chance to stutter her objections. "Your father knew me as Tanaka, and I was loyal to his cause. I put the name 'Stern' in the wing pack that you were to wear so that your father might discover it there. He can be relied upon to be thorough. Now, because he thinks Stern is close by, he proceeds more slowly than he might, with greater caution than is necessary. For the cost of a needle and thread and the time to stitch a monogram, I have bought us a few more hours of time before the battle begins, perhaps even the battle itself. How small the seed, how great the harvest, don't you agree?"

"Battle?" I asked. "Battle?" Another excellent question, I thought, both fundamental and to the point; it won me a smile, a nod of approval, and a raised finger, the signal to wait my turn. Synthetica's mood was dark, dangerous, and in need of first class attention. But each time as she was about to speak, Theo was there with proper words to dissuade her. "My darling child, you have been put into a strange position by forces you didn't even know existed until a short while ago. A life you presumed totally free, subject only to the whims of nature, turns out to have been planned and manipulated to serve a purpose about which you knew nothing at all. Now, rather than face the truth, you pretend to join the forces that used you when the truth is that you have been hurt deeply by a father you loved and trusted."

"What battle? Tell me!" I was more than mildly curious. It seemed to me that if there were going to be such a thing as a battle, we were likely standing near the battle site. Theo ignored me.

"Synthetica, believe me, I am not your father's enemy. I have not, and will not interfere with his cause. I am a shy and easily frightened little man of few capabilities, asking for your trust, because I think that together we can undo some of the harm that is about to be done."

"Ah, excuse me, but when you said battle, I couldn't help but wonder where."

"Shh, Mark, let her think."

There was real need for caution on her account. She was listening, though. And when she seemed content with what Theo had said so far, he laced her up good and tight with the following: "Though your father enjoys the credit, you were *my* idea, the seed of my mind if not my body. I like to think of you as my daughter. Perhaps someday you will think of me as your true father. In the meantime, I am here to protect you and hopefully give you back the life you love, complete with purpose and meaning. If you feel used, then for what it's worth, I tell you that you are not alone. You see, Mark too was created without the slightest knowledge of the role he was created for. I know, for you see, I am *his* father too."

Synthetica took it no better than I, although she'd suffered one rude awakening already and should have benefited from the practice. This was my very first. I tried disbelief with no success at all, not even a moment's worth. He had nothing to gain by lying. This was it and he was the one. Nineteen years and I was face to face with the responsible uncle.

As to resemblance, well, Theo was so much a product of sculptive surgery that he had nothing left unaltered for comparison. None of the other uncles ever guessed, or I'd have heard about it. Mimi Jo had them thinking that they were all equally responsible—that I was a genetic mish-mash resulting from their share and share alike shenanagans. I had Uncle Alexander's eyes, Uncle Rufus' knees, Uncle Calvin's scrotum, and so on. But that half which was not Mimi Jo's was Theo's by his own admission. I'd have held out for someone else. I was in no hurry. I can't say I was too pleased by the implication that Synthetica was in some way sisterly, either. Devastating news, that, but nothing at all compared with the news that I, like Synthetica, was a piece of someone's plot.

I'd learned to live with, and much preferred believing, that I was unintended, a case of spontaneous regeneration of tissue in Mimi Jo's empty tubes, or an implant case put there by a practical joker, for which there were several likely candidates. Or maybe merely a computer misidentification. I preferred anything to the notion that I was a planned child with purpose and destiny: *someone else's* purpose and destiny, that is.

To comfort me over the long long silence that was to follow his announcement, Theo offered these words: "A babe knows nothing of his parents' plans. That's what it means to be a child. You find yourselves involved in the troubles of another generation, but that too is what it means to be a child. We have no debts left between us on that account."

Well, I'm afraid my poor psyche suffered from just one too many blows to the reality center. My heart went pounding like I'd been running all day, and I contracted a severe case of open mouth disease. Synthetica showed some of the same symptoms, and for mindless obedience Mombo Zombie had nothing on us. We were all wax. He invited us aboard and we came. He offered us the couch and we sat. He handed us each a cup of tea, which we held pending the command to sip. I think at times like these, when the foundation upon which one's knowledge rests is cracked, the mind switches over to emergency operation and in the process diverts most of its power to the construction of a new set of basics, shutting down everything the body can do without for awhile, such as dignity and posture.

He left us alone to ponder and heal while he went about the business of preparing for flight. A word to navigation, a coordinate, an altitude, a request to park. The little Liston rose to his bidding.

We weren't in a house in the usual sense. Liston never built a house. Their specialty was little craft, machines built for long-range trips outside the atmosphere, where a good airtight seal takes precendence over swimming pools, patios, porches, and windows. It had one steel door and the rest was solid. The cabin was just large enough for comfort, containing a couch, a folding chair, a table that served as a monitor station, a sink, and a few dispensers for food and liquid. Where windows might have been, Theo had installed two large screens providing the view from two outboard cameras front and rear, so that we could look outside just as though the ends of the room weren't there at all. Otherwise I doubt he'd have gotten Synthetica aboard.

A moment's flight in the high thin air, a good safe distance from the gathering crowd, well out of traffic, with a good view through the rear screen of the expanding cluster. The mother lode hadn't arrived yet, but already there were perhaps a hundred or more little craft jockeying for position close to the vault. I enjoyed some feeling of importance to see the results of my call, even though Theo could as easily have placed the call himself if I hadn't. In the squeeze to be near, respecting legal minimums, they were forming themselves into a dome, with small craft, the first arrivals, making up a nucleus around which larger houses would pack themselves later on. It was already a beautiful formation to my way of thinking, much lovelier than any of the current rash of arbitrary and meaningless compositions that Maynard Pink and the like had been directing. When he won that year's best arrangement award for a random scattering he called "Untitled," I wrote unsigned letters complaining. Abstracts I can do without. Pornographic representations too. Christmas trees are okay, the jack-o-lantern, the Thanksgiving turkey, but for every day, recognizing the possibility of a personal bias creeping in, I wanted to see something regular. The half sphere suited me fine.

"Now, Mark . . ." he said, finishing up with the last of his chores and preparations, "in answer to your question."

"Ah . . . what? Huh?" I was some distance away in thought, and still deeply confused. I must admit, though, that the evidence was all there, albeit unjoined and scattered. Given a few days or a faster intelligence I'd have come to a full unassisted understanding. Apparently Theo was short of time. He was in a rush. He wanted—I should say *needed*—my full cooperation, and to that end my full understanding.

"Monitor one, please. Monitor one . . . excuse me, Mark, would you mind lifting your teacup? Thank you. Monitor one, please."

In response, a small thin black monitor screen shot up from the coffee table and came to life. Its image was fuzzy and flat, as they tend to be when their source is a small self-tracking camera.

"Look at the monitor, Mark, and tell me what you see."

Tiny shiny people, that's what I saw. A high angle shot looking down through branches and leaves upon a small group of people dressed in laser armor, foil suits with chrome helmets and mirrored visors, standing around a hole in the ground receiving armloads of strange-looking equipment from someone down under. Around the opening were stacks of crates and an assortment of evil-looking glass and metal devices, not a one familar to me, but terrifying just the same.

Theo requested screen number two. It rose beside the first with another picture, another location, another group of people, another supply depot. The crates were opened and scattered. From small components people were putting together awesome shapes, the whole more frightening than the sum of its parts.

"Three up, please." And still another group, and a fourth and a fifth to the limit of the monitor screens. "What do you make of it, Mark?" They were Peter Winter's people getting ready for war. I knew they were up to something, of course; a little more time to think and I would have had it. Seeing them live on screen brought me up to date with a kind of impact you can't expect from deductive reasoning. "Well?"

"Holy shit."

"Fair enough."

"Why? I mean . . . what on earth for? I mean. . . ." I meant why so much power for what Dr. Winter described in my own hearing as a "piece of cake?"

"Dr. Winter believes he will encounter powerful resistance from Randolph Stern. I may be partly to blame for having put Stern's name in his daughter's wing pack. As you must know, he and his friends are conspiratorial in nature, much disposed to fears and doubts. They see Stern behind every tree, in every flyer that crosses the sky. These weapons you see them preparing are appropriate for what they believe awaits them. Unfortunately, Mark, neither you nor I nor anyone else has anything to offset such a force."

"Can't we tell them?"

"Tell them what?"

"That Stern is dead and gone?"

Not without some difficulty, I fear. To you Stern is a forgotten name in history, as likely an enemy as Julius Caesar. To them he is real and dangerous. Each of their yesterdays was full of Stern. You were in the vault; you must know that. Now they look up and see flyers converging on this location from all directions. If you tried to tell them the truth now, what would they think?"

"If your name was ever Tanaka, Dr. Winter will trust you. I heard him say so. You're the one who gave him the second combination. He *has* to trust you."

"I've changed physically since Dr. Winter knew me, a disguise he wouldn't accept too readily, I'm afraid. And even if I could convince him of my identity, I wouldn't gain his trust. I was also trusted by Stern, you see. I escaped them both by creating the false impression of a suicide. One lie is all it takes to destroy a trust. No. He'd sooner trust you, and you betrayed him once already when you ran away."

"Well, Jesus . . . I mean . . . Jesus."

"I think you understand the danger. Dr. Winter prepares to meet an enemy who does not exist, with extraordinary weapons he does not need, and neither you nor I nor Synthetica can do a thing to stop him. And that's only the half of it. What use are weapons without a target? So now, if I may direct your attention outside."

And there they were, on the rear screen, the houses of the Free Market, pouring out of the sky by the hundreds along every projectable route, taking up spaces around the first arrivals as fast as they could be assigned. It could have been a replay of the Merit incident, so help me, every bit as spectacular, but knowing what lurked among the trees below, considerably more terrifying. I looked back and forth between the big rear screen and the five little monitors and finally to Theo, who it seems merely wanted my understanding. "Oh Jesus. Oh my God."

"Quite so."

It was Theo's doing, all of it. And yet if the whole plot failed and fingers went pointing, what specifically had he done? His greatest contribution was to stitch a monogram, an utterly innocuous and totally innocent act, and yet it provided Dr. Winter with his only solid piece of intelligence at a critical moment of doubt. And should anyone have asked how the Market community just happened to be at the wrongest possible place at the wrongest moment in a thousand years, there would be one name on the list ahead of all others: M.A. Hornblower. If I am to credit the man with genius, it would be less for what he did than for the clean way he did it, completely without personal involvement, from a carefully protected distance, with a new look and a new name neither side would recall from history. Well, of course, the issue of cause never came up, let alone the issue of guilt. That was and still remains entirely another matter, one I wouldn't consider for some time afterwards. My immediate and overwhelming concern was to stop it before it happened, and to that end Theo gave me his every cooperation. But there again, you see, he knew full well there was nothing I could do. The course of history was set; he had set it, and no power on earth could alter it.

I asked for a phone. He provided. I punched buttons one after another after another, searching for an unoccupied channel, getting only numbers on a screen, one as high as 98, none lower than forty ahead of me. Mayday got me zilch. I accepted position number forty-one on the least popular channel and set the phone aside.

Theo very tolerantly allowed me to run through every possibility, offering to pursue any reasonable suggestion I might come up with. Right away I suggested that since the phones were backed up we should visit the news stations in person. No good. We'd get caught in the parking traffic and never get through, or worse, never get out again. A computer link? Busier than the phones. I was welcome to try. I did. No luck. Flares? Smoke signals? Semaphore? Who would notice? Who would care? One, maybe two at the most. Then what?

"No, Mark, there is no way to get through. No way to warn them."

"But we've *got* to warn them. It's the Market. It's the whole entire Free Market."

"Oh no. In that you are mistaken. It is only a hundredth part. The Free Market is all but dead and gone. It was gone before you were born. What you see outside is the last remnant after a century of suicides, a small population of cowards, really, willing but unable to call it quits on themselves. Even if you could warn them, you would only hasten the slow ones and attract those few who might otherwise stay behind. You haven't lived long enough to understand. I tell you, Mark, if they knew as much as you and I, they would come all the faster, for here is the opportunity to have done unto them what they are afraid to do unto themselves."

"What'll we do? What'll we do?"

"Watch."

"Watch? You mean just sit here?"

"In peace, because it is inevitable."

"In peace because it's inevitable? In peace because it's inevitable? You're crazy. You are! You're crazy!"

"Mark, Mark, take it easy. It's all right."

"My God almighty."

"Mark, listen to me. . . ."

"Oh Jesus. Oh Jesus. Oh my God."

"You're forgetting something."

"I can't believe it. This is horrible."

"Mark, the shelter. Don't you remember? The shelter."

"Oh Jesus God Almighty, oh my . . . shelter?"

"You saw it. Did you not understand? This isn't the end. Not at all. Mark, it's a new beginning."

". . . . ."

"Mark?"

Since that moment when the vault door opened, perhaps before, I'd been hearing a strange psychic sound, a sustained dissonant chord playing on and on, warning me of something wrong, that I was off course in my understanding, incorrect in a basic way.

"Mark, are you all right?"

And yet I had continued on through the vault, through my conversation with Pecan Regent, right into Uncle Theo's little craft, despite this all-prevailing sense of incorrectness.

"You know where the bathroom is. Don't be too embarrassed to use it."

What was wrong, the one thing out of place that led to my ultimate bewilderment was this: little people do not find themselves in the center of a world cataclysm—the very first law of reality, upon which all else rests. There I sat listening to Theo fill in the blanks back to the day of my birth, and the sound got louder and louder and louder until suddenly, in a flash, I was back on course with the correct understanding. Power returned to all parts. I stood up. I smiled. I stretched and massaged my numb appendages. Color returned to my face, and for the first time, really the very first time since I was put out of the house, I was myself again.

"Mark, what is it?"

"What is it? I'll tell you what it is. Bullshit. That's what it is."

23

"Bullshit, bullshit, bullshit."

"Mark, what's come over you?"

Synthetica, who'd been quietly attending the infinite all this time, came back to life with a smile on her face and joy in her heart. "I understand," she said. "There is a purpose and meaning to everything. It *is* a new beginning."

"Aw shit. You're in on it too, aren't you?"

Looking Theo in the eye for the first time since boarding, she rose from the couch, walked to where he stood, and I swear to God, she knelt before him. Choking back sobs, she asked him, head bowed, "Are you the cause?"

Theo awarded her his biggest smile of the day, and better, a direct answer, his highest reward for a good question. "Insofar as I did not interfere with your father's conspiracy, yes. And insofar as I helped plant a few seeds here and there, again yes. But ultimately I would say that those who created the Market were also responsible for its demise, for in creating it they unwittingly programmed it to self-destruct."

"Then you think my father will succeed?"

"Yes. Fabulously. Although he won't realize it for many years to come. In destroying what he believes to be a small contingent of Stern's mighty forces, he will in fact lay waste to all that remains of the technology he hopes to recover. He and his people will be forced to begin again, living off the land. They will have little spirit for that kind of life, and with the exception of your father, little knowledge. It is my fondest hope that you will go to them and help them. Your father will be able to survive and to teach his followers how to do so, as he did with you, but I doubt that he will have the heart for it if he has no goal above and beyond pure survival. It would be up to you to show them that there is joy in living for the sake of living alone."

"I'll go. Oh yes. Oh yes I will," she said, tears streaming down her face. From the look of her you'd think she'd just been kissed by God, full of the mouth. I could have smacked her just for looking that way.

"And you, Mark?"

"Forget it. It won't work. You can both just quit now. I'm not buying. It's all over."

"Oh?" Theo said, not the least put off. "I see. Would you be so kind as to tell me where I went wrong with you?"

"The shelter."

"And?"

"Look, I've *been* there."

"Yes. I don't know how you could have missed it." He had the audacity to wink.

"I was more than just there. I went down inside. I saw it, the people, the cathedral, I set off the alarms, everything. I *know* what it is."

"Well then, I don't have to explain it to you now. Imagine if I hadn't placed the beacon light, how difficult it would be for me now to convince you of its existence."

"Look. I know a fake when I see one. And that's a fake."

"Ah, so that's it."

"You bet. I grew up on shelters. I've seen every episode of *The Survivors* ever produced. I've been through hundreds by remote camera."

"And who do you suppose bought you those cameras year after year?"

"You?"

"Every Christmas."

"Well then, give me credit for what I know."

"So you suppose that the shelter I took such pains to bring to your attention is fake."

"Absolutely. It has Venture Company written all over it."

"And Peter Winter?"

"He's probably a friend of yours. I don't know. Maybe he's an actor. Maybe they're all actors. You tell me."

"I see. Well then, Mark, how do you explain that?" He pointed to the rear screen, certain he had a case there.

"A re-run of the Merit formation of ninety-four. And I wish you'd shut it off. I'm allergic to re-runs."

"A recording? You call that a recording?"

"Why don't you just open the door and let me see it for real?"

"I can't do that. We'd lose pressure."

"Then go down lower."

"It could explode any minute. I don't think it would be too wise to go any lower for awhile."

"*Ha!*"

"And the monitors? I suppose you think those are recorded images?"

"Exactly."

"Would you care to direct the cameras? I have them on voice control. Be my guest."

"All right, it's live. They're actors in any case."

"Mark, you have some gall to suppose that so many people would go to so much trouble merely to tease a child."

"Trouble? What trouble? What the hell else has anyone got to do? The whole Free Market could be in on it, for all I know. Big deal. They got tired of Ted Wasserman and had me. What's a child for?"

"I sympathize with your point of view. I'm as much to blame for it as your mother or any of the others. Still, it is a sad occasion when a man is reduced to such skepticism that he won't believe his own eyes."

"I suppose now you expect me to dress up like the guy in the picture and march into the cathedral looking like a blond Jesus, full of innocence, arms spread, a dumb holy glow on my face, for what? A church full of uncles and aunts waiting there to shrivel me with laughter, well no, sir. I won't do it. Never."

"So you've figured it all out."

"I chose 'D,' didn't I?"

"Very well. Have it your way." He turned from me to the monitor screens. Three of the five images showed people gathered beside monster cannon-like things pointing up through the trees. Two groups were still making ready. "We have very little time. There is a great deal I must tell you. You will listen to me," he said, fully convinced that I would. His tone of voice was such that I had to at least pretend to be interested, regardless of my current state of mind. "I am not asking you to believe, merely to remember. The matter of belief will take care of itself soon enough. I will waste no more time with it. Now you listen."

He launched into what I interpreted as a sort of last-ditch attempt to patch up the whole preposterous scheme by giving it a background of plausible causes. Shelters were the subject, shelters in general and one in particular. He claimed to be the last surviving member of *Le Consortée de l'Anthropologie*, what we of the English-speaking community called the Anthropology Club, an old and venerable institution predating the Market itself, and for many years richer. So he said. The club bought up the last remaining occupied shelters for the purpose of preserving the unique and special character of each society from the overpowering influence of the burgeoning Market system. For starters, they removed the very best of their purchases from the tourist lists, but later, when the folks down under began to show some interest in coming up, the club decided that to protect them from Market contamination, certain measures had to be taken to encourage them to stay down. What they did was to present the shelter societies with certain aspects of Market contamination on a small scale, such as the introduction of cryogenic technology, which is to say, the Martin beam. Of course, Uncle Theo and his associates couldn't just walk right inside a shelter and deliver them the equipment without arousing suspicion among the natives of a better world outside, so naturally they slipped plans down under and encouraged them to build their own suspension systems. How? Religious revelation worked well in a large number of cases, especially among those unique and special cultures with a unique and special religious predisposition toward holy apparitions, and at the same time no familiarity with standing wave holography. And so on and so forth. I got the picture.

I listened to all this with such childish doubt that half of what he told me never registered. He was not unaware of my attitude, so perhaps he told me twice what I needed to know. I gave him the best attention I could muster, salted with "yeah-yeah's" and "uh-huh's" and "why not's," just to keep the ball rolling. Every so often, as it became necessary, I'd throw in a "Look, any idiot would assume as much," to keep him from getting bogged down under a big load of boring details. With my help and encouragement he managed to skip over whole important subjects, such as anything and everything pertaining to his early days, the great movement led by Stern, the counter-movements that generated, and his part in them. All that. A whole history irretrievably lost. I also missed the chance to discover precisely how he tricked Mimi Jo, not that it matters. He did it. That's all that counts. Except I am curious.

While Theo hammered away at me, poor Synthetica could think of nothing else to do but assume a holy pose and maintain it for the duration. She chose the posture of a Hindu monk, sitting cross-legged on the carpet, nose to nose with the rear screen, watching the events outside. I watched too, although with something different on my mind. For her it was to be the triumph of her father over all the evils of the world; for me a technical curiosity regarding special effects. In particular there was the problem of going from footage of the Merit formation to a battle scene without a cut.

"Now Mark, listen carefully. The photograph in the cathedral is mine, taken some time ago, to be sure. Here." He handed me a copy. "I suggest you trim your beard to match this. The hair will do as it is. You'll find robes in the cupboard there, along with sundry supplies. Wings, of course. And you know where my home is if you need anything else. I can't give you step by step instructions because I don't know what you'll encounter. I can only tell you what you must accomplish. I rely on your intelligence, which I find wholly adequate."

"I figured this one out, didn't I?"

"And you escaped the shelter without getting yourself reduced to protein powder and calcium tablets. They are in the habit of eating intruders, an edict against a bygone threat to their sanctity. I suggest you countermand that with something more charitable."

"First thing."

"No. First thing, get them out of there. I suggest you cut a ramp with this." He reached under the table and pulled out what looked for all the world like a nuclear inductor. "It's fully charged, so be careful. Melt the rock, give them a path from the entrance. As they leave, count them. There should be 517. When the last is out, seal off all entrances. Cut them off from their technology. It is for their own good. Do you understand?"

"Back to nature."

"All the way back. Now. In my day I never spoke to the people directly. In that way I avoided the scrutiny of too many doubting eyes. I recommend the same for you. Especially you. Keep your distance. Remain aloof. When you've got something to say, say it to the bishop. He is devout, and as such tolerant of minor errors. You will make mistakes."

"We've met, you know."

"Yes, I do know. You did remarkably well."

"Why, thank you."

"Remember you are not God, nor any close relation. You are a lower-echelon messenger, and as such understandably fallible."

"What's my name?"

"Jones."

"You're kidding."

"Their theology is full of common names. I suggest you read up at your earliest opportunity."

"I will. I will."

"You may wear wings and fly. They will expect you to, but never let anyone examine them too closely. And never, I repeat, never take them off your back in anyone's presence."

"Angel, right."

"Precisely. Vertical ascensions will impress them. You'll have a hard time explaining mistakes, though, so be careful when you fly. You're well-practiced by now, so you shouldn't have any problem."

"No loops, I promise."

"Resist the urge to put on a show. Hide your power. Otherwise you'll end up with a population of lifeless worshippers depending on you for everything. That's not healthy for you, it's not healthy for them. You're not raising plants. These are people. Insofar as it is possible, let them work out their own problems."

"Easy on the miracles. Gotcha."

"Nevertheless, you are their undisputed leader. Maintain your image, not for your sake but for theirs. Allow them to perform ceremonies in your behalf. Accept offerings. Have them give blessings in your name. In your presence, they shall take off their shoes, for where you stand the ground is holy."

"And if they're sitting down, they shall take off their pants. I wouldn't have it any other way."

"Now listen to me. I want you to take them to Michael's farm. They are to walk. The journey will take many days. How well they endure depends on you. There will be hunger and sickness. The old will tire, the young will fear the open spaces. Teach them what Synthetica taught you of natural foods and cures. They will bless you for it. These are a good people. And resourceful. They will settle and prosper. Your duty once they have established themselves is to protect them from anything that might destroy them totally, from within or without. Otherwise leave them alone, do you understand? They can take care of themselves. As time passes, fade into the background. Do what must be done, but go unnoticed. If a change is required, use knowledge, not force. Discover the pivots and make your changes there. A feather's touch in the right places can bring down a world and raise up a new one in its place."

"Hey, I know what you mean."

"You will fall in love with them. I assure you. It is unavoidable. The temptation will be to put aside your equipment, to give up your position, your duties and responsibilities, and join them as an equal. This you must not do. As the messenger of God, you are the foundation of their faith. Do not destroy that trust. Though it breaks your heart, live your life apart from them. You will have my home. It's yours. In time you will discover a community of others like you. Make friends among them. Your attitude toward Synthetica will change. Find her. She will welcome you, as will her father. I am speaking of a distant future. For now, you have only one thing to do. Go to them. Make them dramatically aware of your presence. Instruct the bishop that the time has come. Cut a ramp from the door and lead them into the world. Any questions?"

"Not a one."

"Good. Then let's go over everything again step by step."

"Wait, I got a question."

"Yes?"

"Why don't *you* do it?"

He smiled. "Because I'm tired. And old. Exactly like those people out there." He pointed toward the screen, where "those people" were collecting for the last act in their little play. Only by now I wasn't so sure that it *was* a play.

He turned back to me. "Now," he said. "Let's go over the whole thing again."

"Do we have to?" It seems we did. Over and over again. And in case I forgot anything, in one of the pockets of my robe I would find a small bound reference edition of the *Book of Jones*, wherein all that I was to do had been conveniently foretold. A complete script with timetables, the works.

Theo opened up his closet and laid out all my paraphernalia. My robe was outrageous, a garish sparkle of self-illuminating gold chain mail draped over a luxurious blue silk lining. Inside were more pockets than stars in the sky, each with a miniature gizmo, everything from course plotters to listening devices to bug repellent. And wings, of course, an outlandish set of tapered laminates for me, which I could absolutely guarantee no one would get a close look at, and a fine new 880 pack which Theo set aside for himself.

"You don't expect me to parade around in *that*, do you?"

"They have a photograph, remember."

"Isn't it enough you set me up? You want me to look ridiculous too?"

"Beauty is in the eye of the beholder."

"Along with ugly, silly, and ludicrous."

"These are not a fashion-minded people. Nevertheless, they have certain rigid expectations. You don't want to be mistaken for an intruder again. You *do* understand." I understood. And if it came to that, I resolved to put a never-ending ban on photography.

We were just going over some of the finer points of angel etiquette when something on the monitor caught Theo's attention. It seems the last and slowest of Peter's five groups had finally finished up what they were doing. Their huge cannon stood completed, turning back and forth and up and down to everyone's satisfaction. One by one they went down into their underground supply chamber. Theo directed the camera to close in. They had good shelter. The hole was deep, and as the last of them disappeared a door closed over them, clean and white, the same impenetrable substance of the vault.

"They're frightened to death," Theo said. "They will not attempt to communicate at the risk of their first strike advantage. Even if they should try, they will get no answer. The channels they know have been closed for ten centuries."

"How long will it be?"

"Are you impatient?"

"Oh no. Bored more than anything."

"Then why are you trembling?"

"Huh? Me? No, I'm just cold."

"Here, try this on," he said, handing me the robe.

"Oh, ah, that's okay. You don't suppose maybe I could watch a little TV before it all blows up?" I expected his immediate refusal, and some lame excuse to back it, for TV would give me proof positive. However, without any hesitation he turned over his little screens to me. I went racing through the channels, looking for regular programming. As it is with all matters of faith, though, I found nothing that could not sustain at least two interpretations. Most stations were off the air, either in transit, meaning a bonafide world calamity, or these were simply blanks that Theo's equipment could not fill. Of the twenty or so working channels, all but six carried pictures of me taken from my conversation with Pecan Regent, recordings Theo could easily have made himself. Announcers repeated my story as best they knew it in their rapid-fire newsy kind of way, an easy style for anyone to imitate. The six that weren't running my close-up had cameras on the sunset, an odd thing under any curcumstances.

We had an incredible sunset, unlike anything I'd ever seen. I was perhaps to suppose that it had something to do with the breaking up of the Nimbus system, scattered clouds, free to assume any shape they desired in the evening sun. Or I might have assumed I was seeing very old footage, pre-dating weather control. In any case, there it was as big as life on our front screen, and looking back I could see it reflecting off the houses in formation. If it *was* a hoax, it was well-synchronized. I shut off the monitors, all but channel thirty-eight, which had on an ancient rendition of "Hard Hearted Hannah" in my honor. I let that play and joined Theo and Synthetica at the rear screen.

Theo was standing beside Synthetica, watching the last trickle of traffic drip down from above. After awhile he sat himself down next to her. I couldn't be the odd one, so I sat too.

The sunset was beautiful, but not half so lovely as the city reflecting it. Synthetica had never seen a formation before. This was her first. It was beautiful. Just gorgeous. A hundred hundred silver spheres in perfect array reflecting the sun, each one a fiery red star of the first magnitude in a pincushion universe, resting lightly above the green-black forest.

And yes, I was trembling. I admit. I was crying too, I guess, but not so obviously that I couldn't hide it. I'd yawn and rub my tired eyes from time to time, then casually dry my hand on my sleeve. No one saw me. At least not Synthetica. She was too enraptured and did not notice her company. I'm glad she had the chance just once to face her enemy in all its splendor before the end. It was something she needed to know.

I looked for Mimi Jo's big house among those on the perimeter. We were much too high to distinguish one from another. I looked just the same.

Level by level the houses winked out as the shadow of the horizon rose up from the ground and engulfed the city. We were so high that if anyone cared to look our way, they would have seen us shining like a star, until finally our day ended too.

And then a strange thing. Channel thirty-eight interrupted its broadcast. And by the way, I was wrong before. It isn't "swamp in Alabama," it's "vamp of Savannah." Grey Thacker came on live. It sounded like him, but by the time I turned to look, he was gone. He said, "Ladies and gentlemen, I . . ." He paused, unable to say what he had to say, and then simply concluded: "Good-bye."

And another thing. I don't know if Theo or Synthetica noticed, but I could just barely make out tiny flickering lights emanating from each house. I could be mistaken, but I believe people were lighting candles and putting them in their windows or out on their porches. I'd never seen anything like that before.

We waited. The last trace of pink vanished from the sky, and night was full. I don't know yet what caused the delay—something technical, perhaps—although I like to think that maybe Peter Winter, in spite of tactical risks, tried to get through to someone, and failing that, opened fire.

We'd have been blinded looking through the glass. Laser beams like searchlights fanned the sky from five sources, setting off explosions at each point of contact. As fast as the beams could sweep, houses blew apart. Reactor units in some houses were touched off, causing bright flare-ups every so often, but most fell slowly to the ground, like cinders from a grate. Houses on the inner bottom layers were the first to fall, followed by those above, the beams spooning out the formation like a melon.

It didn't end all at once in a giant explosion as I had imagined; there was enough space between houses that the explosion of one did not trigger the next. Each home had to be dealt with separately. Those around the outside and near the top had protection from the houses beneath. They might have ascended vertically out of range and survived, but they did not. No one made any such attempt. Quite the contrary, as Theo predicted, a few latecomers joined as though there were nothing out of order.

We were in motion. I didn't realize it until later, but we were moving away fast, racing the shock wave across the continent. I couldn't take my eyes off the destruction. I watched as the fires slipped over the horizon, and after that I watched the glow in the sky fade away to the east. When there was nothing left to see I still sat there watching. Synthetica too, right beside me.

Theo was the first to turn away. He had quiet words with the navigator, some parking instructions, and return coordinates for Synthetica. Somewhere in the back of my mind I heard the door open and the wind whistle across the opening. When we stopped, Theo was gone.

Later, as I was putting on my wings, I noticed his were still there. We found a note pinned to them: "Synthetica," it said, "tell your father he is not to blame. It was all my doing." Nothing for me.

But the little Liston wouldn't budge until I got out of it, and there was no place left to go but down. I still had my doubts, I can't deny it. But I went anyway, determined to face either possibility, because if it was to be a joke, it would be a very bad one.

And then some while later I found this passage in the *Book of Jones*: "He will come to you in tears. By this sign you will know it is him and no other."

If I'd come any other way, they'd have been better off without me.

DRAY PRESCOT

The great novels of Kregen, world of Antares.

- ☐ **THE SUNS OF SCORPIO** (#UY1191—$1.25)
- ☐ **WARRIOR OF SCORPIO** (#UY1212—$1.25)
- ☐ **SWORDSHIPS OF SCORPIO** (#UY1231—$1.25)
- ☐ **PRINCE OF SCORPIO** (#UY1251—$1.25)
- ☐ **ARMADA OF ANTARES** (#UY1227—$1.25)
- ☐ **RENEGADE OF KREGEN** (#UY1271—$1.25)
- ☐ **KROZAIR OF KREGEN** (#UW1228—$1.50)
- ☐ **SECRET SCORPIO** (#UW1344—$1.50)
- ☐ **SAVAGE SCORPIO** (#UW1372—$1.50)
- ☐ **CAPTIVE SCORPIO** (#UW1394—$1.50)
- ☐ **GOLDEN SCORPIO** (#UW1424—$1.50)
- ☐ **A LIFE FOR KREGEN** (#UE1456—$1.75)
- ☐ **A SWORD FOR KREGEN** (#UE1485—$1.75)

Fully illustrated.

If you wish to order these titles,
please use the coupon on
the last page of this book.

- [ ] **THE 1979 ANNUAL WORLD'S BEST SF.** The latest "World's Best" with David Lake, C. J. Cherryh, Ursula K. Le Guin, and more. (#UE1459—$2.25)

- [ ] **THE 1978 ANNUAL WORLD'S BEST SF.** Leading off with Varley, Haldeman, Bryant, Ellison, Bishop, etc. (#UJ1376—$1.95)

- [ ] **THE 1977 ANNUAL WORLD'S BEST SF.** Featuring Asimov, Tiptree, Aldiss, Coney, and a galaxy of great ones. An SFBC Selection. (#UE1297—$1.75)

- [ ] **THE 1976 ANNUAL WORLD'S BEST SF.** A winner with Fritz Leiber, Brunner, Cowper, Vinge, and more. An SFBC Selection. (#UW1232—$1.50)

- [ ] **THE 1975 ANNUAL WORLD'S BEST SF.** The authentic "World's Best" featuring Bester, Dickson, Martin, Asimov, etc. (#UW1170—$1.50)

- [ ] **THE DAW SCIENCE FICTION READER.** The unique anthology with a full novel by Andre Norton and tales by Akers, Dickson, Bradley, Stableford, and Tanith Lee. (#UW1242—$1.50)

- [ ] **THE BEST FROM THE REST OF THE WORLD.** Great stories by the master of sf writers of Western Europe. (#UE1343—$1.75)

- [ ] **THE YEAR'S BEST FANTASY STORIES: 3.** Edited by Lin Carter, the 1977 volume includes C. J. Cherryh, Karl Edward Wagner, G.R.R. Martin, etc. (#UW1338—$1.50)

If you wish to order these titles,

please use the coupon on

the last page of this book.

Presenting JOHN NORMAN in DAW editions...

- [ ] **EXPLORERS OF GOR.** The latest novel in the exciting saga of Tarl Cabot. (#UE1449—$2.25)
- [ ] **SLAVE GIRL OF GOR.** The eleventh novel of Earth's orbital counterpart makes an Earth girl a puppet of vast conflicting forces. The 1977 Gor novel. (#UE1474—$2.25)
- [ ] **TRIBESMEN OF GOR.** The tenth novel of Tarl Cabot takes him face to face with the Others' most dangerous plot—in hte vast Tahari desert with its warring tribes. (#UE1473—$2.25)
- [ ] **BEASTS OF GOR.** The twelfth novel of the Gor saga takes Tarl Cabot to the far north to confrontation with the Kurs' first Gorean foothold! (#UE1471—$2.25)
- [ ] **HUNTERS OF GOR.** The saga of Tarl Cabot on Earth's orbital counterpart reaches a climax as Tari seeks his lost Talena among the outlaws and panther women of the wilderness. (#UE1472—$2.25)
- [ ] **MARAUDERS OF GOR.** The ninth novel of Tarl Cabot's adventures takes him to the northland of transplanted Vikings and into direct confrontation with the enemies of two worlds. (#UE1465—$2.25)
- [ ] **TIME SLAVE.** The Creator of Gor brings back the days of the caveman in a vivid lusty new novel of time travel and human destiny. (#UJ1322—$1.95)
- [ ] **IMAGINATIVE SEX.** A study of the sexuality of male and female which leads to a new revelation of sensual liberation. (#UJ1145—$1.95)

DAW BOOKS are represented by the publishers of Signet and Mentor Books, **THE NEW AMERICAN LIBRARY, INC.**

THE NEW AMERICAN LIBRARY, INC.,
P.O. Box 999, Bergenfield, New Jersey 07621

Please send me the DAW BOOKS I have checked above. I am enclosing
$_____ (check or money order—no currency or C.O.D.'s).
Please include the list price plus 50¢ per order to cover handling costs.

Name _____

Address _____

City _____ State _____ Zip Code _____

Please allow at least 4 weeks for delivery